C000046636

Forbidden Fruit

Halfway up the ladder Jonathan swayed slightly and Beth reacted before she could stop herself. As she placed a hand either side of his hips to steady him, she felt a tingle of excitement in the pit of her stomach. Her hands were only inches from his buttocks.

Jonathan immediately stiffened and Beth could see the muscles in his thighs tightening involuntarily. Was he becoming aroused again?

He started back down the steps. As he moved, he twisted round so that one of her hands began to slide across his thigh, towards his crotch. She could see his erection growing harder. Any second now, she would be touching it.

By the same author:

Taking Liberties
A Sporting Chance

Forbidden Fruit
Susie Raymond

BL

Black Lace books contain sexual fantasies.
In real life, always practise safe sex.

This edition published in 2008 by
Black Lace
Thames Wharf Studios
Rainville Rd
London W6 9HA

Originally published 1998

Copyright ©Susie Raymond 1998

The right of Susie Raymond to be identified as the Author of the Work has been
asserted in accordance with the Copyright, Designs and Patents Act 1988.

A catalogue record for this book is available from the British Library.

www.black-lace-books.com

Typeset by Palimpsest Book Production Limited, Grangemouth, Stirlingshire
Printed and bound in Great Britain by CPI Bookmarque, Croydon, CR0 4TD

Distributed in the USA by Macmillan, 175 Fifth Avenue,
New York, NY 10010, USA

ISBN 978 0 352 34189 1

*All characters in this publication are fictitious and any resemblance
to real persons, living or dead, is purely coincidental.*

This book is sold subject to the condition that it shall not, by way of trade or
otherwise, be lent, resold, hired out or otherwise circulated without the publisher's
prior written consent in any form of binding or cover other than that in which it is
published and without a similar condition including this condition being imposed
on the subsequent purchaser.

The Random House Group Limited supports The Forest Stewardship Council [FSC],
the leading international forest certification organisation. All our titles that are
printed on Greenpeace approved FSC certified paper carry the FSC logo
Our paper procurement policy can be found at www.rbooks.co.uk/environment

13 5 7 9 10 8 6 4 2

1

As she pushed her arms through the sleeves of her dress and pulled it down over her head, Beth thought she heard a noise behind her. Alarmed at the idea of someone walking in on her, she tugged the hem down as quickly as she could and spun round.

The door remained closed. Puzzled, Beth took a step towards it and then stopped. She could hear the unmistakable sound of footsteps stealing away slowly and furtively. A few seconds later, she heard the door to the staff toilet slam shut. Her eyes moved down to the empty keyhole, staring back at her like an unblinking eye, and her face flamed. Surely someone hadn't been spying on her?

Staring at the open keyhole, Beth thought back to other Saturdays in recent weeks. This was not the first time she had heard footsteps outside the back room while she was changing out of her overall. Just last week she had opened the door expecting to find Mr Bailey or Jonathan standing outside waiting to come in. Yet, when she had looked, the tiny, dark corridor had been empty.

Beth picked up her things and moved forward to turn the handle. The door swung inwards. There was no one in sight.

As she walked past the staff loo, Beth thought she heard a small sigh almost too faint even to carry through the thin wooden door. Then, the cistern flushed and Beth increased her pace. By the time the toilet door had swung open, she was out in the main shop. Mr Bailey was still at the till, cashing up the morning's takings. He looked up at her and smiled cheerfully.

'You off then? I expect you're ready for your lunch.' It was much the same comment Jack Bailey made to her every day when her morning shift was over.

Beth looked round quickly. Jonathan was nowhere to be seen. Before she could say anything, the door to the back corridor opened again and Jonathan ambled into the shop. Tall and lanky, he reminded her of a young colt. His short blond hair was slightly damp, as if he had just splashed himself with water. Mr Bailey frowned at him.

'There you are, lad. I wondered where you were. How many times do I have to ask you not to disappear when I'm cashing up? I need you to be out here in case a customer comes in.'

'Sorry. I had to go to the loo,' Jonathan muttered. 'I was only gone a few minutes,' he added quickly. Mr Bailey sighed.

'Just see it doesn't happen again, that's all,' he responded mildly. He turned back to examine the shelves and paused a moment before adding, 'I need a few more boxes of cigarettes brought through from the stock room before you go to lunch.'

'OK. No problem.' With a farewell nod to Beth, Jonathan fetched the key and disappeared out the back again.

Beth hurried through the front door and closed it behind her. She turned right, crossed the railway bridge, and set off up the narrow High Street to meet her friends. As she walked, her mind was in complete turmoil.

It was a lovely day. Dry and sunny, with just a hint of spring in the air. One or two shopkeepers had opened their awnings to add a splash of welcome colour to the normally drab, rundown appearance of the street. Even so, one could not help noticing the ever increasing number of empty buildings. Dark, empty caverns with dirty windows, faded sale signs and cobweb-laden doorways. No one seemed to want to shop in the traditional way any more. Not since the huge, sprawling out-of-town shopping centre had opened the previous autumn.

Usually, the sight of all these abandoned, unwanted shops depressed her. They looked so sad; each hiding its own unhappy tale of hopes and dreams swept away on a tide of progress. Today, Beth barely gave them a second thought.

Was she just imagining things, or had someone really been standing outside and peering through the keyhole to watch her change? If so, who was it? It was certainly possible that Mr Bailey might have sneaked in to peek at her. Somehow, Jack Bailey seemed an unlikely candidate for a peeping Tom. For a start, he had to be at least sixty years old! Besides, he just wasn't the kind of man who would ever dream of taking such liberties with his staff. It was inconceivable to imagine him spying on her.

Which only left Jonathan. Yet what on earth would a young lad like Jonathan want to peer through the keyhole at her for? She was more than twice his age – old enough to be his mother. As it happened, Beth even knew Jonathan's mother. She popped into the shop several times a week for her newspapers and magazines. She couldn't be much older than Beth herself, if at all.

Yet Beth was convinced that someone had been outside watching her. Someone's footsteps had crept away before she could open the door. Could it have been a stranger? Beth frowned. How could anyone have sneaked into the shop and walked straight past Mr Bailey? Whoever it was, it was hard to imagine why they would be interested in staring at her. She could feel herself flushing with embarrassment at the thought of anyone looking at her in her under garments. Even before she had lost a bit of weight, they had never done much for her.

She had been meaning to do something about sprucing up her wardrobe for ages.

She soon forgot her embarrassment about her clothing as her mind returned to her other, even more disturbing, thought. The toilet door had slammed shut just after she had heard the footsteps creeping away. It hadn't been Mr Bailey. He had been in the shop. There really was only one possible conclusion. Sixteen-year-old Jonathan Evans had been staring through the keyhole, watching her change.

Beth began to panic. How often had he done it before? Even worse, what had he been doing in the loo afterwards? This idea was so shocking that she could feel her whole body beginning to tremble.

It was no secret that men did that sort of thing. She had even suspected that Tony did it sometimes. What other explanation could there be for those nights when she had felt the mattress shuddering slightly beneath her and heard the sound of her husband's ragged breathing before he crept off to the loo?

They had never talked about it, of course. It wasn't that she was a prude or anything. She had always believed that she had enjoyed the physical part of their relationship as much as anyone ever did. Nevertheless, she had always been grateful that Tony respected the strict, religious upbringing her parents had imposed. Actually, he had always said that he liked her genteel attitude to sex and he had always taken her gently and patiently under the sheets, treating her body as if it might break.

As she had so many times in the four years since Tony had walked out on her, Beth wondered if he treated his new wife with the same respect and reverence. For once, however, she did not dwell on the subject of Tony's infidelity for very long. She was far too preoccupied for that.

What if Jonathan hadn't just been peeping at her through the keyhole? What if he had also sneaked off into the toilet afterwards to fantasise about the sight of her in her under-wear? No! It was unthinkable. She must stop letting her imagination run away with her.

Beth smiled at the sheer stupidity of the idea. A lad like Jonathan couldn't possibly have any interest in her. He would probably be horrified if he knew what was going through her mind. By the time Beth arrived at the coffee house where she had arranged to meet her friends, she had almost managed to forget the whole thing.

Ann and Geraldine, her two closest friends, were already sitting at a small table in the far corner. As she walked through the door, Geraldine looked up and gave her a cheery wave.

'There you are,' she called, as Beth made her way across the lunchtime crowds to join them. 'We had almost given up on you. I thought you must have run off with your boss or some-thing.'

It was a typical remark for Geraldine. Beth and Ann often teased her about her one-track mind where men were concerned. Not that their remarks had any effect on her. Geraldine was the first to admit that she had what she called a 'healthy' attitude towards the opposite sex, and nothing her friends could say made any difference.

At her friend's comment, Beth's suspicions returned. As she slipped into the chair next to Ann and leant forward to give both women a quick peck on the cheek, she was certain that her own cheeks were glowing again. Fortunately, Geraldine was too distracted to notice the guilty flush.

'Look at that young lad serving the table by the door,' she whispered in a voice loud enough to be heard right across the room. 'I wouldn't mind getting my hands on that.'

'Geraldine, hush! He'll hear you,' Ann reprimanded their

friend softly as her cheeks coloured. A middle-aged man at the next table looked up and leered suggestively and Geraldine giggled.

'If he is going to walk around with a rear end as enticing as that, he should expect people to comment,' she protested. 'It's practically a public health hazard.'

Beth followed Gerri's gaze. The lad in question was probably only a year or two older than Jonathan, although it was hard to tell really. Jonathan certainly didn't look as if he were only sixteen. Of course, he was tall and muscular for his age. He was probably nearly six foot already. A picture of Michelangelo's *David* sprang into her mind and she hastily brushed it aside. What was it his mother had once said? Something about him being a top-rate swimmer.

'Mad about it, he is,' Mrs Evans had told her and Mr Bailey proudly. 'Never thinks about anything else.'

In the light of what had just happened, Beth wondered now if that were entirely true and if it had been him peeping through the keyhole . . .

'You're very quiet today, Beth,' Geraldine commented as the waitress scurried off with their orders for coffee and sandwiches. 'Your face has got that dreamy look on it. You're not holding out on us, are you? If you've got a new man in your life, Ann and I want to know all the sordid details.'

Beth smiled ruefully. 'No such luck, I'm afraid. Too much competition,' she complimented her friend. 'What chance has a timid mouse like me got with you around?'

'The quiet ones are always the worst, so they say.' Geraldine smirked, obviously pleased by Beth's insinuation. 'Though, I must admit, I can't see it myself. If you've got something to sell then you need to advertise it.' She stared meaningfully at the high-necked, loose-fitting dress Beth was wearing.

'I thought you said you were going to buy yourself some

new clothes? Why do you always hide yourself like that? You've got a great body. If my waist was as tiny as yours, I'd probably wear a tape measure round it.'

Beth looked embarrassed. She had never found it easy to accept compliments. Actually, she had never had all that many compliments. When she was younger, she had always been a bit on the plump side and it was only since Tony had left her that she had finally managed to shed the excess pounds. Well, it was easy to diet when you were just cooking for yourself. Joining the health club had helped too, of course. That, plus a lot more walking. The car was so expensive to run these days and parking anywhere in town was a nightmare. Still, nothing could really make up for the fact that she was fast approaching the big 'four-o'.

Ann seemed to notice her discomfort and leapt in to her rescue. 'I think Beth's dress is very nice. The colour suits her.'

'I didn't say it wasn't nice. I was just suggesting that she think about showing herself off a bit more. You know, a bit of cleavage and perhaps a belt round that darling waist.'

'When you two have quite finished discussing me,' Beth interrupted her quickly. She waited while the waitress handed out their order.

'As a matter of fact,' she added, as she prepared to bite into her cheese and tomato sandwich, 'I am going shopping this afternoon.' She shuddered again at the thought of anyone staring at her in her plain underthings. 'I've decided that it's about time I bought myself some new underwear.'

Later, after she and her friends had parted company, Beth made her way down the High Street to the only lingerie shop still trading.

Inside, she gazed in amazement at the bewildering array of under garments. She hadn't realised that there was such a variety to choose from. Gingerly, she picked up a hanger displaying a minute, lacy red bra and matching panties. She had to check the size label twice before she could believe that it was supposed to fit her. The material in the back of the panties would barely fit over the crease, far less cover her buttocks. As for the bra, she wasn't convinced it would even hide her nipples.

She quickly replaced the flimsy items and moved on down the rack. A black lacy set caught her eye. Tony had always told her that she suited black. She picked up the hanger and turned the garments over in her hands. They didn't seem much more substantial than the red set.

She must be out of her mind. Jonathan was only a lad. She was a middle-aged divorcee, at least twice his age. If he had been looking at her at all, which was doubtful, he had probably just done it out of idle curiosity. Maybe it was some kind of a dare. Perhaps he and his friends would all be having a good laugh about it later.

Hastily, she replaced the tiny lace garments on the rack. This sort of thing wasn't for her. It was time she got back home and did some ironing. She needed to put all this silly nonsense out of her head once and for all. As she turned to leave, the young sales girl looked up and smiled at her.

'Is everything all right?' she questioned.

Beth hesitated. 'Yes, thank you.' She took a deep breath. It was now or never. She reached out and picked up the black underwear again. 'I'll take these please,' she added quickly, her cheeks still glowing.

Although she had been waiting for it, Beth jumped when the shop door opened the following Saturday morning. She quickly busied herself, pretending to rearrange a pile of magazines on the counter in front of her.

'Morning.' Jonathan closed the door behind him and began to remove his jacket. Beth noticed how his T-shirt stretched tightly across his chest as he moved. She quickly averted her eyes.

'Oh, hello, Jonathan,' she replied breathlessly. 'You're nice and early today,' she added awkwardly.

In the six months or so that Jonathan had been working in the shop on Saturday mornings, Beth couldn't remember ever having any trouble talking with him before. As far as she could recall, conversation between them had always been perfectly natural and carefree. Why was it that she was suddenly finding it impossible to think of anything to say to him? What sort of things did they normally talk about?

Jonathan moved across the shop and disappeared out the back, presumably to get rid of his jacket. Beth followed him with her eyes. 'I wouldn't mind getting my hands on that.' Gerri's words from the previous week sprang unbidden into her mind. Compared to Jonathan, the lad at the coffee house was not such a prize. She decided that she had better make sure Geraldine didn't get anywhere near Jonathan. She would eat him for breakfast!

Startled by her thoughts, Beth was grateful for the distraction of a customer entering the shop. As she put on a friendly smile and busied herself cashing up the items purchased, she was sharply aware that Jonathan had returned and was busy sweeping the floor. As he leant forward, she noticed that he had let his normally short cropped hair grow slightly longer than usual, so that the silky blond strands curled slightly over the back of his neck. She felt an urge to run her fingers through it.

He will be breaking a few hearts before long, she told herself, as she nodded a polite goodbye to her customer. She wondered if Jonathan already had a girlfriend. Probably not. She hadn't ever seen him with anyone or heard him mention dating. As his mother said, he was completely absorbed by swimming. Or was he?

'So, what are you planning to do tonight?' she asked him brightly as she tried to push her suspicions firmly to the back of her mind.

Jonathan shrugged.

'Oh, come on. It's Saturday night. Surely you and your friends are going out to have some fun?' Perhaps he wasn't allowed out on his own at night. Maybe his mother kept him at home watching TV or something. If only she knew more about teenage boys. If she and Tony had ever had children of their own then, perhaps, she would have a better idea. As it was, she realised that she didn't even know anyone with youngsters his age.

'Don't you have a special place where you all get together?' She tried again. 'A club or something?' She was beginning to wish that she had never started the conversation.

Jonathan shrugged again and his face was clearly puzzled. 'I don't have any plans,' he told her softly.

Feeling completely foolish, Beth forced another smile. 'I just remembered something I need to do,' she told him. 'Watch the shop for me, will you? I won't be a minute.'

Out the back, Beth closed the door of the staff toilet behind her and moved across to stand in front of the long mirror on the wall. She peered at her reflection for a moment and then reached up to brush a stray strand of hair back from her cheek. When she saw how flushed she looked, she moved over to the basin and splashed cold water on to her face. After she had wiped her cheeks with a paper towel, she reached for her handbag. She took out her compact and carefully began to reapply her lipstick.

Finished, she dabbed a little powder on her nose and cheeks

and inspected herself again. Her face was still red. She moved the compact from side to side and examined herself critically. She was pleased to see that the laughter lines around her eyes were barely noticeable, although she spotted one or two grey hairs sprouting among her dark locks. She pulled them out quickly and her eyes watered at the sharp sting.

She wondered if Tony's new wife had any grey hairs. Probably not. She was ten years younger than Tony. She felt the usual rush of anger and jealousy that thoughts of her successor in Tony's affections always aroused in her. She pushed them away and peered at herself in the long mirror again. She couldn't resist.

Beth checked to make sure that the door was closed and then slipped her overall off. Her new underwear really did fit her perfectly, although it certainly didn't cover anywhere near as much flesh as her old ones did. It was a good job that she didn't have a suntan or she would have white bits sticking out all over the place. She twisted from side to side and stared at her reflection from all angles.

Did the tiny panties make her bottom stick out too much? She moved round slightly so that she could see her back, then grinned. Actually, it wasn't bad at all. Her rear end was both firm and round, and her thighs were slim and shapely. Her sessions in the gym seemed to have worked wonders for her. Beth stood up on tiptoes and twirled round slowly. Everything looked much better like that. Perhaps she should wear heels more often. They weren't very practical in the shop, of course, but still. She pulled in her tummy and thrust out her chest, surprised and pleased by what she saw.

What would Jonathan think if he got an eyeful of her now? The thought shocked her. For the first time, she admitted to herself that she was actually flattered by the idea of him spying on her.

She heard voices in the shop and pulled her overall back on quickly. She really should get back out there. Mr Bailey didn't like Jonathan to be left alone for too long.

By mid-morning, the shop was quite busy and the time passed quickly. After Jonathan had finished sweeping the floor, he disappeared out the back to make a start on the stocktaking Mr Bailey had asked him to do. This afternoon, their mild-mannered, conscientious boss would probably go through it all again to make sure Jonathan hadn't missed anything. As usual, he would tell the boy that it saved him doing it twice himself, rather than letting Jonathan think he didn't trust him.

'I'd appreciate it if you would keep a bit of an eye on the lad,' Mr Bailey had asked her when Jonathan first joined them. 'Give him the benefit of your experience. I would like to think he does more than just pass the time while he is here. Learning how a small business is run will be good experience for him when he leaves school. At least, that's what he told me when he asked me for a job here,' he had added with a small grin. 'Cheeky young devil. Still, with him here to give you a hand, at least it will give me a few hours to myself on a Saturday morning once the papers are out.'

What else was Jonathan trying to learn about while he was here? Beth wondered, as she remembered her suspicions. Assuming, of course, that Jonathan was actually guilty of spying on her.

The more she had thought about it, the more ridiculous the whole idea had become. Why, Jonathan was almost too shy even to talk with her. It was hard to imagine him in the role of lecher. 'The quiet ones are always the worst.' Geraldine's remark taunted her.

Just then, Jonathan came through from the back with an

armful of stock Mr Bailey had told him to put out on display. Beth quickly turned her attention to tidying up the counter. She watched him surreptitiously as she worked, enjoying the way his muscles flexed and rippled under his shirt as he moved.

The shop door opened and Mr Bailey walked in. He greeted them both warmly, then headed out the back with a heavy box. Beth glanced at her watch. It was almost one o'clock. Another couple of minutes and she could go and get changed. She was meeting the girls again in half an hour to go and see the new Spielberg film everyone was raving about. She had been looking forward to it for days. That was probably why she felt so restless. She fingered the strap of her new black bra.

Supposing Jonathan had been guilty. What if he tried to take another quick peek at her in a minute? What would he think of her new, skimpy underwear? She felt a strange shiver of excitement at the thought. She pushed it away quickly. At least she wouldn't have any reason to feel ashamed of herself if there were a peeping Tom at large. It was funny how she was more upset at the idea of not looking her best than she was at the notion that someone might be spying on her! Well, it was rather flattering and her new under garments did make her look and feel good. No doubt, she had just imagined the whole thing anyway.

A few moments later, the door to the back opened and Mr Bailey returned. He walked round behind the counter and began to fuss absent-mindedly with a display of cigarette lighters. Beth looked at her watch again.

'I'll be off in a minute then,' she muttered. 'I'll just go and get changed.' As she hurried towards the doorway, she saw Jonathan straighten up and follow her with his eyes. His face was flushed and his eyes seemed much too bright. She felt suddenly very conscious of her new underwear, as if he could see right through her overall. She turned her back quickly before he could see her face.

Beth closed the door of the staff room behind her and pulled her overall over her head. She strained her ears for the slightest sound outside, but could hear nothing. She lowered her arms and stood shivering in her lacy black bra and panties. Deliberately pulling her stomach in, she turned slowly and reached out for the dress folded neatly over the back of the only chair.

She thought she heard a faint creak outside the door and her heart started hammering. She picked up the dress and stood upright again, facing the door. When she glanced down, she could clearly see the outline of her nipples poking against the sheer material of the bra. She held her breath. The floorboard creaked again. Now that she was listening for it, it seemed much louder.

Suddenly flustered, Beth pulled the dress over her head and quickly smoothed the soft material down over her breasts and hips. Outside, stealthy footsteps headed rapidly down the passageway and she heard the loo door close with a soft click.

Someone was watching! Someone had been crouched down outside the door with their eye pressed to the keyhole, ogling her body. A wave of indignation swept through her. It had to be Jonathan. Mr Bailey would never behave like that. Dirty little sod. How dare he! Who did he think he was? Hadn't his parents taught him any manners at all? Somebody ought to give him a good hiding. Crafty little bugger. Looking as if butter wouldn't melt in his mouth, when all the time ...

What was he doing now? Surely, he wasn't ... She couldn't even bring herself to put words to what she was thinking. It was too shocking. Beth was shaking like a leaf. She could feel the droplets of perspiration trickling down between her breasts. She was sweating all over. She could even feel a cold dampness between her legs. How dare he upset and humiliate her like this? Why, she had a good mind to march right out there and tell him what she thought of his behaviour.

The lock on the loo door didn't work. As soon as she remembered that, the look on her face changed from indignation to shock. If she gave the toilet door a good shove, it would swing open. She could catch him in the act. What better possible way to punish him? He would be so humiliated and ashamed of himself that he would never dare behave so badly again.

Beth took a small step towards the closed door. An image of Michelangelo's statue formed in her mind again. Jonathan was so tall and muscular. Was he fully mature all over? She had never actually seen Tony like that. They had both always undressed separately or in the dark.

As she placed her shaking hand on the door, Beth swayed slightly and felt suddenly dizzy. She closed her eyes. She couldn't do this. She would die of embarrassment if he were, well, misbehaving.

But she wouldn't be as embarrassed as he would. Someone had to teach him a lesson. It was her duty to put a stop to this. Beth opened the door and walked out determinedly into the dark passage. Out in the shop, she could clearly hear the sounds of coins clinking as Mr Bailey cashed up. So, it was Jonathan.

She stopped outside the loo door, placed her ear up against it, and held her breath. Was he still in there? What was he doing? Her heart began thudding painfully.

It was a standing joke among those who worked at the shop that the only way to guarantee any privacy in the loo was to sing or whistle. Months previously, one of the screws had come loose and fallen out of the catch so that it was impossible to push the bolt home properly. It was something Mr Bailey was always meaning to fix but, somehow, never got around to. After so long, it was so much a part of the routine that no one really minded.

'In fact, it wouldn't be the same, somehow,' Mary, the woman who worked three afternoons a week, had once commented. 'I would miss the dulcet tones of Mr B singing "Moon River" at the top of his voice.' Everyone had laughed at the comment and, so far, the lock had remained unfixed.

Beth certainly couldn't hear any singing or whistling now. As she continued to strain her ear, however, she thought she could make out a much fainter noise. A kind of urgent moan. She stiffened. No one ever entered the loo if the door was closed without knocking first, just in case.

Before she could lose her courage, Beth raised her hand and gave the door a sharp push. There was a gentle click and the door gradually began to swing open. Her eyes widened.

Jonathan was standing in front of the loo. His body was turned sideways to her, facing the long mirror. He appeared totally oblivious to her presence. His jeans and pants were down round his ankles so that she had a clear view of his long bare legs and the swell of his left buttock. Its smooth skin was startlingly white against his sun-kissed limbs. Her senses were so heightened by her emotional state that she could even see the individual hairs on his legs. Soft and blond like threads of finest gold silk.

Breathlessly, she glanced at the mirror. Despite the fact that it had not been cleaned for some time, she could see the reflection of his body quite clearly.

His left hand was holding the bottom of his T-shirt well up above his hard, flat stomach. It was also clutching a small scrap of white cloth, maybe a tissue or a hankie. His eyes were tightly closed and his face was screwed up in a grimace, almost as if he were in pain. She lowered her eyes.

His right hand was wrapped round his fully erect penis and he was moving it up and down so rapidly that Beth could hardly follow the motion. As she watched, mesmerised, his mouth parted slightly and he made a soft grunting sound, whether of pleasure or pain she could not tell. His hand slowed and stopped. The fingers began gently kneading and squeezing the tip and his gasps became more urgent. He began pumping again as his buttocks tightened and loosened in rhythm with his movements.

All thoughts of catching him out and teaching him a lesson fled from Beth's mind. She was powerless to move, unable to take her eyes off the tantalising movements of his right hand and the shockingly erotic vision of his clenched fingers slipping up and down over his hard, erect penis.

The door reached the end of its swing and the handle banged loudly against the wall. Beth jumped and let out a small gasp.

Jonathan opened his eyes and spun round, his face filled with panic. Frantically, he reached out to push the door closed again. The cloth slipped from his fingers and fluttered to the floor. Jonathan made a grab for it and lost his balance. He let go of his cock and placed his other hand on the mirror to steady himself.

Beth gazed in open-mouthed wonder at the sight of his erection thrust out towards her like an accusing finger, pointing. She found herself staring in amazement at the long swell of his cock and the soft roundness of his testicles nestled at its base in their bed of silky curls. She had never seen a man like that before.

When he saw her standing there, Jonathan gasped with horror. He crouched down as far as he could and raised both hands to cover himself. As he clasped his erect cock again, the look on his face changed from horror to despair. Frantically, he grabbed himself as hard as he could, but it was too late. With a small jerk, his swollen penis reached the point of no return and a spurt of hot, sticky fluid burst from its shiny smooth tip to dribble through his fingers and run down his knuckles. His face relaxed completely and he groaned aloud.

Still unable to move or speak, Beth stared, transfixed, as his cock jerked and spurted in his hands and the semen began to ooze through his fingers.

Jonathan's moment of ecstasy passed and the sheer horror of his situation appeared to overwhelm him. He tried to crouch even lower to reach for his pants and jeans. He raised his bottom slightly as he struggled frantically to pull them up. His feet became entangled and he lost his balance yet again, stumbling backwards.

At that moment, Beth suddenly realised where she was. Scarlet with embarrassment, she began backing out of the doorway. Her breathing was ragged and her heart was thudding. What should she do? What could she do? In desperation, she blurted out the first words that came into her head.

'I'm sorry. I should have knocked first,' she whispered hoarsely as she turned and fled.

2

Beth had no memory of the journey home. Her mind was a complete blank from the moment she had fled from the loo until now, as she leant back against the inside of her front door with her heart thumping.

She must have said goodbye to Mr Bailey. She must have crossed the bridge, walked up the High Street and turned along Raleigh Avenue. She must have gone by the house where Jonathan lived with his mother, and then on down past the park fence and round the corner until she had come to her own home. She remembered none of it. Her mind was completely filled with the images of what she had just seen.

All thoughts of meeting Ann and Geraldine had been swept away. By now, they must have realised that she was not coming and wondered what had happened to her. She would have to worry about that later.

Weak at the knees, Beth headed into the kitchen and filled the kettle. What she needed now was a good, hot, strong cup of tea and two aspirin. While she waited for the water to boil, Beth perched on a kitchen stool with her elbows propped up on the work surface and her throbbing head resting in her hands.

Confused images of Jonathan's erection and taut, white buttocks flashed through her mind. She closed her eyes. She could still see every detail. The pictures were so vivid that she could almost smell the dampness of the corridor, the sharp aroma of the toilet cleaner and the perspiration of her own body.

She trembled visibly as she remembered the strange sounds Jonathan had made as his semen had pumped from him and seeped through his clenched fingers. Oh God, the look on his face when he had spun round and realised that she was standing there watching him! Like a fox turning to face a ravenous pack of hounds bearing down on him, or a trapped fly sensing the vibrations of an approaching spider. Whatever must he have been thinking?

Although Beth knew little about the opposite sex, the look on Jonathan's face had made it quite clear how mortified and humiliated he had been by her presence. He must have felt much as she would have done if he had walked in and caught her taking a pee. Despite the fact that she had failed to reprimand him verbally, as she had intended, she was quite sure that he had been well and truly punished for his behaviour.

'Quite right, too. He should be thoroughly ashamed of himself, the dirty little sod,' she muttered aloud. At least she needn't worry any more about him peering through the keyhole at her in her undies. If his expression were anything to go by, he would probably have trouble looking at her at all in future.

All things considered, everything had probably turned out for the best. She made the tea and sat back down. As she remembered the words she had whispered as she fled, she felt another rush of embarrassment. Of all the stupid, pointless, inadequate comments to have made . . .

Mind you, under the circumstances, it was difficult to imagine what words might have been any more appropriate. 'Feeling better now?' Or perhaps, 'If you're quite finished, maybe I could use the loo?' She giggled softly at her thoughts and then frowned. Perhaps she should have stood her ground and given him what for. Maybe she should have told him just how dirty and sordid his actions were.

The trouble was, it was difficult to apply those words to what she had seen. Although she had been half expecting it, the sheer impact of what she had witnessed had quite literally taken her breath away. Her body had felt so weak that, if she hadn't grabbed on to the doorway, she might have fallen. At that moment, what he had been doing had seemed neither dirty nor sordid. It had been natural and pure, almost artistic.

She wondered what would have happened if he hadn't noticed that she was watching him. What if he had been allowed to finish what he had been doing, naturally, without any interruption? Would he have come just then or would he have carried on even longer? She felt a sudden shiver of excitement tinged with regret at the idea.

For goodness sake, pull yourself together, she chided herself. The boy had taken unacceptable liberties and she had caught him out. That was it. Finished. It was time she forgot all about it and did something useful.

She glanced around the kitchen and decided that it was well overdue for a good clean. She had been meaning to empty out the cupboards and scrub the shelves for some time. Now was as good a time as any. She had nothing better to do now that she had missed out on the film. She must remember to call Ann and Gerri later and apologise for letting them down. She would have to say that she had had a bad headache or something. It was sort of true.

It was nearly five o'clock by the time Beth had replaced the last of the items in the now spotless cupboards. Just one last drawer and she would have a nice long soak in the tub. She picked up a washing-up brush and her hand slid up its slender handle. She closed her eyes.

Jonathan was standing in front of her with his hand

wrapped round his erection. She slid her own hand back down the handle. Is that what it would feel like? She had never really touched Tony there, except maybe by accident under the sheets. Certainly, she had never grasped it in her hand. Her movements quickened and she felt her nipples harden. Beth dropped the brush as if it had suddenly bitten her.

She hurried upstairs into the bathroom and put the plug in the bath. She turned both taps on full, then stripped off her dress and slipped out of her underwear. She fingered the soft, lacy material and smiled. Why had she never realised before how nice it was to wear such things? After work on Monday, she would go and buy herself several more sets. Maybe even those tiny red ones.

The hot water felt great on her aching shoulder muscles. Lazily, Beth picked up a bar of soap and soaped the bath sponge thoroughly. She lifted her arms and began to wash herself gently, stretching to reach down her back.

As she ran the sponge across her breasts, she watched her nipples spring up. Her breasts were actually very nice. Small and firm, thanks to the regular exercise in the gym. She moved the sponge lower, pushed it under the water, and slipped it between her legs. She closed her eyes and began to rub herself gently. Her whole body tingled. The phone rang.

Damn! Beth dropped the sponge guiltily. She stood up quickly and reached for the bath towel. As she swung her legs over the side, the water drained down her body and splashed into the tub. 'All right, I'm coming,' she muttered angrily.

The phone was in the bedroom. As she lifted the receiver, she noticed that her hand was still dripping with soap bubbles. Like his hand had been dripping. 'Hello?'

'Beth? Is that you? What happened? Gerri and I were worried about you.'

'Ann. I'm sorry. I was going to call you both later. I was just having a bath. I'm really sorry. I – I got delayed at the shop. Mr Bailey was late so I had to stay on,' she lied quickly. 'I really am sorry.'

Ann sighed with relief. 'That's OK, Beth. It wasn't important. We were just afraid that something might be wrong.'

'No, nothing's wrong.' Beth was suddenly glad that she had not said she was feeling unwell. 'How was the film?' She used her free hand to mop up the drips still running down her legs.

'Oh, it was all right. Gerri spent most of the time ogling the young lad selling ice creams. You know what she's like. As if the boys she drools over would be interested in her. Talk about cradle-snatching.'

Beth shuddered. 'Look, I'd better go. I'm dripping puddles all over the carpet. I'll see you at the club on Monday. I really am sorry about today.'

'Don't worry about it. I'll tell Gerri you're all right, shall I? I've got to ring her anyway to tell her that I've found her earring. Sorry to have got you out of the bath. Bye.'

Beth replaced the receiver and finished drying herself off. She returned to the bathroom to let the water out of the bath, then slipped into a dressing gown and made her way downstairs to get something to eat. The scene at the shop had put all thoughts of food from her mind earlier and she hadn't eaten anything since breakfast.

Surprisingly, she found she still wasn't very hungry. After she had picked at her food for a while, she gave up and tried to watch some TV. She couldn't concentrate on that either. Finally, she gave up and decided to have an early night.

It must have been about three o'clock in the morning when she awoke with a start. She had been dreaming about something, but the images were too muddled to remember properly.

Whatever it was, she must have been sweating profusely. She could smell her own body odour under the sheets, harsh and musky. She slipped her hand underneath her. Both her nightie and the bottom sheet were sopping wet.

Grimacing, she got up and slipped the nightie off. She found a clean one in the airing cupboard and donned it quickly, shivering at the chilly air on her still damp skin. She really needed a shower. It would have to wait.

It was a long time before she managed to get back to sleep again.

By the following Saturday morning, Beth was a complete mess. How could she possibly face Jonathan as if nothing had happened? In all honesty, of course, he should be far more embarrassed by what had happened than she was. So, why did she feel so awkward about it?

She wondered if she should say anything to him or just act as if nothing had happened. That would be the easiest, but it might not be the right thing to do. Maybe he needed more punishment than that? She thought about taking him to one side and telling him that he was never to behave so badly again. Maybe she should consider having a word with his mother about him.

Mrs Evans had been into the shop twice during the week. Both times, Beth had managed to avoid her. What could she say? 'Did you know your son is a dirty little pervert who spies on women through keyholes? Did you know that he has got a strong, muscular body and adorable little white buttocks ...'

She had been up far too early for work, so she found that she had plenty of time to get ready. She spent twice as long as usual doing her make-up, even using a little mascara and eyeliner the way Geraldine had shown her. She was delighted with the result. It made her eyes stand out and emphasised their colour. She brushed her long dark hair until it shone and, for once, left it hanging loose down her back instead of tying it up.

Excited, Beth took off her robe and slipped into the new red undies. She stood in front of the long mirror in the bedroom and twisted from side to side. Dressed in the skimpy red bra and panties, she found it hard to recognise herself. She was only just beginning to appreciate how much effect regular exercise and sensible eating had had on her. Tony would probably hardly know her.

She ran her hands over her breasts and down into the curve of her tiny waist, then out again around the flare of her hips. She looked great. She felt a sudden rush of confidence in herself and her body. For the first time, she began to understand what Jonathan might see in her.

Emboldened by what she saw, Beth strutted up and down. She thrust out her breasts and pulled in her tummy, then slipped the new blue dress over her head and smiled at the way it clung to her figure, emphasising all her curves. Feeling faintly foolish, she practised pulling the dress slowly over her head and then slipping it back on again in what she thought might be a seductive manner. What would Jonathan think if he could see her now?

As she walked down the road half an hour later, she had a sudden awful thought. What if Jonathan had been so humiliated by what had happened that he didn't come back to work again at all?

She took the long way round, so that she wouldn't have to pass his house. Even so, she was still far too early at the shop. Mr Bailey had not even finished sorting the morning papers. He gazed at her in astonishment.

'You're up with the birds today, Beth. Perhaps you would like to make us both a nice cup of tea while I finish up here?'

Beth nodded, glad to have something to do to pass the time. Jonathan wouldn't be in for at least another hour. If he came in.

'Did you have a word with Mrs Evans?' she asked Mr Bailey. He looked puzzled.

'You know. I suggested that you ask her to remind Jonathan how important it is that he doesn't let me down today.' Her voice sounded strange, almost desperate. Mr Bailey nodded.

'Yes. I told her.'

Beth smiled happily. As she disappeared out the back, Mr Bailey frowned.

Jonathan had been awake most of the previous night. He had just lived through the worst week of his entire life. If anyone had asked him to describe the most horrific thing that could ever happen to him, his worst nightmares would not have come close to the way he had felt when he looked up and saw Beth standing there.

Oh God, why did she have to come in just then? Had she guessed what he was doing and followed him? If only he had stood with his back against the door. How long had she been watching him?

And, then, to go and lose it like that! Come all over himself. No hole would have been too deep if, at that moment, the ground had opened up and swallowed him. Nothing that could ever happen to him, ever again, could be as bad. Except perhaps, one thing.

Beth might decide to tell someone about what he had done. What if she told Mr Bailey, or if any of his friends ever found out about it? He groaned aloud in utter despair. What if she decided to tell his mother?

In his more optimistic moments, which were few and far between, Jonathan had tried to tell himself that Beth would not say anything to anyone. She would be too embarrassed. But what if she did tell anyone? Would they believe her? Jesus! Of course they would. If only she hadn't been wearing those black lace undies. He had been watching her all that morning, his mind filled with thoughts of what he would like to be doing to her that night.

He had seen the way her shop overall stretched tightly across her buttocks when she moved. Usually, he could see the outline of her panties through the thin material and picture how she would look later, without the overall. With those black things on, the telltale outline had not been visible. For a while, he had thought that she wasn't wearing anything at all under her overall.

He remembered her standing there. Even now, he could still see her nipples in his mind. If she had been completely naked, he didn't think it could have excited him more. Oh God, why hadn't he leant against the door? He wondered if he could ever face her again.

As Saturday drew closer, he became increasingly desperate. Maybe he should phone in sick. Yes, that was it. He was feeling pretty sick. But then, if she was on her own and he let her down, she might be so angry that she would tell someone the real reason he wasn't there.

If only he had heard her come in sooner. He had been so wrapped up in his fantasies he wouldn't have heard a stampede of elephants! If only she hadn't been wearing that black underwear.

If she had been going to tell his mum she would have done it by now, wouldn't she? His mum often popped into the shop during the week. Maybe she was just going to pretend it had never happened at all.

Round and round, over and over, Jonathan agonised endlessly over his situation. One minute, he managed to convince himself it would be all right, the next minute he was plunged back into despair as he remembered the expression on her face.

Once or twice, he had even managed to convince himself that she had not been all that angry or shocked. She hadn't shouted or screamed or anything. She hadn't lost her temper and told him what she thought of his behaviour. She had been perfectly calm and reasonable. After all, she was an experienced woman, not a silly little girl.

Despite his humiliation, Jonathan hadn't been able to stop himself from continuing to fantasise about Beth. She was the most desirable woman he had ever seen. Compared to her, the girls at school were nothing. It was impossible to keep his thoughts from what he would like to do to her. He only had to think about her in the sexy black bra and panties she had been wearing that day and he could feel himself growing hard. He had found it completely impossible to concentrate at school all week.

As he stood in the bathroom that Saturday morning brushing his teeth, Jonathan pictured her again as he had seen her through the keyhole with her nipples showing through the delicate lace of her bra. He started to imagine what it would be like to kiss those nipples and to run his hands over her breasts. He put his hand over his groin and began to rub himself gently.

'Jonathan. Are you up yet? Get a move on. I promised Mr Bailey he could rely on you today.' His mother's voice made him jump. Quickly, he put one hand down the front of his jeans and tried to make himself more comfortable. His heart began pounding at the thought of being alone with Beth all day.

How would she treat him? What would he say to her? With a small sigh, he headed downstairs for breakfast. His feet dragged like a condemned man's.

Of course, it was hopeless to imagine that she might be the

slightest bit interested in him, he told himself moodily as he tried to force himself to eat something. He had to act normally. He didn't want his mother wondering if he was sick. She might even say he couldn't go in to work.

The best he could possibly hope for was that Beth would just forget the whole thing. Just, please, don't let her tell anyone.

And, just so long as she didn't make it impossible for him to watch her any more. He was already desperate to see her again. Whatever the cost, the humiliation, Jonathan knew that he would still spy on her. His cock began to harden just at the thought of her and he shifted uncomfortably on the kitchen stool, hoping his mother wouldn't notice anything.

When he finally arrived at work that morning, he found Beth was standing alone, behind the counter. As he walked through the door, he saw her blush from head to toe.

'Hello, Jonathan. How are you?' She smiled feebly at him.

Jonathan stopped in the middle of the shop. His face went bright red and he found he was having trouble swallowing. He couldn't stop himself from staring down the front of her overall. She had left the top two buttons undone and he could just see the swell of her breasts.

Mr Bailey came in from the back room. 'Hello, lad.' He peered at him curiously. 'Been running, have you?' he questioned him. Jonathan shrugged. Mr Bailey turned towards Beth. 'Now, you are quite sure you don't mind working this afternoon, Beth? I don't want to spoil your weekend.'

'No. It's fine, really. I don't have any special plans. It's no trouble, honestly. Besides, the extra money will come in useful.'

'Thank you. I must say my grandson and I are really looking forward to the match.' Mr Bailey beamed. 'Well. I'm all done here so I'll be off then, shall I? Don't forget, now. Just ring out for a pizza for your lunches, or send the lad to get you both something. My treat. After you have locked up this evening, post the keys through the letterbox. I'll pick them up when I get in.'

'Yes I will.' Beth nodded. 'Have a good time and don't worry about anything here.'

As soon as Mr Bailey had gone, Jonathan headed out to the stockroom and started to unpack a new supply of stationery that had arrived the previous day. He took his time, still uncomfortable at the thought of being alone with Beth.

As the hours went by, however, he felt himself growing increasingly optimistic. Obviously, she hadn't said anything to Mr Bailey. If she had intended to speak to his mother then she would probably have done it by now. It was still possible that she might take this opportunity to tell him off, yet even that was becoming less likely as the morning wore on. It looked as though she had just decided to forget the whole thing.

Perhaps she hadn't actually realised what he had been doing. If she had only been at the door for a couple of seconds, maybe she hadn't really seen all that much. Had he been worrying for nothing?

As the morning progressed, his fears receded further. Of course, with Mr Bailey away, there was no chance of watching her change at lunchtime, but since Beth was locking up that night, the shop would have to be closed before she went out the back to get changed. If he worked things carefully, maybe he could still be here too, with no one else around to disturb them.

His thoughts filled with unlikely yet delightful fantasies about what she might let him do to her.

It was around twelve o' clock by the time Jonathan had finished the unpacking and returned to join her in the shop.

Beth had spent the morning trying to collect her muddled thoughts. She was still wondering if she had done the right thing by saying nothing, but kept trying to convince herself that he had learnt his lesson. The poor kid had probably been living in terror all week at the idea she might tell someone. The kindest thing she could do was to be as nice to him as possible so that he realised that he needn't worry about it any more. After all, there had been no real harm done, had there? Apart from giving her a few restless nights.

She jumped when Jonathan came through from the back with a box of confectionery. Wordlessly, he began restocking some of the shelves.

'Don't forget to put it in from behind,' Beth reminded him, giggling to herself at the vivid image the words conjured up in her mind.

'Make sure the fresher ones are at the back,' she corrected herself quickly. She decided that didn't sound much better either. She looked away and hoped that he wouldn't realise why she was smiling.

As he worked, Beth watched him surreptitiously, noticing the way his eyes kept straying towards her. She was certain that, given half a chance, he would try to peep at her again. She was astonished at the idea. Was she really so attractive to him that he would risk it again, just to see her? The image of his erect cock sprang into her mind. She had done that to him. Her body had aroused him so much that he had been unable to help himself from ...

Could she arouse him that way again? It was a strange thought. Exhilarating. It made her feel strong and powerful.

Around one o'clock Beth sent Jonathan out for his lunch and gave him some extra money to bring her back a sandwich. Despite what Mr Bailey had said, the idea of sharing pizza with him was too uncomfortable, somehow. What would they talk about while they ate? She didn't even know what sort of things he was interested in. Swimming. What else? Music? Fashion? Football? She knew nothing about such things.

When he got back, Beth left him to manage the shop while she headed out the back to take a break and eat her own lunch. While she was there, she remembered that they were running short of cigars.

As soon as she had eaten, she fetched the key to the storage cupboards. She unlocked the doors and slid them open. The cigars she wanted were up on the top shelf of one of the cupboards, well out of reach. Beth cursed and went out into the passageway to find the stepladder.

The skirt of her overall was too tight to climb the steps properly. Angrily, she pulled it up over her knees and tried to struggle up on to the first step. It was hopeless.

'Jonathan?' she called. 'Do you think you could come and give me a hand for a minute, please?'

When he walked into the back room, Beth was still balanced precariously on the first step. Her overall was pulled up well above her knees, exposing her long, shapely legs and a tantalising glimpse of stocking top. She saw his eyes widen.

'I can't reach the cigars,' she explained as she stepped awkwardly back on to the floor beside him and smoothed down her skirt.

In the confined space between the two rows of facing cupboards, they were forced to stand so close together that she could feel the warmth of his breath on her face. She noticed that his eyes were now glued to the swell of her breasts and her excitement mounted.

'They're up there on the top shelf,' she told him. 'Next to the matches.' She stepped back out of his way and her feeling of power over him was so intense it made her feel light-headed.

As Jonathan began moving slowly up the steps, Beth stood below and followed him with her eyes. The sight of his buttocks enchanted her. She remembered how white they were and how soft and smooth his skin was.

What would he do if she reached out and put her hand on him there? Would he be excited by it, or would he think she was out of her mind? She was old enough to be his mother. Did he know that? He must know. Perhaps it didn't matter to him.

Jonathan moved up another step and leant out to reach for the cigars. His body swayed slightly and Beth reacted before she could stop herself. She reached up and placed one hand either side of his hips, as if to steady him. She felt a tingle of excitement in the pit of her stomach. Her hands were only inches from his buttocks.

Jonathan immediately stiffened and Beth could see the muscles in his thighs tightening involuntarily. Was he becoming aroused again too?

'Are you all right? Have you got them?' Her voice sounded strange again. Deep and husky. The tingle inside her grew stronger.

Without answering, Jonathan took hold of the box of cigars and started back down the steps. As he moved, he twisted round slightly so that one of her hands began to slide gently across his thigh towards his crotch. She could see his erection growing harder. Any second now, she would be touching him.

Beth quickly removed her hands and took a small step backwards. Terrified that he would see the flushed look on her face, she turned her back on the stepladder and slid another door open. As she pretended to rummage for something inside the opposite cupboard, she could feel her hands shaking. He was hard. As he had turned round, she had clearly seen the tightness of his jeans over his crotch. Just the touch of her hands on his hips had been enough to turn him on!

As he reached the ground, Jonathan swung round so that he was standing right behind her and her bottom was only inches away from him. Although there was not really enough room for him to move past her, she made no effort to get out of his way.

What would he do? If she moved at all, he would brush against her. The temptation to push herself back on to him was almost more than she could bear. Just one push and she would be able to feel his erection pressed against her. She held her breath.

Jonathan leant forward slightly and slipped his hand between her body and her arm as he placed the cigars on the shelf in front of her.

'There you are,' he told her, his voice cracking. He made no attempt to withdraw his arm.

Beth froze. His hand was hovering so close to her that she was afraid to move. He only needed to sway his body slightly and his fingers would be against her breast. There was nothing she could do to stop him. She found that she was almost willing him on.

Carefully, she edged backwards so that the material of her overall brushed against the front of his jeans. Jonathan gasped softly and pushed himself against her. His hand was still hovering in the air beside her.

Beth slid out from his embrace.

'Thank you. Would you put the steps away for me, please?'

Back in the shop, Beth stood shivering. She realised that she was holding her breath again and she released it with a long sigh. She had actually felt his erect penis pressed against her. There could no longer be any doubt whatsoever that she had turned him on again. What power! She had never had that effect on a man before. Certainly not on Tony.

Well, yes, obviously, she must have turned Tony on, but it had not been the same, somehow. She couldn't define it. With Tony, everything had always been, well, almost mechanical. This was different. Just a touch. That was all it had taken to arouse him! Just one touch. She had never been in control with Tony. Not like this.

Beth took another deep breath. He had deliberately tried to get her to touch him there when he had turned round on the steps. She had certainly been tempted. Afterwards, when he was pushed up against her, she had been certain he was going to put his hand on her breast. Her skin tingled as she imagined what it would have felt like. She could feel her nipples rubbing against her overall.

What was he doing now? Perhaps he was in the loo masturbating again because of her. Surely, he wouldn't risk her catching him a second time, would he? Her heart began pounding. She was already turning towards the door to the passageway when the front door opened and a customer came in. Disappointed, she turned back behind the counter. Five minutes later, Jonathan joined her. She thought his face looked strangely flushed, but she couldn't be sure.

By late afternoon, Beth had begun to feel as though the long day would never end. Fortunately, there was a constant stream of customers and she barely had time to look at Jonathan, let alone speak to him. It was almost five thirty before things quietened down. She checked her watch hopefully as the shop finally emptied. Close enough.

Beth walked across the shop, turned the OPEN sign round to CLOSED, and pushed the bolts across. Without saying anything to him, she headed out the back towards the staff room.

Once inside, she pushed the door to and thankfully removed her overall. She moved over to the chair, picked up her dress, and pulled it over her head. With one foot raised on the chair, she reached up to adjust her stocking. A floorboard creaked outside the door and Beth stiffened. Slowly, deliberately, she twisted round slightly towards the door and raised the hem of her dress. She checked to make sure that she was standing so he could see right up her skirt and then reached round to adjust her stocking again.

As the top of Jonathan's head touched the door it swung open, just as Beth had hoped it would when she had deliberately failed to shut it properly. Jonathan put out his hand and tried to pull it closed again. His fingers slipped and he stumbled into the room.

Without lowering her leg, Beth turned to face him. She stared openly at the hand now covering his groin. Her skirt was still raised so that he could see everything. She noticed with a small thrill that this was exactly where he was looking.

'I should have thought that you would have learnt your lesson last week,' she chided, trying her hardest to sound and look serious. 'You should be thoroughly ashamed of yourself.'

Jonathan stood completely still. His face looked as if it were carved from stone. His gaze never moved from between her thighs.

Beth smiled. 'What is it going to take to satisfy you?' she demanded, remembering the way he had felt pressed up against her. Boldly, she reached up and took hold of the zipper at the front of her dress. Slowly, she pulled it down below her breasts as her eyes stared straight into his.

'Go on. Have a good look,' she commanded. 'That's what you want, isn't it?' She pulled the two sides of the dress apart so he could see the tiny red bra.

Jonathan raised his head and she saw that his face was now filled with longing. Her feeling of power grew stronger. She could do anything she wanted to with him. He was like putty in her hands.

'How would you like it if I were to speak to your mother about your behaviour?' she suggested. 'What do you think she would say if she knew that her son was nothing but a peeping Tom?'

Jonathan's eyes filled with fear.

'No. Please don't do that,' he begged. 'Please. I'm sorry. I'll do anything you say, only please don't tell my mother.' His voice was squeaky with fright. Suddenly, he looked like a little boy who had been caught shoplifting.

Immediately, Beth felt guilty. It was cruel to torture him like this. The poor kid looked completely terrified. But, oh the power she had over him. Her eyes narrowed. With a feeling almost of disappointment, she saw his erection was now noticeably smaller.

'Can you give me one good reason why not? Don't you think you should be punished for spying on me? Don't you think you should be punished for what you were doing in the loo the other day?' She paused, then, when he didn't reply, added, 'Well, if I don't tell your mother, what else shall I do to punish you?'

'Anything,' Jonathan whispered desperately. 'Do anything you want. Just, please don't tell anyone.' He sounded almost as though he was about to burst into tears.

Beth smiled mischievously. 'All right then. Perhaps I won't tell anyone if you really don't want me to. Perhaps I can think of another way to teach you a lesson.' As she spoke, she raised her hand to her breasts and touched the soft lace of her bra with her fingers.

A spark of hope and longing flashed across his face. Beth glanced down. To her astonishment, he appeared to be growing harder again. God, she would love to see him doing it to himself again. To watch his hand moving up and down his cock and to see that look on his face, hear those sounds he made.

'I'll tell you what. Why don't you come round to my house one evening when I have had time to think up a suitable punishment for you?' Even as she spoke, she could hardly believe the words coming out of her mouth.

Jonathan stared at her. 'Come round to your house?' he stammered.

'Yes. You know where I live, don't you? It's not all that far from where you live. I've seen you cycling past sometimes.'

Jonathan flushed. 'When?' he squeaked.

Beth grinned, suddenly certain that it was no coincidence she had seen him near her house. He had probably been trying to spy on her there, too. Was there nothing he wouldn't do for a chance to watch her? She glanced down at his crotch and realised that his penis was beginning to strain against his pants again as the significance of her words sank in. She shivered.

'How about after work next Saturday?' She had been going to say 'tonight', but it suddenly occurred to her that it would do him no harm to sweat it out for another week, wondering what punishment she would think up for him. It would also give her a chance to think about it, too. She knew what she wanted to make him do, but would she ever find the courage to say it?

'Well? Will you come, or do you want me to have that little chat with your mother?'

'I'll come,' he whispered. 'I could come tonight, if you want,' he blurted out desperately.

Beth grinned. 'Next week will be fine,' she repeated softly. She zipped her dress back up and moved over to check that the back door was locked. Satisfied, she picked up her handbag and walked past him without another word.

Back in the shop, she quickly removed the cash from the till and placed it in the safe. After she had set the alarm, she looked around carefully to make sure that everything was as it should be.

'Time we were off home, Jonathan,' she called.

As soon as they were both outside, she locked the door securely and bent down to post the keys through the letterbox. She smiled to herself as she sensed him crouching down behind her, as if tying a shoelace. She could practically feel his eyes burning into the skin of her legs as he tried to peer up her skirt again. She straightened slowly and turned round. Jonathan stood up quickly.

'I'll see you next week, then,' she told him calmly, doing her best to keep her eyes off the bulge in his groin. 'I would walk with you, only I'm meeting some friends.' This was not entirely true, but Beth felt the need to get away from him as quickly as possible so that she could think about the implications of what she had just done. As she walked away, she could feel his eyes burning into her back again.

3

The following Friday lunchtime Beth met her friends outside the pub, as arranged.

It had been a strange week. In some ways, the days had seemed to drag by as if the weekend would never come. In other ways, however, the time had flown by. Only one more day to go and Jonathan would be coming round to her house.

She would see him before then, of course. He would be at work tomorrow with her, as usual. How would she behave towards him? Should she remind him about their arrangement or say nothing?

Probably better just to say nothing. Beth wondered if he had thought about it at all during the week. Was he worrying about what she might do to punish him or hadn't he even been thinking about it? Most probably, he was just wishing it were over and done with so that he could forget all about it.

If she could have been a fly on the wall in Jonathan's bedroom during the past week, she would have been left in no doubt at all just how much he had been thinking about her.

Once the four friends had ordered and paid for their drinks, they found themselves a table in a corner. Ann kept giving Beth funny glances as if sensing that there was something on her mind. Fortunately, she didn't say anything.

As soon as they had sat down, Gerri launched into a complicated and highly improbable tale about a young man from the health club who had been eyeing her up in the gym.

'His tongue was practically hanging out,' Gerri giggled. 'You should have seen him. If he had stared any harder, his eyes would have popped out.' She pulled a face that was, presumably, supposed to resemble the way the man had been staring at her. Ann and Sally laughed politely. Beth felt a sudden rush of annoyance.

Did Geraldine really think she was the only one who had anything worth looking at? She examined her friend objectively. Gerri was quite attractive, in a bold, brassy sort of way. Short red hair, pretty green eyes. Her figure was good too, although Beth thought her breasts were a bit on the large side. Did Jonathan like large ones? Perhaps he thought she was too small and skinny. Would he like the short, tight dresses Gerri wore and the tops that left practically nothing to the imagination?

He probably would. Gerri had told her often enough that she should show a bit more breast and exaggerate her curves. What would she wear when he came round tomorrow? Maybe she could go shopping on the way home.

'I think the Saturday lad at the shop has got a bit of a crush on me,' she announced suddenly. 'He's always staring at me.' As soon as the words were out, she regretted them. Why did she have to go and call him a 'lad'? She didn't want everyone to think she was only attractive to children. There was nothing childish about Jonathan's body or behaviour.

Gerri grinned. 'Good for him. What's he like? Has he got a nice bum?' She leered suggestively.

'He's very nice, actually.' Beth sprang to Jonathan's defence. 'Tall and slim and very mature for his age.'

'I hope you don't encourage him,' Sally commented. 'I think it's disgusting the way some young boys behave. Undressing you with their eyes.' She seemed to shiver with distaste. 'Just see you don't let him take any liberties with you.'

Beth flushed, remembering the way he had seemed to stare through her overall. 'It's not like that,' she insisted, more to convince herself than anyone else.

'I think it's quite sweet,' Ann interrupted. 'It must be very flattering to be admired by someone young like that. Not that there's any reason why he shouldn't find you attractive, Beth,' she added. 'You don't look anywhere near your age and you've got a lovely figure.'

As quickly as she could, Beth changed the subject. Soon, they were all absorbed in a heated political discussion in which everyone was siding against Gerri's typically outrageous views. Beth couldn't help noticing the way Ann kept looking at her, as if she had guessed that there was something else on her mind. Maybe she would say something to her later. She needed to talk things over and get her mind sorted out. Before they left the pub, she quietly asked Ann round that evening for dinner. That afternoon, she went window shopping for a new dress.

Later that evening, after the two women had finished their meal and cleared the dishes away, Beth poured them both a drink. Back in the living room, they settled down beside each other on the settee. With their feet curled up comfortably underneath themselves, they began to chat contentedly together about what they had been doing lately.

As usual, Ann was full of amusing stories about her colleagues at the bank where she worked part time. Although Beth did not actually know these people, she had heard so much about them from Ann that she was always interested to catch up on the latest gossip.

Tonight though, she was having trouble concentrating. Her thoughts kept returning to Jonathan and what she was going to do when he came round. Finally, she became aware that Ann was obviously waiting for her to respond to something.

She realised that she had no idea what her friend had been talking about.

'I'm sorry, Ann. I was miles away.' Beth put her drink down and leant back, her face troubled. Ann placed her own glass on the table in front of them and looked at her friend meaningfully.

'Come on, then, out with it. I know you've got something you are just dying to tell me. You've been acting funny for days. It's a man, isn't it?'

'No!' Beth exclaimed quickly. She grinned nervously and reached for her glass. Her heart was hammering painfully and the palms of her hands were becoming damp and sweaty. She looked back at Ann thoughtfully. Would her friend understand or would she be completely horrified, as Sally obviously would? Supposing she was so shocked that she never spoke to her again. Maybe it was better not to say anything.

On the other hand, though, she just had to tell someone what had happened. She needed to talk about it and sort out her own feelings before tomorrow night. She would burst if she kept it to herself much longer. I've known Ann for years, she reminded herself firmly. She's my closest friend. I can trust her with anything. Even this.

'What then? Oh, come on, Beth,' Ann pleaded.

Beth swallowed hard. 'You're right. I have got something I need to tell you,' she began, then stopped again. What did she say now? Guess what? I've been letting this sixteen-year-old boy ogle me in my underwear until he is so turned on he does it to himself in the loo while I watch. Oh God. How pathetic and sordid that would sound! She couldn't. Some things just couldn't be put into words.

Ann groaned. 'Spit it out, Beth, for goodness sake. I'm practically wetting myself with curiosity. Whatever it is, it can't be all that bad.'

Want to bet? Beth took another deep breath. She wouldn't say anything about tomorrow. She would just tell Ann about what had happened in the loo.

'Well, it's about Jonathan.' She paused again.

'Jonathan? The lad in the shop? The one who has got a crush on you? What about him?'

Beth giggled awkwardly, then forced herself to look serious. 'You have got to swear you won't breathe a word of this to anyone, Ann. Not ever. I mean it. Promise me?'

'Just tell me!'

'Swear it! No one. Especially not Geraldine.'

'Yes, yes. All right. I swear it. For goodness sake, just tell me!'

Beth giggled again. She could feel her face beginning to grow pink. 'Well, I think he has got more than just a bit of a crush on me. I think he really fancies me.'

Ann grunted impatiently. 'Is that all? I thought it was something terrible with all the fuss you were making. Young boys are always dreaming about the opposite sex. It's the way they are made. Just ignore it. He'll soon get over it.'

Beth felt a sudden rush of fear. She didn't want him to get over it. Not yet, anyway.

'What do you mean?' she demanded anxiously.

Ann grinned wickedly. 'Just that young boys are always fantasising about older women.'

Beth frowned. 'Very funny!'

Ann shook her head. 'No, I mean it. I read it somewhere in a book.' She flushed slightly, then grinned again. 'So what did he do? Did he make a grab at you, or what?'

'He's been spying on me in the shop,' Beth confessed. 'When I go out the back to get changed after work. He's been creeping up to the door to peer at me through the keyhole.' There. It was out. There was no turning back now.

Ann laughed. 'The dirty little sod.' Her eyes widened. 'Did you give him a good eyeful?'

Beth stared at her friend in amazement. It was true that they had both had a couple of drinks already. She had needed something to give her courage. Even so, Ann was not reacting the way Beth had expected her to. She seemed almost excited by the whole thing. Certainly not shocked.

'Well?' Ann demanded. 'What else happened? Does he know that you are on to him?'

Beth nodded and her face flamed as the scene in the loo rushed back into her mind. 'Oh yes, he knows all right. I caught him at it.'

Ann laughed again. 'I bet that taught him a lesson! I hope you gave him a good telling off. Or did you slap him?' She grinned mischievously. 'Perhaps you should have put him over your knee!'

Beth looked startled. 'Is that what you would have done?'

She began to picture Jonathan sprawled face down across her knees with his little white buttocks striped red from her slaps and his erect cock pushed hard against her thighs. She sighed heavily at the idea and shifted her own buttocks slightly, so that the heel of her foot was pressed between her legs.

Ann shook her head. 'Me? God no. I would have been too flustered to do anything. I just wondered. Mind you, I seem to remember reading that some men actually like being spanked, so maybe it wouldn't have been such a good idea.'

Beth was beginning to wonder which section of the library her quiet little friend spent most of her time in. Her own reading material was nowhere near as interesting as Ann's appeared to be. The quiet ones are always the worst, she remembered again. She forced her mind back to their conversation.

'Anyway. You don't understand. That's not what happened.'

She hesitated, then took another deep breath. 'I mean I caught him, at it,' she whispered, emphasising each word carefully. She knew her face was already glowing again. 'You know. In the loo. At it.' Beth moved her clenched hand up and down just above her groin to demonstrate.

Ann stared at her for a moment, her face puzzled. Suddenly, her eyes widened and she gasped aloud. 'No! You're kidding me! You mean he was actually...' Her own hand mimicked Beth's and she, too, began to blush.

Beth nodded. There was a moment's stunned silence and then both women began to giggle helplessly. Beth could feel the relief sweeping through her now that she had finally confessed. Well, it was kind of funny when you stopped to think about it.

Eventually, Ann stopped sniggering and wiped her eyes. 'Oh God. I can't believe it,' she spluttered. 'How? I mean, when? What exactly? Oh Jesus. Start at the beginning and tell me absolutely everything!'

Now that her own inhibitions had been released by her friend's positive response, Beth realised just how desperately she needed to talk about this.

'Well, it was a couple of weeks ago,' she began quickly. 'While I was changing, I heard the floorboards creaking outside the door again so I knew he was there. Then, when I heard him heading for the loo, I decided to see just what he was up to.'

Ann gazed at her friend, wide-eyed. 'You didn't!' she squealed. 'Good for you. I didn't think you had it in you! Go on. What happened next?' Ann's face was flushed with excitement and her eyes were sparkling. She had curled up in the same position as her friend and was squeezing her thighs together tightly.

Beth smiled to herself. Apparently, she wasn't the only one who had learnt how good that could feel.

'Well, I sneaked up and listened at the door,' she replied softly.

'And?' Ann whispered breathlessly as she squeezed her thighs together even more tightly.

'And, I could hear him making strange little moaning noises.' Beth smiled at the memory.

Ann put her hand over her mouth.

'Before I had time to lose my courage, I reached out and pushed the door.'

'Oh my God, you didn't?' Ann whispered.

Beth leant back and closed her eyes. She found that she could still picture the scene almost as clearly as if she were watching it all over again.

'There was a slight click and then the door swung open slowly. Jonathan was standing sideways to me, facing the mirror.' She sighed at the thought. 'Oh God, you should have seen it, Ann. His jeans and pants were down round his ankles and his eyes were tightly closed. He had absolutely no idea I was there.'

'What was he doing?'

Beth opened her eyes and glared at her friend impatiently. 'What do you think he was doing? His left hand was holding his T-shirt up above his stomach and his right hand...' She paused, then rushed the words out as quickly as she could: 'His right hand was wrapped round his thing and he was moving it up and down.' Without realising what she was doing, Beth began moving her own clenched fist up and down in front of herself again.

Ann gasped again. 'Did you see it?' she demanded. 'How big was it?'

'Of course I saw it. He was fully hard and rubbing it right in front of my eyes. I couldn't help seeing it! Side on and in the mirror!' Beth closed her eyes again and allowed the vivid images to wash over her. She was tingling all over just at the memory of it. No words seemed adequate to describe the pictures running through her mind. She remembered how it had felt when he had brushed against her more recently and the throbbing sensation between her legs grew more urgent. She placed her hands in her lap.

'I couldn't believe how quickly he was moving his hand,' she whispered softly, almost as if she were talking to herself. 'He was grunting to himself as if he was in pain.' Her mind filled with the images of the way Jonathan's buttocks had been tightening and loosening spasmodically as he had pumped, almost as if he had been pushing against something.

Ann's eyes were enormous. 'So, what did you do?' she demanded impatiently. 'I think I would have run as fast as I could before he saw me.'

Beth opened her eyes again. 'I couldn't move,' she confessed. 'I was completely mesmerised. I never imagined it would be like that. It made me feel, well, like when Tony and I were first together and he would hold me close and we'd kiss.'

'You mean, you got horny?' Ann savoured one of Geraldine's favourite expressions. She looked thoughtful. 'I suppose it must have been pretty exciting,' she admitted enviously. 'It's making me feel sort of funny, just talking about it.'

Beth sat up and threw a cushion at her. 'Horny, you mean?' she asked. 'Go on, admit it.'

'Well, all right, yes. I admit it is very erotic,' Ann agreed as she ducked the cushion. 'In fact, to be honest, it's the most erotic thing I've ever heard. I know women do it in front of men sometimes but I've never heard of it the other way round,' she admitted.

Beth looked startled. It had never even occurred to her that anyone might deliberately do something like that in front of someone else. She felt another shiver run through her body.

'Still, if it had actually happened to me,' Ann continued, 'I'd have been so embarrassed I probably wouldn't have known where to look. I don't suppose he happens to be good-looking too?'

Beth grinned. 'Which bits?' she questioned, and Ann blushed.

'You know what I mean,' Anne protested weakly.

Beth nodded. 'He's got a gorgeous body,' she admitted dreamily. 'Like Michelangelo's *David*. He's already got a slight suntan, except for where his trunks normally cover him, of course. He looked like he was wearing tiny white pants.' She shivered again at the memory.

'He's so hard and muscular,' she continued softly when Ann said nothing. 'Especially his – his – you know what! You should see his little bum! Geraldine would die for a handful of that. If I hadn't been frozen to the spot, I would have grabbed it myself. I could have stared at him like that for ever.'

'You did leave, didn't you?' Ann demanded suspiciously.

'Before I could move, the door handle banged against the wall,' Beth continued. 'It must have only been a couple of seconds, but it felt like an eternity.'

Beth picked up the cushion she had thrown at her friend and placed it between her legs. Without consciously being aware of what she was doing, she tightened her thighs around it.

Ann stared at her. 'Don't tell me he saw you?'

'He started like a frightened rabbit,' Beth told her. 'His eyes opened and he swung round, reaching out to push the door closed. He was standing front on to me so that I could see everything.'

Ann gulped and grabbed Beth's arm, then let go again and hugged herself in excitement. 'What on earth did he do?'

'When he realised I was there he tried to cover himself with both hands. He was just crouching there with his erection clutched in his hands, squeezing himself.'

Ann clenched her own legs even more tightly together and heaved a sigh. 'Poor little sod.' She smirked. 'I bet he must have felt a right prat. Did you give him what for?'

Beth shook her head. 'He made a small groaning sound,' she whispered. Her hand began gently moving the cushion between her legs as she pictured the image in her mind. 'Louder than before, as if he was really hurting. I could see his erection between his fingers. It was huge, like a balloon about ready to burst.' She looked thoughtful.

'You know, I don't think I ever saw Tony like that. Not properly. We always did it in bed where I couldn't see him.' She sighed gently, then continued. 'Anyway, before he could do anything else, he started to come. Right there, in front of me. He was crouched down as low as he could get and it just sort of pumped out between his fingers. I think he was trying to stop himself, but he couldn't.'

Beth was panting slightly now and she could feel beads of perspiration forming between her breasts. The material of her bra felt rough and harsh against her nipples.

'It was the most incredible thing I've ever seen, Ann. I just can't explain it. I wanted to walk forward and grab him. Pull him upright so I could see exactly what was happening.'

Ann was staring at her friend in silence as if too stunned to speak. Finally, when Beth remained silent, she found her voice.

'God. I wish I could have been there.' Her own voice was deep and husky. 'What happened next?' she asked.

Beth giggled. 'He tried to take a step backwards,' she muttered breathlessly. 'He was leaning forward trying to grab his jeans and pants to pull them up. His feet somehow got tangled up and ...' Beth's body quivered with mirth. She hadn't allowed herself to stop and think about how ridiculous it had been until now.

'He lost his balance and fell over backwards into the loo bowl,' she howled helplessly.

'Oh my God, he didn't!' Ann, too, began to laugh.

'He did! His legs went up in the air and his hands flew out to the sides to try and save himself. I had a full view of everything. He wasn't so hard any more, but it was still quite firm. I could see the individual hairs curling around the base of it, sort of wet and sticky. Like his hands. He was wet and sticky everywhere, come to think of it.' She stopped laughing and looked thoughtful again. Then, with a small sigh, she reached for her drink. She found that her hands were shaking so much she could barely hold the glass.

'I still wish I could have seen it,' Ann confessed again later, when they had composed themselves and Beth had poured them both another gin and tonic. 'I have always wondered what it would be like to watch a man doing that.' She stared at her friend thoughtfully. 'What has he been like with you since? Has he learnt his lesson or is he still spying on you? Maybe you should still punish him?' She grinned. 'Or, you could let me do it,' she suggested cheekily as she licked her lips.

'I don't know what to do.' Beth coloured slightly. Should she tell Ann anything else? Should she confess the way she had deliberately teased Jonathan the following week? How she had watched him bulging with desire for her and felt him pressed against her? Should she tell her friend that he was coming round to her house the following evening to be punished? Or what she intended his punishment to be? Perhaps she had better wait and see how it turned out first.

Ann was staring at her curiously. 'He's still interested in you, isn't he?' she demanded. 'Jesus. I bet he is so hot for you that he'll do anything you ask him to. Especially if you threaten to tell anyone. Just imagine what you could do with him if you wanted to! At that age, boys are so desperate for it they can hardly think about anything else.' She lowered her voice. 'I read once that they can just keep doing it, over and over, if they want to.'

'Ann! You're worse than Geraldine is,' Beth exclaimed in mock horror. 'Honestly, I never would have suspected it of you.' Beth realised that she was feeling so much better about everything that she was almost tempted to confess her plans. Ann might have a few ideas about how she should handle the following evening. On the other hand, maybe it would be better to keep it to herself for now. After all, Jonathan might not even bother to turn up.

'Drink up,' she said. 'I feel like getting really merry this evening. There's a good movie on later I thought we might watch. Gerri says it's supposed to be quite naughty in places.'

4

By nine thirty the following morning, Beth knew that she couldn't kid herself any longer. He wasn't coming in to work that day. Maybe he wouldn't come in again at all. Perhaps she would never see him again.

The shock and disappointment were so deep that Beth could feel the tears burning behind her eyes. She must have been mad to think that he was seriously interested in her. What a fool she had made of herself flirting with him the previous week. How he and his friends must have laughed about it.

'You don't seem quite yourself today, Beth. Is something wrong?' Mr Bailey's face seemed full of concern.

'No. I'm fine. Just a bit of a headache,' Beth lied quickly. 'Isn't it time you were on your way? I'll be quite all right on my own.'

Mr Bailey shook his head. 'Since Jonathan can't make it in this morning, I thought I would stay on and give you a hand. Things can get quite hectic here on a Saturday.'

'Is Jonathan sick?' she asked as innocently as she could. 'I wondered why he's a bit late.'

'Didn't I tell you? Sorry. It must have slipped my mind. Jonathan has got a swimming contest or something for the county. He won't be in until after lunch.'

The relief was so great that Beth felt her legs turn to water. She had to put her hand on the counter to steady herself. Mr Bailey peered at her worriedly.

'Are you sure you're all right? You've gone quite pale.'

'I'm fine,' Beth assured him. Jonathan hadn't disappeared without a word. He might still be coming round this evening, after all! Her hands began shaking at the thought. Quickly, she put them behind her back and grinned.

'Honestly. My headache's almost gone already. I'll just go and make us a good strong brew, shall I?'

While she waited for the kettle to boil, Beth tried to picture what Jonathan would look like in his swimming trunks. Were they the loose, boxer-shorts type, or was he wearing a pair of those tiny little nylon things which showed every bulge? He would need to be careful not to get aroused wearing a pair of those or his tip would poke up out of the top. It must be a bit awkward for him at times. As she lifted the kettle, she had to use both hands to stop the water from spilling everywhere.

The morning dragged by. It was funny how empty the shop seemed without him. Beth had never noticed before how boring her job could be.

As soon as lunchtime arrived, she escaped quickly to do some shopping. She had already had a quick look the previous afternoon and had spotted two or three dresses that might do. One in particular had caught her eye, but she hadn't managed to pluck up the courage to go in and try it on. Now, she paused outside the window and examined it again.

The dress was black and made of some kind of clinging jersey material. It had a low neckline and long, off-the-shoulder sleeves. The waist was fitted and the skirt flared out in a prettily fluted hemline. She doubted if it would come halfway down to her knees.

Beth plucked up her courage, opened the door and went inside.

'May I help you?' The saleswoman was around her own age. She was dressed in a no-nonsense tweed skirt and jacket with a high-necked, lacy blouse. She looked plump and middle-aged.

'Yes, please. I'd like to try the dress in the window. The black one.' Beth was certain she was turning red.

'The black one?' The saleswoman managed to make the request sound faintly ridiculous.

'Yes. It's for a cocktail party,' Beth lied. 'You know. The trusty little black number.'

'We have got quite an extensive range of cocktail dresses,' the saleswoman informed her smugly. 'Perhaps I could show you some of them?'

'I'll just try the black one,' Beth insisted stubbornly, her face glowing.

'Certainly, madam. This way please.'

She was ready far too early for him. While she waited, Beth twirled in front of the mirror in her bedroom and peered at herself from all angles. The dress fitted her to perfection and showed off every curve, just as Geraldine had advocated. The material was so fine that she could almost see the outline of the mole on her stomach through it. Thank heavens she had been too nervous to eat anything all day or her tummy would be sticking out as if she were four months gone.

Beth giggled as she remembered the look on the saleswoman's face when she had tried it on. Although she had pretended to look disapproving, Beth had detected a slight trace of envy in the stare. She tried to imagine the saleswoman dressed like this with her flab bulging out everywhere. She smiled happily at the sight of her own slender figure in the mirror.

Was it too short? Beth examined her legs critically and was pleased to see how shapely they looked in the high heels. She would have to be careful how she bent over or Jonathan would see the tops of her stockings. In fact, if she even so much as twirled too quickly, he would have a pretty good view.

She leant forward to get a look, bending from the waist to

show her figure to best advantage. Her breasts swelled at the low neck and she adjusted the top carefully. She had never worn a dress with shoulders like this before.

'I bet that would get him going,' she said aloud, surprised at how good she was feeling about herself. It was amazing what new clothes could do for your self-confidence.

Beth moved over to the dressing table and checked her make-up for the umpteenth time. She hardly recognised the face staring back at her from the mirror. Her long dark hair framed her face nicely, freshly washed and gleaming from the brushing she had given it. Her eyes looked huge with her lashes carefully thickened with mascara, and her cheeks were glowing with more than just the gentle brush of blusher. She had never looked better in her life. If Tony could see her now, he would wonder what he ever saw in Janet. Tony's new wife might be a few years younger, but she was definitely a bit on the plump side.

Maybe Tony likes his women plump. Perhaps that wasn't why he had left her. Was she too thin now? Perhaps she would be better off wearing a dress that didn't show her figure quite so clearly. As she hovered anxiously, filled with indecision, the doorbell rang.

Beth jumped visibly. Her heart felt as if it had abandoned its normal resting place and lodged itself in her throat. She struggled to take a breath. Was it possible to suffocate with fear? Was this what having a heart attack felt like? The bell rang a second time and Beth managed to force some air into her lungs. As if sleepwalking, she made her way out of the bedroom and down the stairs.

As she opened the door, Jonathan was just reaching up to push the bell for a third time. His face looked pale and anxious and Beth wondered whether it was caused by fear of what she would do to him or worry that she was not at home.

'Hello, Jonathan. Come in.' Beth stood back and held the door open wide for him. Her voice had the same husky tone she had noticed before. She cleared her throat quickly.

'So. Did you win your swimming contest?' she asked, as she closed the door behind him. 'Straight through there,' she added, pointing along the hallway towards the living room.

Jonathan looked around nervously for a moment then rested his gaze on her slim, shapely figure in the short, tight-fitting dress. He grinned nervously.

Beth put a hand on his arm and led him along into the living room. She thought she could feel him trembling at her touch, but her own hands were shaking so much that she couldn't be sure.

'Have a seat.' Beth indicated the chair opposite the settee. 'Can I get you something to drink?' The polite phrase sprang to her lips automatically. She and Tony had once done a lot of entertaining. She was good at it. The role of perfect hostess gave her confidence.

When she noticed the strange look he was giving her, Beth suddenly realised how ridiculous her behaviour must seem to him. Boys his age didn't go calling on people for a social chit-chat. He probably didn't even drink! Oh God, why hadn't she thought to buy a bottle of coke or something?

She tried again. 'Sit down, Jonathan,' she commanded firmly. 'I'll just make us a cup of coffee and then we will discuss what we are going to do about your behaviour.' There, that was better. More as if she was one of his schoolteachers or something. Did he have female schoolteachers? Maybe he fantasised about them too. She felt a sharp twinge of jealousy at the idea.

Automatically responding to her tone, Jonathan sat down quickly on the chair. He said nothing.

Beth hurried out into the hallway and headed for the kitchen. She had noticed the way he watched her skirt floating around her when she moved. She liked the looks he had given her.

As she stood in the kitchen waiting for the kettle to boil, she rested her arms on the work surface and tried to compose her thoughts. Suddenly, she sensed his presence behind her. Before she could turn round, Jonathan had moved across the room and put his hands on her waist.

Beth jumped and her body went rigid. Jonathan moved closer and pressed himself against her. His hands slid round over the soft material of her dress until his fingers were gently caressing the sides of her breasts. She shuddered and closed her eyes. She had never felt like this with Tony. She fought the urge to turn round and press her lips against his.

'I bought you something.'

Beth jumped at his words, then jumped again as she felt his fingers place something cold round her neck. His hands moved round further and began to slide down the wide neck of her dress. She felt a rush of longing as her nipples began to harden. Frightened that he would feel them through her dress, Beth shrugged her shoulders and pushed him away with her elbows so that he stumbled backwards. She looked down.

Jonathan had placed a gold, heart-shaped locket round her neck. Its centre was filled with a dark-red stone of some kind that shone as the light caught it. Although it was obviously only cheap costume jewellery, she was touched by the thought behind it. Was this his way of apologising, or did he hope that it would stop her punishing him?

'Thank you, Jonathan. It's lovely.' Beth picked up the kettle to make the coffee and then turned round, a mug in each hand.

'It doesn't get you off the hook, though. Let's go back through and have that little chat, shall we?' Beth deliberately avoided looking down at his groin. She knew how aroused he was. She had felt him quite clearly through her dress.

Visibly quivering with desire, Jonathan followed her back into the living room. At her insistence, he sat back down on the chair and she saw him wince. She smiled at the way he crossed his legs and placed his hands in his lap as if to try to hide the bulge in his jeans.

Still smiling, she placed the steaming mugs on the small table and sat down on the settee in front of him. She crossed her own legs slowly and Jonathan took a long, shuddering breath. His eyes began to roam restlessly around the room as if he were trying to get his mind on something else. He shifted uncomfortably from one buttock to the other, uncrossing then recrossing his legs.

Beth stared at his face thoughtfully and noticed how flushed he was and how bright his eyes looked. Slowly, she lowered her gaze. His jeans looked as if they were about to split open. She could almost imagine the noise of the stitching as it began to give under the strain. She licked her lips and squeezed her thighs together tightly. She was so damp that she was afraid she would stain her new dress.

'So. Have you had a chance to think about your behaviour?' she demanded. 'What do you think I should do about it?'

Jonathan didn't answer. His eyes continued to look around nervously. His mouth was clamped tightly closed as if he were gritting his teeth.

Beth grinned and wondered why she had been so nervous about this. He was obviously captivated by her. Given half a chance, he would probably rip off her clothes and make love to her right now. What further evidence did she need? Her power over him was absolute. As Ann had suggested, he would probably do anything she asked him to. What else was it Ann had said? 'They can just keep doing it, over and over, if they want to.'

Maybe that was what he wanted. Was he so turned on by her that he would be willing to do it for her now? Just like he had done it in the loo? Beth could feel her own desire building up inside her, urgent and demanding, almost as if she needed to go for a pee yet, somehow, different. She squeezed her thighs together again and the pressure grew even more intense.

Jonathan watched her avidly, like a leopard watches its prey.

'Why don't you come and sit over here,' she said invitingly as she patted the cushion beside her. 'We'll have a little talk about what to do with you.'

Jonathan appeared to need no second invitation. Within seconds, he was perched beside her with his arms hovering awkwardly in front of him as if he didn't know what to do with his hands.

Beth placed her hand on his thigh and was thrilled to feel how much he was trembling. Almost absent-mindedly, she began to move her fingers slowly up his leg towards his groin. Her fascination with his arousal was drawing her like a magnet.

Jonathan shuddered and put his right arm around her shoulder. He pulled her towards him and placed his lips on hers. His left hand reached up and cupped her left breast. He squeezed it gently and Beth sighed with pleasure.

Jonathan pushed his tongue against her lips and forced them open. He thrust it inside her mouth, seeking her own tongue. Beth shuddered and pulled back in surprise. She had never been kissed like that before. Jonathan squeezed her breast harder and raised his head to kiss her again. As he did so, he dropped his hand from her breast and began to slide it up her leg under her skirt.

Beth pushed him away quickly, terrified he would feel how

wet she was. She shifted herself along to the far end of the settee and laughed breathlessly.

'Jesus. You're like an octopus,' she complained. 'In case you've forgotten, you are supposed to be here so that I can punish you.'

Jonathan continued to say nothing. His face was still flushed. He was breathing heavily. Beth had a feeling that he was about to grab her again. She felt a brief tinge of fear. Supposing this got out of hand? Would she be able to stop him from forcing her? Would she want to?

'Get up!' In her fear, the words came out loud and commanding. He stared at her in confusion.

'What?'

'You heard me,' she repeated loudly. 'Stand up.'

Jonathan stood up. His jeans were bulging in front of him, almost level with her eyes. To her delight and amusement, he quickly lowered his hands to cover himself from her penetrating gaze. Beth smiled and fingered her new locket.

'Bend over my knee. Let's see if a good spanking will teach you how to behave.' Ann had said that men enjoy being spanked. Well, she would soon see.

Jonathan stared at her as if she had gone mad. Beth pursed her lips.

'I thought we had agreed that you were going to let me punish you?' she reminded him. 'Of course, if you prefer, we can always leave it to your mother.'

A look of fear crossed his face. 'No!'

Slowly, he began to bend down over her knee.

'Not like that. Take your jeans down. I want this to sting so that you will remember it.'

Jonathan stood up again and stared at her blankly. Beth sighed.

'All right. I'll do it for you, then.' As she spoke, she took hold of the top of his jeans with both hands and undid the button. As she began to pull the zipper down, she marvelled at the sight of his swollen cock bursting out through his underpants. As the zipper came all the way open, she wondered how he ever managed to fit it in that tiny space at all.

Gently, she eased his jeans down over his buttocks then began to remove his underpants. Jonathan gritted his teeth and struggled to control himself. His hands moved round to cover himself again. Playfully, Beth slapped them away.

She almost gasped aloud as his erect penis burst free from his clothing and stuck out proudly in front of him. She didn't remember it being so big or hard the last time she had seen it. Beth resisted the urge to reach up and fondle it.

'Now bend over,' she said softly.

Jonathan screwed his eyes tightly closed and leant forward across her legs. She could almost see the struggle going on within him. It was as if he was torn between the excitement at the idea of his prick touching her practically bare skin and the utter humiliation of exposing himself like this in front of her. His face was scarlet with embarrassment.

'Right down.' Beth raised her left hand in the air.

Before she could strike him, Jonathan's cock made contact with her leg. They both gasped. He was so stiff. Beth wanted him to push himself against her as hard as he could. Without thinking about what she was doing, she lowered her hand on to his buttocks and pushed down, forcing him against her. At the same time, she moved her legs slightly underneath him and tightened the muscles of her thighs.

Jonathan quivered from head to toe. He thrust once against the smoothness of her stockings and then lost it completely. His come pumped out of him in waves. He groaned with pleasure and then lay still, panting.

Beth froze. She was shaking all over with the emotion of

the moment. She could feel the wetness soaking through her stockings and the pressure of his cock against her. She ran her hand over the smooth whiteness of his buttocks and shivered at the way his muscles jumped and flexed at her touch. A sudden wave of disappointment ran through her. It was all over and she hadn't actually seen him come.

She raised her hand and gave him a sharp, stinging blow. The white skin turned as red as his face and Jonathan jumped violently. She pushed him off.

'If you've made a mess on my dress you are going to wish you had never been born,' she threatened softly as she pulled the skirt up away from the dampness so that her stocking tops were exposed.

'Get up. Go and clean yourself up. The bathroom is at the top of the stairs.'

Jonathan straightened up. His eyes were fixed on the bare skin above her stockings. Beth cleared her throat. He turned his head away quickly and reached down to pull up his clothes, still keeping his head carefully averted.

Beth reached out, put her hand on his arm, and pulled him round towards her. 'Leave your clothes here, Jonathan. I'm not finished with you yet.'

Wordlessly, Jonathan removed his shoes and slipped his feet out of his jeans and pants. Still without looking at her, he turned away and headed for the stairs. Beth watched him leave. He should have looked ridiculous in just his T-shirt and socks with his white buttocks striped red where she had slapped him. Yet, ridiculous was not the word that sprang to mind.

She stood up, undid her soiled stockings and slipped them off. She rolled them up into a ball and took them out to the kitchen bin. As she headed back out into the hallway, she met him coming down the stairs. He stopped, embarrassed. Immediately, his hands moved round to his groin to cover himself.

Beth frowned. She moved up on to the first step, reached out and pulled his hands away almost roughly. She wanted to look at him.

His penis was curled up limply against his damp body hair, like a puppy curled up in its basket. His testicles were hanging loosely underneath and swaying slightly from side to side as he moved. Before she could stop herself, Beth reached out and placed her hands on his thighs. Slowly, she slid them up on to his hips. Gradually, she began moving them towards each other across his stomach. Immediately, his cock stirred, twitching at her touch as if it had a life of its own. She moved her hands closer and he began to swell.

'I don't think you have quite learnt your lesson yet, do you?' she whispered, entranced at her power over him. Already, he was almost fully erect again. Reluctantly, she removed her hands before she gave in to the overwhelming temptation to stroke him.

She walked back into the living room with Jonathan following. His hands had automatically moved round over his crotch again and, as she watched, he began to fondle himself. His erection reached full size again.

Beth picked up the blanket that was lying over the back of the settee and spread it out on the floor in the middle of the room. She heard Jonathan's breathing quicken.

'Lie down there and do it,' Beth commanded.

Jonathan stared at her in confusion. 'Do it?' he whispered. 'Do what?'

'Lie down and do what you were doing to yourself in the loo. Maybe that will teach you to behave. From now on, every time you feel like playing with yourself, perhaps you will remember me watching you. That should be a good lesson for you.'

When he still hesitated, Beth smiled. She ran her hands

slowly over her breasts and down her body. 'Perhaps you need to watch me first to get you in the mood,' she suggested boldly. 'The way you watch me at work.' She put her hand on her leg and began to move it slowly up under her skirt.

Jonathan's eyes widened. As though unable to resist, he wrapped his hand round his cock and began to move it up and down. Red-faced, he sank to his knees in front of her with his buttocks resting on his heels. He hunched forward slightly, trying to hide himself from her gaze.

Beth removed her own hand and stared down at him. Jonathan's hand began to move more quickly. He closed his eyes and turned his head away from her. She moved round slightly and pushed him right back on to his heels so that she could see him better.

As she watched, his face tightened and his expression changed. His lips parted and he began panting softly as he kneaded and squeezed himself. A dribble of liquid appeared on the tip of his penis.

Jonathan groaned loudly and resumed pumping up and down rapidly. His other hand reached down between his legs. His eyes were still tightly closed and she had the feeling that he had now forgotten where he was, totally absorbed in what he was doing. He caressed the skin under his balls and his face twisted as if he were in pain.

Beth sank back on to the settee. Her own breathing was shallow and rapid. She felt as if her body were on fire. Her nipples were so hard that they were almost painful and her stomach felt as if it were tied in knots. Unable to stop herself, she pushed up her skirt and placed a hand between her legs. Her panties were dripping wet, as if she had peed herself. She crossed her legs so he could not see what she was doing, slipped her fingers inside, and ran them across her pubes. She shivered as the waves of longing washed over her.

Jonathan suddenly stopped pumping and squeezed himself tightly. His face relaxed and several jets of come shot out of the tip of his penis and landed on the blanket. Jonathan moaned, then slumped forward on to his thighs with his buttocks raised slightly into the air.

Beth removed her own hand quickly and smoothed down her dress. She felt keyed-up and restless, as if unsure of what to do next. She knew some women did it, but she had never felt comfortable about the idea of masturbating herself. She had always been taught that it was not something 'nice' girls did.

She glanced down at Jonathan. Perhaps it was a bit late to be worrying about what nice girls did or didn't do. Her mother would have a fit if she could see her darling daughter now. Maybe it was about time she did a little experimenting with pleasuring herself. She could always ask Ann about it. She had probably read a book on the subject. Beth giggled.

'I think you have been punished enough for now, Jonathan, don't you? Perhaps it's time you went home.'

Jonathan nodded and began to replace his clothes. His face was already flaming again. Neither of them spoke.

As soon as he was dressed, Beth showed him out. As she closed the door behind him, she let out a long, deep sigh. She went back to the living room and rolled up the soiled blanket, then headed into the kitchen. What she needed now was a long, stiff gin and tonic. She could feel her panties wet and cold between her legs and she sensed a strange burning deep inside her.

Shuddering, Beth lifted her dress and began peeling the damp underwear down her legs. She pretended that he was standing there watching her and pictured how his body would respond. She stepped out of them, stooped down to pick them up, and popped them into the washing machine with the stained blanket.

If Jonathan was going to be allowed to come round and entertain her again, she would have to overcome her inhibitions about masturbation or she would go mad. Well, there were plenty of those sorts of books and magazines in the shop. Perhaps it was time she did some reading of her own. Thoughtfully, Beth began fingering the golden locket again.

5

It was around mid-morning the following Monday when Mr Bailey announced he was popping out for half an hour to run a few errands. As soon as she was alone, Beth hurried over to the magazine section.

The adult magazines were on the top shelf and Beth found that she could not reach them properly. Cursing under her breath, she hurried out the back and fetched the stepladder. When she returned, she propped it up below the shelf and looked around quickly to make sure no one was watching her. At least she could pretend that she was stocking the shelf or something if a customer should come in. She hiked her skirt up and began to climb.

They were all girlie magazines. Apparently, there wasn't much call around here for pictures of naked men posing in all their glory. Even if there had been, she doubted if Mr Bailey would have stocked them. With so many schoolchildren in and out of the shop every lunchtime, she knew some of their customers weren't very happy about him having these here, either.

Beth chose one at random and opened it curiously. Soon, she was engrossed. How did these girls ever find the nerve to pose like that? Didn't they realise what men might do to themselves while they were looking at them? Beth pictured Jonathan fondling himself at the sight of the erotic pictures. She pushed the thought away quickly, unwilling to admit to the feelings of jealousy it aroused in her.

She turned the page and studied a series of shots of a dark-haired beauty set against a jungle backdrop. In each picture, the images became more explicit as the girl undressed. First her skirt and top then her bra, until finally, in the last pose, she wore nothing but a long gold chain round her neck.

Beth examined the final photo avidly. The girl was lying on her back on a rug with her eyes closed and her face serene. She appeared completely relaxed and at peace with herself. She had one leg bent at the knee and her hands were straight down by her sides. Her skin was golden brown all over and she had a few drops of moisture on her breasts and stomach, as if she had just been for a swim. Shafts of sunlight were falling across her body, accentuating the areas of shadow at her breasts and thighs.

Her breasts were tiny and rounded, the nipples hard and erect and the skin puckered slightly around their darker-coloured tips. Beth's eyes moved on down her body. She drew a sharp breath. The girl was shaved cleanly between her legs so that her clitoris and vagina were clearly visible.

Beth examined the shaved area between the girl's legs. Her sex-lips were pink and moist and the tiny clitoris looked like the bud of an exotic flower. Beth put her hand over her groin and rubbed herself gently, feeling her own thick pubes under the material. She had never thought about shaving herself there.

Excited, Beth turned the page and avidly examined a large-breasted redhead who immediately reminded her of a younger version of Geraldine. The model in these photos hadn't shaved herself. Her whole pubic area was covered with a mat of thick, wiry red curls. Beth was shocked by a sudden longing to run her fingers through it.

In the final picture, the girl had her hand down between her thighs so that her fingers were gently caressing her outer lips. The girl's face was flushed, her eyes closed and her mouth slightly open. Her facial expression reminded Beth of the way Jonathan had looked just before he had exploded, and the burning sensation inside her intensified.

Beth closed the magazine and reached for another one. This time, she paused to read the letters page. Within seconds, her face was beetroot. How could people write such things? Perhaps they weren't real and the magazine just made them up. Even so, someone must have written them.

She lingered over one explicit account of a man who had made his girlfriend masturbate while he and his best friend had watched. Her flush deepened. How could the girl have found the courage to do it? Yet, it was only what she had made Jonathan do in front of her. Where was the difference?

She knew that some men liked to watch women doing that. Ann had said that she knew of some women who did it as part of their regular love-play with their boyfriends. Would Jonathan enjoy watching her playing with herself as much as she enjoyed watching him? Intrigued, she began to concentrate more closely on the description of what the woman had done to herself. The shop door opened and the bell rang loudly.

Beth jumped and hastily replaced the magazine on the shelf. Quickly running her fingers through her hair, she took a deep breath and then hurried down the steps. As she moved, she made a careful note of which magazines she had been looking at. When she left the shop later to meet her friends, they were carefully folded inside a cookery magazine in the bottom of her shopping bag.

As soon as they had finished their lunch, Beth and her friends piled into Geraldine's car and headed for the swimming baths. Normally, they swam at the pool belonging to the health and fitness club they all belonged to, but today it had been emptied for cleaning.

'Thank goodness for an excuse not to have to work out first,' Ann commented. 'Usually, by the time I've finished in the gym, I'm too exhausted to enjoy it.'

'Talking of enjoying things, has anyone thought any more about our holiday? If we don't do something about booking it soon there won't be anything left,' Sally chided them.

They had been talking for weeks about arranging a summer holiday together but, so far, no one had been able to agree on where or when they wanted to go.

'I think it's already a bit late now,' Beth muttered. If she was honest, she wasn't really all that keen on the idea. Although she was very fond of Gerri, it was easy to have a bit too much of her boisterous company. Two full weeks might be more than she could stand.

'Some of the best bargains are on offer if you leave it to the last minute,' Ann chipped in. 'One of the girls at the bank saved a small fortune like that last year.'

'Why don't we just forget about the summer and book something for Christmas?' Gerri suggested. 'I've always fancied having a go at skiing. We could go to Switzerland or even Italy.'

'No fear.' Sally shuddered. 'I'm not paying to freeze to death. I want somewhere hot and sunny.'

'Not too hot and sunny,' Gerri argued. 'You know how easily I burn.'

'People get burnt skiing too, you know.'

Beth slumped back wearily in her seat as the other three continued to argue. They would never agree on anything. It had been exactly the same last year. It was a shame she couldn't take Jonathan away on holiday with her. Now, that would be fun. She shut her eyes and tried to block out the heated voices as she allowed her imagination to run riot.

It had been Geraldine's idea to go to the public baths. It was only after they had arrived and changed into their swimming things that Beth realised why. She had forgotten that it was half term that week. The pool was swarming with students of all ages.

Geraldine rolled her eyes expressively and made a great show of licking her lips. 'Just feast your eyes on all those healthy young bodies,' she announced loudly as she examined one well-built lad of about nineteen. 'What a banquet!'

Beth and Ann laughed and looked around with feigned enthusiasm. Sally frowned with disapproval and pulled her beach robe round her more tightly. Gerri grinned.

The women made their way down one side of the pool towards a row of sun loungers. They pulled four of them together and settled themselves down to catch up on each other's news and gossip.

Over on the far side of the pool, by the deep end, a group of older boys and girls were gathered together around the low diving board. With a sudden jolt, Beth realised that one of them was Jonathan.

Quickly, she reached out to grab her sunglasses from her bag then hunched down on the lounger and prayed he wouldn't see her. Thank heavens none of her friends had ever been into the shop on a Saturday morning. If any of them had recognised him after what she had said, they would have teased her to death. Especially Ann. Beth shuddered as she recalled her recent confessions to her friend. But even she didn't know the half of it!

Beth lay back as if dozing. She turned her head slightly to one side and watched Jonathan surreptitiously over the top of her glasses.

His swimming trunks were not the loose, boxer-short type and, as she had imagined, he looked fabulous in the tiny black trunks. They were obviously not the only pair he had. His suntan mark was larger than the area covered by these skimpy things, so that a line of white flesh showed all around them. For some reason, the image excited her.

When she had first spotted him, he had been standing with his back to her. Now, as she watched, he turned round towards the diving board and Beth barely stifled a gasp as a surge of longing shot through her.

Even unaroused the trunks barely covered him and the tight, shiny material left little to the imagination. She was shocked to realise how much she wanted to run her hands over his exposed flesh and watch him expanding and growing until the trunks could no longer contain him and his tip peeked out over the top.

Jonathan walked out on to the diving board and raised his arms above his head. Every muscle in his body stretched taut. He looked like a young Greek god. Transfixed, Beth watched him dive. She was filled with admiration at the grace with which he cut through the surface of the water, barely making a ripple. She held her breath until he surfaced, then watched breathlessly as he struck out strongly across the pool back towards his friends.

As he clambered up the side with the water streaming down his bare skin, Geraldine spotted him. She grunted appreciatively. 'Look at those,' she marvelled, ogling his buttocks. 'Just like a pair of ostrich eggs.'

Sally and Ann ignored her, already deep in conversation about a new lipstick that Ann had just bought. Beth felt her heart hammering. She had no desire to get into a discussion with Gerri about Jonathan's assets!

'Fancy a swim?' she suggested quickly, desperate to distract her friend in any way she could.

'Why not?' Gerri stood up and peeled off her towel to reveal her voluptuous figure in its too skimpy two-piece swimsuit. 'I could do with cooling down after an eyeful like that.'

Down by the diving board, Jonathan and his friends were laughing at something one of them had said. A pretty blonde girl held out a bag of crisps and offered him one. Smiling, Jonathan grabbed the bag from her, then turned away and hurried off.

Squealing in mock rage, the girl chased after him. She threw her arms round his neck and jumped up on to his back, wrapping her legs around him. She began pummelling his shoulders with her fist. Jonathan put one hand behind his back and grabbed her round the waist, tickling her. The girl squealed even louder and began kicking at him with her legs.

Beth examined the girl more closely. She must have been about the same age as he was, perhaps slightly older, with long blonde hair falling halfway down her back and a perfect pink and white complexion. She was dressed in a minute red bikini, the top of which barely covered the slight swell of her immature breasts. Her hips were as slim as his were and her stomach was almost concave.

Beth's own stomach knotted. She could feel the jealousy eating away at her insides and her whole body started to tremble with emotion. Did Jonathan lust after her too? Of course he did. Even Ann had told her that lads his age couldn't get enough of it. Was this his steady girlfriend?

'Come on then, if you're coming.' Gerri moved towards the side of the pool. 'Stop ogling the talent like that or someone might trip over your tongue.' Gerri grinned at her own wit and jumped into the water with a loud splash. Water droplets flew up into the air and splattered Beth from head to toe. It felt icy cold against her burning flesh.

Hardly aware of what she was doing, Beth lowered herself

into the cold water. Holding the side, she twisted round and looked back towards the diving area.

The pretty blonde had retrieved her bag of crisps and was now busy flirting with a dark-haired lad, her lips pouting seductively at whatever he was saying to her. Beth sighed with relief. At least she wasn't draped round Jonathan's neck any more. Where was he?

Seconds later, she spied him again. He was back in the water. Two more girls were busy trying to duck him under, giggling and screaming as they splashed around, their hands seemingly all over him. Although neither of them was as pretty as the blonde girl, they were both quite attractive and both dressed in tiny bikinis that showed off their young bodies to perfection.

Beth frowned with irritation. Why didn't the pool attendant put a stop to it? Touching him all over like that in public. Little tramps. Someone should tell them to behave themselves.

Did Jonathan like them doing that to him? Was he turned on by their lithe bodies and skimpy attire? Had he got an erection? Could they feel him pushed up hard against their bodies?

She could feel her heart thudding in her chest. Torn between jealousy and desire, she discovered that she was having trouble breathing. She wanted to go across and pull him away, drag him off home and spank his bottom until he was raw. 'Just you wait,' she threatened him under her breath.

She pictured herself peeling the tiny trunks down his legs and imagined the way his hard cock would spring free, trembling at the soft touch of her hands on his naked thighs. Another shiver of desire tore through her. She had to get away from here before anyone noticed that there was something wrong.

'I'm not feeling very well,' she told Gerri. 'I must have eaten something at lunchtime that disagreed with me. I think I'll just get dressed and catch the bus home.'

By the time Beth arrived home, she had recovered a little of her composure. She could hardly believe the effect the sight of him at the pool had had on her. She had even been jealous of his companions. Ridiculous! She knew how much he lusted after her. She had him totally under her spell. She could make him do anything she wanted just by snapping her fingers. Those other girls didn't stand a chance against her.

After she had made herself a cup of coffee, Beth settled down on the settee and opened one of the girlie magazines. As she scanned the letters page, her heart began pounding again. Apparently, Ann was right. There wasn't anything all that unusual about younger men lusting after older women. From what she read, it appeared that they were attracted to the idea of a woman's maturity and experience.

Well, clearly, since she had once been married, she was undoubtedly more experienced than he was. She felt sure that Jonathan was still technically a virgin. Is that why he was interested in her? She laughed. If he only knew how unsure she felt about everything herself.

Beth turned back to the letter that described in detail what one woman had done to herself to entertain her boyfriend and his companion. She reread every word avidly. When she had finished, she turned back to the final photo of the red-haired girl who was fingering herself for the camera. She stared at it thoughtfully.

Was she really doing it, or just pretending? The girl's face certainly looked intent enough. Yet, surely she wouldn't do it for real with the camera pointing at her? Would she?

Beth's thoughts returned to the little blonde girl at the pool. That silly teenager wouldn't dare do it in front of him.

She pulled a face. Or, maybe she would? Beth pictured the girl posing for Jonathan and imagined his reaction. She studied the photos again carefully, then got up and headed upstairs.

She rummaged around in the bathroom until she finally located a hand mirror. Excitedly, she moved into the bedroom and stripped off her clothes. Beth lay on the bed with her head propped up on two pillows. She opened her legs and placed the mirror between her thighs. She reached down with her other hand, parted her outer lips, and examined herself critically. Eventually satisfied with what she saw, Beth dropped the mirror and lay back with her eyes closed.

Slowly, hesitantly, she placed her hand back over her mound and began to caress herself gently, delighting in the rough feel of her pubic hair against her palm. Experimentally, she used her fingers to seek out her clitoris and squeezed it softly. She was stunned by the shivers of desire that were soon coursing through her whole body. She summoned up a picture of Jonathan in his skimpy trunks with his erect penis poking seductively out of the top.

After a while, she began to remember what it had been like making love with Tony. It certainly hadn't felt as good as what she was doing to herself now. For the first time in her life, she wondered if she had ever actually had a proper orgasm and, if not, what it would feel like to have one. Her thoughts returned to Jonathan and her fingers began moving more swiftly.

By Tuesday afternoon, Jonathan knew he could wait no longer. He didn't want to go and see a film and he couldn't concentrate on anything his friends were talking about. Who cared which group made the number-one spot next week or who won the next round of the cup? He had to go into the shop and see

Beth. He had to try to get himself an invitation to go round to her house again.

'I think you've been punished enough, for now, Jonathan.' Those words were becoming increasingly significant to him every time he thought about them. It had to mean that she wasn't finished with him, yet. It just had to. He made excuses to his friends and hurried into town.

As he walked, he pictured the way she had looked when he had seen her at the pool. The way her hips had swayed from side to side as she moved and the swell of her buttocks beneath her costume. He blushed again as he remembered how the girls had been fooling around. Had Beth seen him with them? What would she have thought, seeing him playing about so childishly?

By the time he arrived at the shop, he was too nervous to think straight. Maybe this wasn't such a good idea after all. Perhaps it would be better just to assume that she was expecting him again on Saturday. If he actually said something to her about it, she would have the chance to tell him not to go, that she didn't want him there again. He hesitated, undecided. He wanted to see her.

When he walked in, Mr Bailey was nowhere to be seen and Beth was busy sorting through a new pile of magazines that must have arrived that morning. She was so engrossed in something she was reading that she didn't look up immediately when the doorbell jangled.

Jonathan stood just inside the shop and examined her intently. As before, the top two buttons of her overall were undone and, when she leant forward over the counter, he could clearly see the lacy top of her bra. Immediately, he remembered what it had been like when he had put his hands round her tits in her kitchen, and the all-too-familiar thrill of excitement raced through him.

Beth looked up. When she saw him, her face flushed pink. Hastily, she picked up another magazine and placed it over the one she was reading.

'Jonathan. What are you doing here?' Her voice had that same deep, husky note he had noticed more often lately when she addressed him, and his excitement grew.

'I was just, I mean, I thought I'd come in and ... My mother asked me to collect her magazines,' he lied desperately, with a sudden flash of inspiration.

Beth smiled. 'That's strange. She was in here herself just half an hour ago. Perhaps she forgot that she had asked you to collect them.' It was quite clear from the look on her face that Beth was not the slightest bit fooled by his excuses. Jonathan reddened and he began twisting his hands together in front of himself.

'I suppose she must have,' he mumbled.

Beth's grin widened. 'Well now you're here, why don't you make yourself useful and put the kettle on for me? My tongue is hanging out for a cuppa.'

Jonathan smiled nervously, relief flooding through him as she supplied the excuse he had been searching for to stay a bit longer. Hastily, he hurried out the back before she could change her mind. As he moved, he slipped his hand down inside his jeans to adjust himself.

Beth followed him through a few moments later. Jonathan finished stirring her tea and turned round to hand it to her. She took it from him with a quick smile of thanks and perched herself on the edge of the only chair.

'So, how are you enjoying your half term?' she asked. 'I suppose you and your friends are getting up to all sorts of things?'

Jonathan shrugged awkwardly and sipped his own drink. Beth frowned.

'I expect you spend a lot of your time swimming, don't you?' she continued cheerfully. 'Your mother has told me how keen you are on it.'

Jonathan reddened at the mention of his mother. He hated the thought of them being too chummy. He lived in constant fear that Beth would say something to her about his behaviour. Besides, his mother could say such embarrassing things sometimes. He didn't want them chatting together about what a sweet baby he had been. It was totally humiliating.

'You haven't got very much to say for yourself today, have you?' Beth commented sharply. He noticed that her voice had taken on a different tone now. She sounded more like one of his teachers. What did she want him to say? He shrugged again and shook his head.

'What's wrong?' Her eyes narrowed. 'I hope you haven't been doing anything you shouldn't have been doing.' As she spoke, she leant forward casually and brushed something off her right shoe. The top of her overall gaped open so that Jonathan could see straight down to her almost transparent white bra. He stared hungrily at the darker shadow of her nipples and imagined running his tongue over them. His cock tingled and began to swell again.

Beth lifted her head and stared at his rapidly tightening jeans. 'Because, if you have,' she threatened, 'I shall be forced to punish you again, won't I?' As she spoke, Beth licked her lips and wiped her palms slowly down her thighs.

Out in the shop, the doorbell jangled demandingly and Beth sighed. She stood up and picked up her mug to carry it through with her.

'I can't sit and chat with you now,' she told him. 'Some of us have got work to do. I'll see you on Saturday.'

'Saturday night?' Jonathan blurted out quickly, before he could stop himself.

Beth looked startled. 'I meant here in the shop,' she replied. She glanced at his face, then ran her eyes down his body. He was certain that she could not fail to notice the extent of his excitement and arousal. Suddenly, she smiled.

'It looks as though we've still got some unfinished business to tend to, haven't we?' she whispered, as she stared as his throbbing groin.

It wasn't exactly an invitation, but it was close enough. Jonathan licked his lips and nodded enthusiastically.

As she turned to walk away, he sighed with disappointment. Saturday suddenly seemed an awfully long way off.

This must be the last time, Beth promised herself, as she bathed and dressed the following Saturday evening. I'll just get him to entertain me once more, so that he is in no doubt about who's in charge, then I'll tell him that's the end of it, once and for all.

She was not really surprised when Jonathan turned up at her house slightly earlier than the first time. She had been ready for over twenty minutes herself.

'You know where the living room is,' she told him as soon as she had closed the front door behind him. There was no need for her to play at being the perfect hostess any more.

As she followed him down the hallway, Beth smoothed down her new black skirt and reflected that it was probably just as well that this would be the last time. Her bank manager would have a fit if she didn't stop splashing out on new clothes soon!

Without waiting to be asked, Jonathan sat down on the settee and stared up at her hungrily.

'Do you want a coffee?' she asked him as she pretended to ignore the way he was already undoing the buttons on her blouse with his eyes.

Jonathan shook his head and reached out to take hold of her arm. Before she could stop him, he had pulled her down on the settee beside him. He pushed her back against the cushions, placed one arm either side of her, and leant forward to kiss her. His full body weight pushed against her so that she couldn't escape.

Beth closed her eyes and lay back, enjoying the feel of his lips against hers. When he pushed them open with his tongue this time, she did nothing to resist.

As he increased the pressure of the kiss, Jonathan moved his hands down on to her breasts. He ran his fingers across her nipples and she felt them spring up in response to his touch.

Beth whimpered softly, thrilled by the feel of his hands on her body. She imagined his penis growing harder and pushing up against his jeans. When he began opening her buttons, she still did nothing to stop him. She shivered with anticipation at the idea of feeling his hands inside her clothing and against her skin.

She jumped as his fingers slipped inside her top and began to caress her hardened nipples through the flimsy material of her bra. Her breasts were aching to be fondled. She was almost tempted to reach up and pull her bra out of the way herself.

Jonathan seemed to be almost pulsating with desire. As he leant over her, she could actually feel the hardness of his erection. He seemed even more turned on than last week by the feel of her breasts and the pressure of her lips against his. As he sucked urgently on her tongue, she shivered with pleasure at the sensation.

His hands visibly trembling, Jonathan slid his fingers down her stomach and into the waistband of her skirt. Beth moaned softly and raised her bottom slightly off the settee. Jonathan's excitement seemed to increase even more. As he pushed his hand down under the elastic of her panties, she noticed he was squeezing his own thighs together tightly as if to control himself.

His fingers made contact with the top of her pubic hair and he sighed with a mixture of success and anticipation. Beth flinched and Jonathan sighed again. Slowly, his fingers began to slide down into her panties. Beth stiffened. Any second now, he would be touching her there. He would feel how wet she was and know how excited he had made her. This wasn't what she had planned at all.

Almost reluctantly, Beth reached down and grabbed his arm. She pulled his hand up out of the top of her skirt and pushed him away.

'No,' she whispered. 'That's far enough.' In her excitement, her voice sounded much harder and angrier than she had intended.

Jonathan sat up guiltily, his excitement visibly receding. He stared at her in shock and confusion. 'What? Why?'

Beth wriggled out from underneath his arms and stood up. Her top gaped open and she saw his eyes lock on to her erect nipples.

'I definitely think it's time we had some coffee,' she suggested shakily. 'Stay here,' she commanded over her shoulder as she left the room. She certainly didn't want him following her again. She needed time to pull herself together.

Jesus! She had almost let things get out of hand that time. How could she possibly hope to control Jonathan if she couldn't even keep control of herself?

When she returned a few minutes later carrying two mugs of coffee, her face was still flushed and her eyes were unusually large and bright. She saw the look of disappointment cross his face as he noticed that she had rebuttoned her top.

Without speaking, Beth leant over beside him to place the

coffee on the table, careful to bend from the waist as she had practised. She glanced sideways to check his expression and smiled inwardly at the look on his face. She knew how high her skirt had ridden up.

'As I said the other day, I think that you are going to have to be punished again, Jonathan,' she told him, as she straightened up slowly and sat back down beside him.

Jonathan gazed at her silently. When she saw the look of resignation on his face, Beth sighed with relief. She was certain he already knew what she was going to make him do. She was also certain that he would not be able to refuse her. However embarrassing it was to do it in front of her, his desperate desire was more urgent.

She had taken command again. She was back in charge of the situation. She was still scared at how close it had come to getting out of control. Just a few more seconds and she might have let him do whatever he had wanted with her.

Beth turned towards him and reached down to undo the button of his jeans. Using both hands, she started slowly pulling down the zipper. Jonathan closed his eyes.

Gradually, Beth peeled back the edges of his jeans as if she were unwrapping a birthday present. Excitedly, she examined the bulge in his pants. There could be no doubt about what she was doing to him.

'Lift yourself up and pull them down,' she commanded hoarsely.

With his eyes still closed, Jonathan obeyed her. His erect penis stuck up in the air in front of her, its shiny tip already wet. Beth marvelled silently at how hard he was.

Without taking her eyes off his erection, she raised her skirt and turned to straddle him so that she was perched across his knees, facing him, with one leg on either side of his thighs. She could feel Jonathan trembling at the silky touch of her stockings against his bare flesh. He opened his eyes and stared excitedly at the tantalising glimpse of her panties, just inches from his cock.

Beth raised herself and leant forward to lift the bottom of his T-shirt. His eyes were now staring straight down the front of her top and the lace of her panties was just inches above his quivering erection. As if by instinct, Jonathan raised his own buttocks and thrust himself upward.

Beth pushed him firmly back down on to the cushion and raised his shirt higher, forcing his arms up into the air as she pulled it up over his head. She ran her fingers lightly down his chest, loving the way his skin twitched and fluttered at her touch. She sat back and ran her eyes over his erection again. Gently, she tightened the muscles of her own thighs so that she was pressed hard against him. Jonathan lay rigid, as though hardly daring even to breathe.

Slowly, Beth lifted one leg and climbed off him so that she was kneeling beside him on the cushion. She heard his sigh of disappointment. Hesitantly, as if half-afraid it might bite back, she reached out with one hand and closed her fingers round the shaft of his penis.

Jonathan drew a sharp breath and his cock lurched sharply in her hand. Beth stared at it in surprise. She hadn't expected it would be able to move like that. It was almost as if it had a life and mind of its own. A strange tingling sensation ran down the back of her thighs.

Fascinated, she moved her hand slowly down the shaft until her little finger was resting against the soft pubic hairs around its base. Jonathan shuddered from head to foot, his face screwed up in a tight grimace. His cock twitched again.

The feeling of power returned and intensified. Beth felt exhilarated by the effect she was having on him. Her face intent with concentration, she moved her hand gently back up towards the tip then down again, trying to imitate the way she had seen him move his own hand.

Jonathan parted his lips and took a couple of deep, ragged breaths. He began moving his head slowly back and forth, his face twisted. Beth looked back down and noticed that he was clenching his thighs tightly together and rolling his hips from side to side as if he was desperate for a pee. She knew what that felt like.

Smiling with pleasure, she increased the speed of her pumping, using her fingers to squeeze him gently as her hand slid up and down the length of his cock.

Suddenly, his whole body went rigid. He raised his hand and placed it urgently over hers.

'No,' he whispered, trying to stop her hand moving.

Thinking he was trying to push her away, Beth instinctively tightened her grip, squeezing him even more firmly between her fingers and totally unaware of the devastating effect her vicelike grip was having on him. Hesitantly, she put her other hand down between his legs and began to fondle the base of his testicles as she had seen him doing.

Jonathan groaned again. His penis was twitching violently in her hands, obviously only seconds from exploding. Still she didn't release him. His whole body squirmed. He groaned even louder and Beth squeezed him again.

'Oh God, please,' he begged softly.

Shocked by his submissive tone, Beth relaxed her grip.

Immediately, a spurt of fluid burst out of him and flew up into his face. As Jonathan moaned with relief, the first spurt was rapidly followed by another. He reached down to grab himself.

With a strength she didn't know she possessed, Beth caught his hands and pinned them back to his sides, her fingers digging into his arms in her urgency not to miss what was happening. Jonathan sank back and let himself go. His muscles continued to tense then relax as each spurt tore from him and his chest grew damp and sticky with his spunk.

Finally, it was over. Jonathan slumped down against the cushions, totally spent. His bottom had slipped down over the edge of the settee and his legs were slightly apart. He began wriggling up.

'Lie still,' Beth commanded as she placed her hands on his chest to push him back. She wanted to see how quickly his erection went down.

Obediently, Jonathan stopped struggling. He closed his eyes. Almost as if he could feel her eyes watching his prick shrinking, he started to blush. Pushing himself with his heels, he renewed his efforts to sit up.

Beth lifted her hands off his chest and stared at the warm white come covering her fingers. She smelt its faint, not unpleasant, odour. She sighed softly, reluctantly accepting that it was all over.

'I expect you can still remember your way to the bathroom, can't you?' she whispered, as she stood up and headed out to the kitchen to wash her own hands.

6

Long after he had cleaned up and gone home, Beth sat quietly on the settee and sipped her drink. What had she been thinking of? There was no way that what she had just done to him could be considered a form of punishment. Worse, she had let him go without saying anything about her decision that it was time to put an end to the whole thing.

Beth squirmed guiltily and her face reddened as the vivid images of her actions raced through her mind. It was one thing taking it upon herself to punish him for his behaviour towards her – although, even then, if she were completely honest with herself, the way she had gone about it was somewhat debatable! She blushed deeper at the thought of him lying, half-naked, across her knee with his buttocks in the air and his erection pressed against her thighs. And, as for what she had just done to him ...

The truth was, she had been indulging herself at his expense. Satisfying her own curiosity under the flimsy pretext of teaching him a lesson. The fact that he appeared to be enjoying the experience as much as she was, was no excuse. She had been shamelessly taking advantage of him. At her age, she ought to know better.

Beth sighed heavily. Why did it all seem so sordid and depraved in retrospect? When he was actually there with her, it seemed so natural and harmless. Like a teacher coaxing a willing student. Even if, in some ways, the student was more advanced than the teacher.

What a mess. Beth finished her drink and went out to the kitchen for a refill. What should she do now? Would Jonathan accept it if she just told him it was over, or would he make a fuss? Perhaps he actually believed himself to be in love with her. Young emotions could be so intense and the last thing she wanted to do was to hurt him. She wasn't ready to let him go yet, either.

They could hardly have a proper relationship though, could they? Beth couldn't help smiling at the idea of the two of them going out to dinner together, perhaps on to the theatre to take in a play. And Ann had accused Gerri of cradle snatching!

No, whatever Jonathan might feel for her or she for him, she had to face the fact that their relationship could never be considered normal or acceptable. It would be far better just to finish it before it led to real trouble.

She decided that she would just say nothing. She could act friendly but distant at work and let things take their own course. He would get the message. Before long, he would find a girl his own age and forget all about her. She felt a sudden rush of jealousy at the idea of him with that young blonde girl. Her own Saturday evenings were destined to be pretty dull and boring from now on. Beth sighed again.

As Jonathan lay in his bed that night, his mind was going round and round in circles. What had he done wrong? Why had she suddenly become so angry with him? He had been so sure that she was going to let him. He had been certain that she wanted it as much as he did. He had felt the way she was trembling, seen the flush of her skin and felt how hard her nipples had become under his fingers.

Everything had been all right until he had tried to put his hands inside her panties. Despite his confusion, Jonathan shivered at the memory of the feel of her pubes. He had never touched a woman there. God, he had been so close.

And, as for the way she had pleasured him like that with her hand! His cock jerked against the duvet and he put his hand down quickly to hold himself. Christ, the way it had felt when she had held him like that, stopping him letting go. He would never forget it. It was as if his prick had been about to burst wide open with the pressure. Why hadn't he known about that? Did all women know how to do that to a man? Holding it off until he had thought he would die with the agony and the ecstasy of it.

Why had she done that, but not let him have her? Perhaps he had been in too much of a rush. Maybe she had wanted him to move more slowly. Slowly! He sighed again at the thought of how close he had come. He wanted her so much.

As soon as he walked through the door of the shop the following week, Beth knew that she was in trouble. All her careful rationalising, which had seemed so obvious and logical at the time, had taken no account of the way she felt when he looked up at her hungrily and began undressing her with his eyes.

'Hello, Jonathan,' she said breathlessly, feeling immediately flustered by his eager gaze. 'There's a big stack of boxes out the back that Mr Bailey wants you to take care of this morning,' she added quickly.

Jonathan nodded. 'OK. I'll see to them in a minute,' he replied as he walked across to stand beside her. He looked around as if to make quite sure that they were alone then took her arm to pull her towards him. Beth stiffened.

'What do you think you're doing?' she hissed angrily.

Jonathan ignored her and began running his hands all over her body.

'Let go of me.' Beth pulled away from his roaming fingers and stared at him furiously. 'Don't ever do that again,' she shouted, her fear feeding her rage. 'Not here in the shop where someone might see us. Now, go and take care of those boxes.'

Jonathan smiled triumphantly and turned away to head out the back. Beth rested her elbows on the counter and struggled to get herself back under control. Things had got more out of hand than she had realised. How dare he try to grab her like that in the middle of the shop? A customer might have walked in and seen them. What if his mother had walked in? It might be a good idea to take care not to be alone with him at work for a while.

She decided that she really would have to give him a serious talking to. Do something to make quite sure he understood his position with her. When he came round to her house later, she would have to teach him a lesson he would never forget.

When she left the shop that lunchtime, she had another magazine in her shopping bag. There was an extremely interesting article in it about bondage that she was looking forward to studying more closely later. Coupled with what she had recently read at the library, one or two ideas were already forming in her mind on that subject.

By seven o'clock that evening, she was ready and watching for him out of the kitchen window.

As he opened the gate and strolled casually up the front path, Beth examined his face, trying to gauge his mood. She didn't like the hungry, almost cocky, expression in his eyes. It was the same expression he had worn in the shop earlier. Her own face hardened. No matter what happened tonight, she was determined that he would be left in no doubt who was the boss. After she had finished with him this time, he wouldn't even dare look at her in the shop without permission.

She opened the door at his second, impatient, ring.

'Jonathan?' She feigned surprise. 'I don't remember inviting you round tonight.' She suppressed a grin at the sudden look of insecurity on his face. That's it. Start as you mean to go on, she congratulated herself. She licked her lips and hesitated.

'Well, now you're here, I suppose you might as well come in.' She struggled to suppress another smile as the look of fear on his face changed to one of hopeful expectation.

As Beth led the way into the living room, she was very aware of him following closely in her wake with his eyes locked on the swing of her hips. She smiled happily to herself, knowing that she was looking good.

She was dressed, as last week, in her short black skirt and button-through jumper, and her hair was fluffed out around her face and hanging loose down her back. She knew that she had never looked more desirable. Let him look, she told herself. That was all he was going to do. If he thought she was going to give him any opportunity to take advantage of her tonight, he had another think coming. For once, she was going to have all the fun while he looked on.

She quickly stifled the panic already rising inside her and reminded herself of the effect of what she was going to do was sure to have on him. 'The power is all mine,' she muttered to herself. 'I am in control here. I can do anything I want with him.'

Jonathan hovered awkwardly in the middle of the living room. She could see that he was already feeling less sure of himself than the last time he had been there. The cold way she had greeted him had obviously had the intended effect. Now she needed to push her advantage before she lost it.

'OK. Strip.' Beth was standing by the settee, just out of his reach, with her hands on her hips. Her face was completely expressionless. She didn't want him to have any idea about what was going to happen to him until it was too late.

'I said, strip,' she repeated loudly, when he made no move to obey her. She forced herself to look stern. Jonathan stared at her in silence, his eyes huge.

'Well? What are you waiting for? Or do I have to do it myself? I would have thought you were a bit big to need help undressing.' Beth found she quite liked the idea of doing it for him. She took a step towards him.

'What are you going to do to me?' he questioned, his voice high-pitched with apprehension.

Beth shook her head. 'Nothing,' she replied. 'I'm not even going to touch you.'

Jonathan cringed. Beth was certain she knew exactly what was going through his mind. He thought she was going to force him to do it in front of her again. Was he ever in for a surprise!

Wordlessly, Jonathan turned away from her and began to remove his clothes. The blood was already rushing to his face again. Beth smiled triumphantly and her eyes narrowed as she watched his outer clothing disappear. She would never tire of looking at his body.

Reduced to just his pants, Jonathan hesitated again. Beth looked down and noticed that, for once, he wasn't already hard. Perhaps the idea of stripping off completely while he was like that was more embarrassing than when he was ready. Did he fear that she would make fun of him?

'Everything off, Jonathan,' she whispered, excited by the sight of his red briefs against the tanned flesh. She remembered the thrill she had felt watching him harden in front of her on the stairs. She wanted to see that again.

With obvious reluctance, Jonathan pulled down his pants and stepped out of them. She noticed that he was careful to keep his head down and turned away from her. His penis and testicles hung down loosely between his legs, as if imitating his head and expression. As before, Jonathan moved his hands round to cover himself.

Beth turned her back on him and picked up a longish piece of cord that was lying, ready, on the settee. She moved towards him, took hold of his hands, and pulled them up towards her. Swiftly, she tied his wrists together securely.

'That should ensure that you keep your roaming hands to yourself.' She grinned as she reached round to pat him gently on the bottom.

Jonathan flinched at her touch and stared at her in confusion.

'What are you going to do to me?' he repeated, with a note of fear creeping into his voice. She saw his penis stir slightly as if remembering how good it had felt when she had taken him in her hand. She quickly suppressed her own sigh of anticipation.

Beth took his arm and guided him back slightly. Still holding the end of the rope in one hand, she climbed up on to the side of the chair and raised his arms. Jonathan twisted round so that he could watch what she was doing. His breathing quickened at the sight of her long legs almost level with his face. As she stretched up towards the ceiling, her skirt lifted so that he could see the tops of her stockings. He moved his head round to get a better look. She glanced down and saw that his cock had already begun to harden.

Beth looped the rope round a heavy hook fixed into a wooden beam that ran across the length of the ceiling. As he watched her, she tied the end securely to the hook.

'It used to hold a chandelier,' she explained conversationally. 'An old family heirloom of my ex-husband. I never did like it. This is a much better use for the hook.'

Beth climbed down off the chair and moved round so that she was standing in front of him. She looked down at his groin again and smiled happily at his growing enthusiasm.

Jonathan flushed and moved one of his legs round in front of the other, twisting his hip forward as if to try to cover himself. Beth laughed, fascinated to see that his penis seemed to be shrinking again as his discomfort increased. Well, she would soon do something about that.

Her own inhibitions at what she was planning seemed to subside a little at the sight of his obvious embarrassment. They were both nervous. It wasn't just her. If he could put up with all this for her sake then, surely, she could overcome her own fears?

Beth walked across to the doorway and turned the dimmer switch on the sidelights right down until the room was in semi-darkness. The centre lamp now illuminated Jonathan perfectly, almost as if he were standing under a spotlight. The shadows increased her confidence further. It was almost like the setting for a play: the two of them merely actors playing out their parts according to the writer's script. According to her script.

Beth turned back to face him and walked forward until she was standing about a foot in front of him. Trembling from head to foot with fear, she crossed her hands in front of her and took hold of the bottom of her jumper. Slowly, she began drawing it up over her head.

Jonathan drew in a deep breath and his eyes widened at the sight of her stripping in front of him. He stared greedily at her breasts, watching them change shape under the bra as she raised her arms.

Beth turned sideways to him. She bent forward from the hips, tightening all her muscles, then leant over and placed the garment on the settee. She had already practised this in front of the mirror and she knew that she looked every bit as good as the models in the magazines.

She straightened up and spun round slowly on her heels

until her back was turned to him. She lifted one hand and undid the top button of her skirt with a flick of her finger. Gradually, she began undoing the zipper.

Jonathan drew another deep breath. He shivered slightly at the sound of the button popping open, then gasped as the zipper came undone.

Praying that she was doing it right, Beth wriggled her hips from side to side and slowly pulled the skirt down until it came free and fell in a heap at her ankles. She stepped out of it and pushed it aside with one foot.

She was now standing in front of him, clad only in her black bra and thong and a matching black suspender belt, stockings and high heels. The tiny strips of lace and nylon framed her round buttocks perfectly and the white of her skin was shockingly erotic against the black material. She heard him swallow. Slowly, she turned back round to face him.

Jonathan was standing completely still with his arms raised above his head by the rope and his face filled with longing. She looked down. His penis was sticking out in front of him, straight and hard, as if saluting her performance. As she watched, it twitched slightly, bobbing up and down as if caressed by unseen fingers. A rush of confidence flowed through her body, a feeling of such power and such control that her legs turned to jelly. A shiver ran down her spine and her final inhibitions vanished. She was in total control now.

Smiling provocatively, her lips parted, Beth placed her hands on her hips and moved towards him. She stopped in front of him and eyed him up and down critically, like a sergeant inspecting the troops. Jonathan stood to attention. She moved on, passing by and circling round behind him.

Jonathan twisted his head round, desperately trying to follow her with his eyes. Finally, he could turn no further.

Quickly, he whipped his head round to the other side and she saw him wince at the pain in his shoulder and neck muscles.

Beth circled right round and then stopped in front of him again. She looked down at his groin. His penis was twitching rhythmically up and down as he involuntarily tensed and relaxed the muscles in his excitement. Beth felt an almost overwhelming urge to reach out and fondle it. She moved back a few paces and turned her back on him again. She could feel his eyes devouring her body.

Trembling with anticipation, Beth raised her hands again and unhooked her bra. As the back strap fell free, she held the bra in place over her breasts. Jonathan gasped again at the sight of the bare skin of her back. She could almost feel him throbbing for her.

Almost beside herself with fear and excitement, Beth spun round on her heels again so that he could see only her hands were preventing her bra from falling free. She slipped the straps off each arm in turn and lifted her hands to allow the garment to drop to the floor in front of her. Her breasts bounced free, their dark nipples already hard and erect.

Jonathan's body shook as if he had been slapped. He was staring at her bare breasts like a starving man eyeing a table set for a feast. His mouth was gaping open so that he seemed to be practically drooling. He leant forward and strained against the ropes holding his wrists. His erection seemed to grow even harder and Beth could hear him moaning softly under his breath. She could clearly see the beads of perspiration standing out on his forehead.

Enflamed by his reaction, Beth began to circle him again, strutting proudly in her high heels with her breasts swaying delightfully at every step. Once again, she moved round to stand behind him and, once again, Jonathan twisted his head awkwardly so that his eyes were riveted on her bare breasts.

'Face the front, Jonathan.' To her surprise, the command was firm and uncompromising, betraying nothing of her emotions. Jonathan's head jerked round as if it were on strings. He reminded her of a puppet. Her puppet. She gazed downwards.

His buttocks were so tense and rigid that they looked as if they were made of porcelain. She experienced an almost irresistible urge to lean down and bite him, to watch him jump. She cupped one cheek in her hand and fondled it gently. Jonathan trembled violently and twisted his head back round over his shoulder. His arms strained against the bindings again.

'I said, face front.' Beth removed her hand and waited for him to turn away.

'You know I still owe you a spanking,' she threatened softly, and was delighted at the way his buttocks immediately stiffened and twitched as if he expected to feel the sting of her blow at any moment. She waited silently, revelling in the sight of his whole body tense with anticipation. Finally, she walked back round and stood just in front of him again.

Beth rested her foot on his thigh and leant forward to begin undoing the suspenders holding up her stockings. Her breasts swung down in front of her, wobbling gently back and forth as she moved. Jonathan squirmed again. She realised that he had probably never seen a woman like this before.

Slowly, she began peeling one stocking off.

'Please,' Jonathan whispered desperately as he writhed from side to side against his constraints. His whole body was shuddering. His cock was as hard as she had ever seen it. He was shifting first on one leg and then the other, squeezing the tops of his thighs together as he desperately sought a way to rub himself.

She was certain that any inhibitions he might have about

masturbating in front of her had vanished. Right now, judging by his expression, if he could only get his hands free he would have done it in front of a whole roomful of watching eyes. The extent of his desperation was intoxicating. She felt certain that if she so much as touched his penis with her own fingers he would come.

As if totally unaware of his plight, Beth finished removing her stockings and slipped her feet back into her shoes. She stood back up and slid her hand down inside the tiny triangle of lace covering her pubes. She could feel the dampness of her own excitement on her fingers.

All her senses were heightened. She could feel a slight breeze from the open window running icy fingers over her skin, hear the sound of the clock ticking on the far wall, and even smell the warmth of both their bodies.

Beth closed her eyes, ran her fingers through her pubic hair, and touched her clitoris with the tip of one finger. She jumped at the intensity of the feelings that immediately rushed through her. She raised her other hand and ran it across her nipples, sighing gently at the shivers of pleasure running down her spine. She opened her eyes again and examined his reaction curiously.

Jonathan was going wild. He was so aroused that he, quite obviously, didn't know what to do with himself. With a desperate groan, he strained forward again, moving his legs and hips from side to side as he twisted and turned in vain. His face was bright red and his eyes were bulging out of their sockets. His throbbing cock twitched and jerked in front of him like a wild animal.

Beth licked her lips and stared at him hungrily. She wondered if she dared bend forward and kiss its burning tip. Would he be able to contain himself?

'Please,' Jonathan whispered again. 'I can't, I want ...'

'What do you want?' she teased him softly as her fingers began once more playing with herself. 'Tell me. Do you want this?'

As she spoke, Beth removed her hand and pirouetted round on her heels again. She raised her hands and began to peel down the back of her panties to reveal the curves of her buttocks. She turned back, placed her hands just below her navel, and lowered the front fractionally to reveal a few of her curls. She stopped and waited, then slid the material a little lower.

She couldn't believe how much she was enjoying herself. She would never have dreamt of doing anything like this for Tony. Perhaps she should have. Maybe she still should.

As she lowered the material over the bottom of her crotch, Beth continued to study Jonathan's response carefully. He just couldn't keep still. His whole body was juddering and twitching and his penis looked hot and swollen, as if it were ready to split open. She had never realised that it could become so dark and hard.

Beth bent her knees and slipped her panties down over her ankles. She stepped out of them and straightened slowly, then used her right foot to flick them up into the air. They landed against his chest and slipped down to brush his erection before dropping to the floor. Jonathan jumped and lunged forward, straining desperately against his bonds. His soft cry was full of desperation.

She stood facing him, with her hands on her waist and her legs slightly parted. Jonathan had stopped wriggling, his eyes now riveted on the dark shadow of her pubes. He almost appeared to have stopped breathing. Beth reached round and unhooked her suspender belt. It dropped softly to the floor so that, probably for the first time in his life, Jonathan was staring at a completely naked woman standing just a few inches in front of him. His whole body shuddered again.

'Is this what you want?' Beth whispered as she placed her hand on top of her mound.

Jonathan groaned loudly, a desperate moan of total frustration and anguish. His cock pumped up and down in the air and his thighs tightened. Suddenly, his face contorted and a stream of come spurted violently from his tip and flew up into the air. His orgasm was so powerful that the fluid shot across the space between them and landed on her bare leg.

Jonathan groaned again as spasm after spasm of come burst from him. He slumped forward with his chin resting on his chest and his eyes closed. His penis was still twitching, almost as if it wanted to spurt more, yet he had nothing left to give.

Beth walked across to the table and picked up a box of tissues. After she had wiped herself carefully, she picked up the dressing gown lying over the back of the settee and slipped it on. Although she was still tingling with desire, she felt a deep sense of satisfaction at what she had achieved. He had been so excited at the sight of her naked body that he had lost it, just looking at her!

Calmly, she walked over to the chair, climbed up on to the arm and untied him. Her gown gaped open, hiding nothing.

She climbed down again and quickly undid his hands. She suffered a slight twinge of guilt when she saw how red and chafed his wrists were from straining against the rope.

'I think you had better go and shower,' she suggested softly as she examined his damp, sweat-streaked body. 'I'll make us both some coffee.'

Ten minutes later, when he had still not returned, Beth felt her curiosity aroused. What was taking him so long? She tiptoed up the stairs, pushed open the bathroom door, and peered inside.

Jonathan was standing under the shower, facing her,

surrounded by a cloud of steam. He had closed his eyes against the spray and he was soaping his chest with a damp sponge. She ran her eyes slowly down his body. God, he was gorgeous: so tall, so muscular. For a moment, she was tempted to slip out of her gown and join him. She shivered at the thought of how it would feel to wash him herself, to run the sponge gently across every inch of his exposed flesh.

Clearly unaware of her presence, Jonathan moved the sponge down between his legs and carefully soaped his genitals. As she watched, he dropped the sponge, and started to rub himself with his hand. His cock immediately began to stiffen.

Beth stared in astonishment. He was already aroused again! Even after what had just happened, he was already wanting more. It would seem that Ann had been perfectly correct about the stamina of youth.

Beth felt suddenly irritated. Why should he keep having all the fun when she was still keyed up and unsatisfied? It was time she exercised her authority again.

She waited until he was really hard again and had begun to pump himself urgently up and down. God, she loved watching him do that. She took a deep breath.

'It's time you got dried off now, Jonathan,' she announced loudly as she moved into the room and picked up a bath towel. 'It's getting late. You should be off home before you get into trouble.'

Jonathan stopped pumping and opened his eyes. His cock stuck out straight in front of him again, hard and stiff. Beth feigned total indifference.

'Come on. Get a move on. If you are too late getting home, your mother might not let you out next week.'

She hadn't meant to say that. She hadn't consciously planned anything more than what she had just done. Wasn't she supposed to be putting an end to all this?

Beth shrugged, finally admitting to herself that she had no intention of putting an end to it. She was having far too much fun for that. Oh well, she would just have to think up something else to remind him who was the boss, wouldn't she? She waited for him to dry off and get dressed, amused by his obvious discomfort and his still half-erect penis.

Her loosely tied gown continued to gape, taunting him.

It was only after he had gone that Beth realised he had not tried to cover his erection from her gaze. In fact, he had actually turned round to make sure that she could see it. Was he finally losing his embarrassment in front of her and becoming too sure of himself? Or had he just wanted to show her that he was ready again?

It had been a good idea to send him home still not fully satisfied. As long as she kept him on his toes, maybe she would have less trouble keeping him under her control in future. She wasn't so sure about her ability to control herself.

7

Beth found that she was still much too keyed up and excited by what had happened to go to bed. She tried to read a book, but the words just seemed to run together on the page. Her eyes kept returning to the hook in the ceiling as images of Jonathan's naked body squirming beneath it danced around in her mind. Restlessly, she got up and wandered around the living room, straightening cushions, moving ornaments about.

Upstairs, she wiped around the shower then picked up the still soapy sponge and held it to her nostrils. She could smell the scent of his body and his come over the slight perfume of the soap. She pictured his fluid shooting across the room on to her leg. Her skin was still tingling where it had landed.

She smiled. She had kept her promise. She hadn't even touched him. Well, apart from when she had fondled his tiny white buttocks for a second or two. Yet, still he had come. Tied up and helpless, so that he had not even been able to touch himself, far less rub or fondle it, still he had been unable to stop himself from letting go just from looking at her. The feeling of power surged through her again and pumped the adrenaline round her body. She felt so alive she wanted to sing and shout, to run round in circles just for the hell of it. She felt like a little girl on Christmas morning.

Beth put the sponge down and moved restlessly into the bedroom. She stood in front of the mirror, removed her robe, and looked herself up and down as she tried to imagine what he had been thinking while he was watching her. She must have seemed to him like one of those girls from the magazines, come alive. She had felt like one of them. Sexy and desirable.

She lay down naked on top of the cover, lifted her head, and gazed down at herself. Her nipples were still dark and swollen and the area between her legs was warm and tingly. She ran one hand over her breasts and felt the shivers of desire running all through her body. What would it feel like to let him run his hands over her like that? To watch the longing in his face and see the effect that touching her body was having on him.

Beth took one nipple in between her finger and thumb and squeezed it gently. To her amazement, she felt a strange sensation between her legs, almost as if a muscle had contracted and then relaxed again. She remembered the way Jonathan's penis had moved up and down while she was walking around him, almost as if it were trying to follow her. She clenched herself and felt another ripple deep inside her.

Still teasing her nipple with her fingertips, Beth placed her other hand between her legs. Her fingers sought out her tiny nub and she rubbed it slowly, then gasped. It was too sensitive to touch. Last time she had fondled herself there, it had felt good. Now, the sensation was almost more than she could take. She noticed that the tiny bud seemed harder and larger than before. She moved her hand down further.

Hesitantly, Beth opened her outer lips and slipped her middle finger inside her vagina. The skin felt smooth and slippery to her touch. She was still wet. Experimentally, she began to move the finger in and out, slowly at first then faster. She closed her eyes and imagined herself moving her hand up and down his cock.

She could feel herself growing even wetter and she pinched her nipple hard, moaning at the curious combination of pain and pleasure it caused. She could sense the pressure building up inside her, like a tidal wave rising towards the shore. This must be how Jonathan had felt, not wanting it to end yet desperate for the moment when the wave finally broke. Her breathing quickened and she began to move her hand even more urgently.

Sweat covered every inch of her skin and she was trembling with the need for release. She could feel that she was right on the verge of coming. Every part of her body was crying out for it. Desperately, she pushed her finger back inside her and squeezed her nipple even harder. She touched her clit again and cried out with the intensity of it. She was more turned on than she had ever been in her life. She plunged her finger back inside and began to move her hand even quicker.

She felt a tingle run through her limbs as the wave broke. Gradually, the urgency drained away. Slowly, she moved her hands to her sides and a peculiar exhaustion enveloped her. She sat up.

As Beth made her way wearily into the bathroom to wash the sweat away, she couldn't help feeling as if she had just missed something. It had been nice, yes, but somehow it hadn't met up with her expectations. She had seen the look on Jonathan's face when he came. What he had felt must have been more than what she had just experienced. Suddenly, she remembered the book she had been reading in the library. One sentence in particular sprang into her mind.

'Some women find their climax is much more intense using a vibrator.'

There were several advertisements for sex aids in the back

of the magazines that she had brought home. Excitedly, Beth pulled her robe round her and hurried downstairs to the cupboard where she had hidden the magazines.

Before she went to bed that night, Beth took a short stroll past the postbox. Her hand was shaking as she took an envelope out of her pocket and checked the address carefully. She ran over the advertisement again in her mind.

'Send off today for our free colour brochure. Every conceivable item for your personal pleasure and fulfilment. Satisfaction guaranteed. All orders sent by return in a plain package.'

Before she could change her mind, Beth quickly pushed the envelope into the waiting slit.

By the time Jonathan arrived back home, it was quite late. His mother was waiting for him in the front room.

'Where do you think you've been?' Madge Evans demanded angrily, as soon as her son walked through the door. 'I've told you before that I expect you to be in by eleven o'clock unless I know where you are. What have you been doing?'

'Nothing.' Jonathan stared at the carpet, his face burning.

'Nothing? Look at you. You're a complete mess with your shirt hanging out like that. Why is your hair wet? It's not raining, is it?'

'I suppose it must be,' Jonathan muttered.

His mother's eyes narrowed suspiciously. 'If you've been doing anything you shouldn't be doing –' she began angrily, then stopped. 'You had better get yourself on up to bed,' she told him. 'You're looking a bit tired and peaky. A good night's sleep will do you the world of good.'

Jonathan headed upstairs gratefully, relieved that his mother hadn't questioned him any further. He would have to be more careful about coming home from Beth's with wet hair.

As soon as he had brushed his teeth, he stripped off his

clothes and climbed under the duvet. His thoughts and emotions were in utter turmoil. Every time he closed his eyes, he could see Beth standing naked in front of him. Even now, he still couldn't believe what had just happened. His mind began to conjure up the unbelievable images he had so recently witnessed. How often had he dreamt of just such a moment? He thought of the many nights he had lain under the covers, wanking himself to just such a hopeless fantasy. He had seen her breasts and her pubes! He had even watched her touching herself.

He ran his gaze over the mental image of her body. He remembered the way her breasts had changed shape as she had moved around and how her fingers had slipped under the tiny scrap of material over her pubes, touching herself there right in front of him.

And as for when she had pulled down her panties and stood there with nothing on but her shoes! His hand reached down and took hold of his cock. It was already rigid. He moved his fingers slowly down its length and shivered as he remembered the way her hand had felt when she had done it to him. Perhaps he could do that to himself. He tightened his grip and began squeezing himself. Maybe he could make it last even longer if he tried.

Jonathan began moving his hand up and down, losing himself in the pictures he could see of Beth in his imagination. Once, he had done this just thinking about watching her through the keyhole. Now he had seen her completely naked. He had kissed her and touched her breasts.

God, he wanted to do it to her so much. He would do absolutely anything she told him to, if only she would let him go all the way. He pumped harder and groaned with the pleasure. The door of his bedroom opened.

'Jonathan? Are you all right? I thought I heard you making

a noise. You're not ill, are you?' His mother opened the door further and a flood of light poured in from the landing, illuminating the bed and the posters on the wall behind him.

Jonathan let go of his cock and quickly rolled over on to his stomach. He lifted his head and turned it towards her.

'Mum? What do you want? I was asleep.'

'I'm sorry, love.' Madge moved across the room and stood by the side of the bed. She placed her hand on his forehead and ruffled the front of his hair tenderly in that irritating way he so hated. He twisted his head away from her touch.

'I didn't mean to wake you. I thought I heard you moaning. I was worried that you might be sick.' She smiled. 'You don't feel as if you've got a temperature,' she admitted. 'I suppose I must have imagined it.'

'I'm fine.' Jonathan was having trouble making his voice sound normal. Beth was still dancing naked in front of him.

'Well, good night then. Sleep tight and sweet dreams.'

As soon as she had closed the door behind her, Jonathan pulled the pillow under his chest. He began groping the corner, pretending it was Beth's nipple. At the same time, he started to move his body up and down and rub his penis on the bottom sheet, imagining that she was lying underneath him. Within seconds, he was stiff again.

Recklessly, he threw back the duvet so that he was lying naked with his muscles tightening and loosening as he practised his stroke and tried to imagine what it would feel like the first time. Beth's naked body writhed tantalisingly in front of his eyes and he felt himself approaching climax. Desperately, he pushed her image away and forced his mind to think about something else. He relaxed slightly and his erection became less urgent.

When he was sure he had calmed down a little, he turned over on to his back and began kneading his tip and fondling his balls. He pretended that she was lying on top of him, urging him on.

'Yes, Jonathan, oh yes. Hold on until I tell you that you can come. Oh yes. I've waited all my life for a man like you.' He took his hands away quickly and lay panting. Slowly, he moved his fingers back and fondled himself softly. Beth had touched him there. Could he make her take him in her mouth? He knew some women did that, but would she?

Jonathan moaned again and rolled back on to his stomach, then pushed himself down hard against the softness of the sheet. It was no good – he couldn't control it. His thoughts of Beth were just too strong and vivid. He couldn't make himself think about anything else.

He stretched out one hand and grabbed for the box of tissues under his bed. He pictured Beth wiping his spunk off her leg. Oh Jesus, he couldn't hold it. Desperately, he thrust his other hand underneath him and held himself tightly. As he lifted himself up off the mattress to push a handful of tissues under him, he saw Beth's tits swaying and jiggling in front of his eyes, the nipples hard and swollen.

Almost immediately, he lost it, biting his lips to stop himself crying out as jet after jet of hot come pumped from him into the tissues. By the time he was finished, he was so exhausted that he could barely find the strength to get up and walk to the loo to flush the tissues away.

Even then, he still couldn't sleep. Although he was now completely spent, his mind was still filled with images of her naked body standing in front of him. He just couldn't get his thoughts off her. What would his mates at school have said if they could have seen it? Tossing and turning restlessly, Jonathan struggled to think about something, anything, else.

Half an hour later, he had to admit defeat. He moved his hand down between his legs and took hold of himself yet again.

He was not surprised to find he was already hard and desperate once more.

He closed his eyes and conjured up an image of Beth, bound and helpless in front of him. Yes, he would tie her up to the hook in the ceiling. Fully clothed, not naked as he had been. He would undress her slowly until she was begging him to stop. Begging him the way he had begged her when she gripped him like that. He would show her no mercy. He began rubbing himself.

He would start at her legs and slowly move his hands up her while she stood rigid with her arms tied above her head so that she could do nothing to stop him. He imagined sliding his hands up past her knees on to her thighs and then, slowly, under her skirt and over the top of her stockings. As he moved, her skirt would lift, just showing the outline of her buttocks. Slowly, so slowly, he would raise her skirt higher to reveal her round bottom framed by her suspender belt and red thong. He quickened his pace and his cock began to throb.

Deliberately, he slowed again, fighting the urge to fondle himself and waiting for the urgency to pass. He didn't want to end this fantasy too soon. His fingers squeezed the pillow, pretending he was rubbing the slip of material in her crack.

He would kneel down behind her and run his tongue from the top of her stocking over her bum up to her suspender belt. He could see her shivering. Perhaps he would nibble her cheek. Not hard enough to hurt, just enough to let her know he was tasting her. Then he would pull down her panties while she clenched herself and tried to stop him.

He could clearly see her in his mind as he gradually peeled her panties over her taut buttocks. She would writhe with passion, desperate for him to take her, yet afraid of her desire for him. Once he had taken her then she would be in his power for the rest of her life – wanting nothing more than to be his sex slave.

Yes! He would only ever let her wear a skimpy strip of cloth just long enough and wide enough to cover her. Maybe an inch wide and tied with a bow in her crack? Perhaps he would let his friends fondle her while he made her stand and pose. She wouldn't like it, but she would do anything he said.

Jonathan's hand began pumping more urgently as his fantasy took over. He wouldn't pull her panties off. Not yet. He would leave them just above her stockings and then he would turn her round and lift up the front of her skirt to reveal her there. A few of her pubes would be showing and he would lower the panties further, revealing all.

He pursed his lips and imagined himself leaning forward to blow gently across her mound as she twisted and writhed. Another tremor of desire tore through him. No! He would rip her skirt off. She would have buttons right the way down it and he would pull them off, one by one.

As the last imaginary button flew off, Jonathan knew he was in trouble again. Quickly, he reached down for his tissues, but he was too late. Groaning with ecstasy, he spurted violently into the air. He wiped himself wearily, too tired even to be bothered to go and flush the evidence away.

He pulled the cover back up and tried to sleep. Every time he closed his eyes, he could see her panties coming down. That had been a good fantasy. He would have that one again. After all, Beth hadn't begged him to take her. Not yet, anyway.

The following Tuesday evening, Beth went round to have dinner with Ann. After they had eaten, Beth and Ann stacked the dishes into the dishwasher and moved back into the living room. They settled themselves down side by side on the settee and leant back contentedly to enjoy an after dinner drink.

After they had chatted for a while about nothing in particular, Ann turned the subject to work. She had a new supervisor at the bank who had been giving her a bad time of it just lately and she felt the need for some sympathy.

'Nothing I do seems good enough for her,' she grumbled. 'I'm too slow, or I'm too careless, or I take too long over my coffee break. Honestly, there's just no satisfying her.' Ann sighed. 'I think I shall have to find myself a new job if she doesn't let up a bit. Who needs that kind of hassle?'

'Umm,' Beth responded. It was obvious that she wasn't really concentrating.

'You're so lucky having a boss like Mr Bailey. He's such a dear. I bet he never grumbles at you, does he?'

'Umm,' Beth mumbled again.

Ann examined her friend's face surreptitiously over her glass as she sipped the cool wine.

Beth looked different lately. It wasn't just the clothes she had started wearing, although Ann had to admit more than a twinge of jealousy at the way Beth looked in the new dress she had on that evening. Gerri had been quite right. Beth was stunning when she made a bit of an effort with herself. She was wearing more make-up than usual, too, and had started wearing her hair loose. It suited her somehow. Enhancing her eyes and softening her features.

It was more than that, though. Her whole face was lit up with a sort of inner glow. Her skin seemed softer and her hair shinier. She looked ten years younger. It had to be a man. Ann flushed. Surely, it couldn't be because of Jonathan, could it?

'You haven't been listening to a word I've been saying have you?' she accused.

'What? Of course I have,' Beth insisted.

Ann was not fooled. 'So, tell me. How's your little peeping

Tom these days?' she questioned cautiously. 'Has he been up to any more mischief in the loo again lately?'

Despite her misgivings, Ann couldn't help smiling wistfully as the memory of that story rushed back into her mind. She had fantasised enough herself about catching him at it. She had even made a point of dropping into the shop last Saturday afternoon to see for herself what Jonathan was like. She had not been disappointed.

Beth flushed and took a quick sip of her drink.

'He still fancies me,' she admitted slowly. 'Even after the way I punished him.'

Ann immediately perked up. 'Punished him? You didn't say. When? What did you do? Oh Beth, you didn't speak to his mother about him, did you? The poor sod. How could you be so cruel?'

Beth shook her head. 'I'd never do that.' She faltered.

Ann immediately sensed that it was confession time again. She sat up excitedly.

'Well? What then?'

'I asked him round to my house so I could give him a piece of my mind,' she replied.

Ann stared at her in astonishment. 'Really? Whatever did you say to him?'

Beth smirked. 'It wasn't so much what I said,' she responded, 'as what I did. Actually, I took your advice.'

'My advice?' Ann looked puzzled.

Beth nodded. 'Yes. As you suggested, I gave him a spanking.'

Ann swallowed her drink the wrong way and started to choke. By the time she had recovered her breath, her eyes were streaming and her face was scarlet.

'Do you mind,' she spluttered hoarsely. 'You almost choked me to death. For a minute there, I almost thought you were serious.'

'I am serious,' Beth retorted. 'I asked him round, made him take his pants down and put him over my knee. Just like you said.'

Ann's watering eyes bulged. 'Jesus, Beth! How could you? I didn't mean it. I was just joking. What did he do?'

'He came all over my legs before I could even raise my hand.' Beth giggled. 'You were quite right, Ann. It seems men do like the idea of being spanked.'

It was a long time before Beth had finally satisfied all Ann's eager questions.

After Beth had finally gone home, Ann emptied the dishwasher and stacked the dishes away. Then she headed upstairs and began to get ready for bed.

Her mind kept running over their conversation. She could still hardly believe most of what Beth had told her. It was like something out of a book or a film. That sort of thing just didn't happen in real life.

Ann removed her outer clothing and glanced down at herself. She had a nice body. Not full and voluptuous like Gerri, of course. In fact, she was probably even skinnier than Beth and her hips were almost boyish. Would Jonathan be interested in her, too? If he had worked in the bank with her, instead of at Beth's shop, would he have sneaked around, spying through keyholes at her body until he was unable to contain himself?

Ann laughed. No one ever had any privacy at the bank. The whole idea was ridiculous. Still, what if it had been her working at the shop, instead of Beth? She sighed, wondering if her friends knew how long it was since she had last been with a man.

Ann sat down on the bed and lay back. She closed her eyes and began thinking back over her various experiences with the opposite sex over the years. She never seemed to meet anyone these days. Why was it that, for longer than she cared to remember, her only gratification had come from pleasuring herself?

Her thoughts turned to what Beth had suggested to her before she left. Did she dare? She felt a shiver of excitement run down her back. Her hand slipped down between her thighs. As she began to caress herself softly, she closed her eyes and lost herself in her fantasies.

8

Beth could hardly contain her excitement as she drove home. It had taken her quite a while to finally convince Ann that she was not just pulling her leg. By the time she had finished, Ann had no longer been red. In fact, if anything, she had looked quite pale and shaken and Beth wondered if she had gone too far. Maybe it would have been better if she had not confessed quite so much.

Still, it had been necessary. If she was going to pull off what she had in mind next, she was going to need Ann's complete co-operation. Although she hadn't actually agreed, Ann hadn't said no either. Beth had sensed that the idea excited her friend. She had listened in silence and her eyes had grown bigger and bigger with every word. Was Jonathan ever in for a surprise!

As Beth turned the car into her driveway, she found herself wondering why Ann had never married. She was certainly attractive enough, in a quiet, unobtrusive sort of way. Not really beautiful perhaps, but certainly not ugly. Beth felt a sudden moment of doubt. Perhaps she was too attractive. Perhaps Jonathan would think that Ann was even more desirable than she was. Supposing he fell for Ann and forgot all about her?

Supposing Ann fell for Jonathan and decided she wanted him for herself? She seemed so much more knowledgeable about things than Beth was, even if she had never been married. She must have had lots of boyfriends over the years. Jonathan would be bound to sense how much more experienced Ann was.

Beth frowned. Now that she thought about it, she couldn't remember Ann ever speaking about a man in her life. Beth hadn't even ever seen her with anyone. Ann couldn't be a lesbian, could she? No. She had enjoyed Beth's story about Jonathan far too much for that. She had seen the dreamy look on her friend's face and noticed the way she had clenched herself. Perhaps she was bisexual, or maybe she just didn't like sharing her men with anyone?

Beth could certainly understand that point of view. She felt another twinge of doubt about her plans. But what she had planned would be so much fun. Jonathan would be completely at their mercy. He wouldn't know whether he was coming or going. The whole thing was just too irresistible.

She would just have to make sure that she kept control of both of them.

Jonathan was even more keyed up and nervous than usual. He was in such a state that he could hardly think straight any more. His whole life seemed to be filled with thoughts of Beth. Of what she had done to him and of what he wanted her to let him do.

He had almost failed to get away from home at all. His mother was growing increasingly suspicious about what he was up to every weekend and concerned that he was not spending enough time on his studies. He had exams coming up soon and his mother had made it more than clear that he was going to have to stay in more and do some work.

He knew that she was also angry because he was being so secretive about what he was doing on Saturday nights. She had actually threatened not to let him out at all unless he told her exactly where he was going.

Jason had saved the day. Jonathan had told his mother he was going round to his friend's house to play computer games and Jason had backed him up. Of course, it had meant telling Jason a bit about what he was really doing.

It was funny how he had always been more than happy to boast about his conquests when there hadn't really been anything to boast about. Beth was different. For some reason, he didn't want to talk about her like that. Maybe it was because he already knew that no one would believe him anyway. He still couldn't really believe it himself.

He had been right about Jason's reaction.

'Yeah? You wish! In your dreams. You don't really expect me to believe that, do you?'

The jeers and taunts had incensed him. By next week, the whole school would probably be talking about his fantasies over what he claimed to have done with the woman he worked with. If only there were some way that he could prove it to them. If only Jason and Mark could actually see him with Beth and watch what she let him do. That would shut them up!

Come to think of it though, he wouldn't want to let them see some of the things she had done to him. He would be a laughing stock if they ever found out. He cringed at the thought of the time she had been going to spank him and he had come all over her legs. Or, when she had caught him in the loo at work. Maybe he didn't want to boast because it wasn't anything to boast about. He rang her bell.

Beth opened the door immediately, almost as if she had been lurking in the hallway, waiting for him. Jonathan eyed her greedily, already excited by what he had in mind.

She was dressed as if she had just been playing tennis. Jonathan shivered at the sight of her long bare legs under the short white skirt and the tiny sleeveless top that stopped just short of her waist, exposing a tantalising glimpse of bare skin. His eyes moved on up her body. She wasn't wearing a bra and her nipples showed quite clearly through the thin, clingy material. He wanted to grab them with both hands.

'Hello, Jonathan. I'm glad you're early.' Her voice was deep and husky and Jonathan's excitement grew. As she turned to walk into the living room, he caught a quick flash of her white panties and saw the curve of her buttocks. His cock sprang to attention.

'I'm glad you're early,' she repeated over her shoulder as he followed her down the hallway, 'because there is someone here I want you to meet.'

Before Jonathan could take this comment in, she had opened the door and led him into the front room.

Another woman was sitting on the chair opposite the settee. She stood up quickly as they entered and her face was flushed.

Beth smiled. 'Jonathan, this is a friend of mine. Ann, this is Jonathan.'

As Jonathan stared at Beth in confusion, his thoughts raced. What was going on here? His disappointment was burning into him, so that he could hardly think straight. Why was this other person here? He wanted Beth to himself. He had hoped and prayed that, this time, she would let him . . . His excitement vanished.

Maybe she wouldn't stay long. Or was this part of his training? He was almost sure now that that was what Beth was doing to him. He had heard about older women doing that sort of thing. He forced himself to look at Ann.

She was dressed in the same way as Beth and, despite his initial disappointment, he couldn't help noticing how attractive she was. Not as pretty as Beth, of course. Her face was a bit on the plain side, but still. He examined her slim figure carefully and noticed that her tennis skirt was even shorter than Beth's. It barely covered her crotch. He resisted the urge to lean forward to get a better look.

'Hello Jonathan. I'm pleased to meet you. Beth has told me all about you,' Ann murmured breathlessly. He noticed her glance down at his body and saw her eyes widen as her gaze reached his groin. Even though he wasn't turned on, he knew that she would be able to see the slight bulge of his penis. Quickly, he moved his hands round to cover himself.

Jonathan could feel his ears burning bright pink, both as a result of her gaze and of her remark. Surely Beth hadn't said anything to her friend about what they had done together? Girls didn't talk about that sort of thing, did they? These weren't girls though. They were women. What did women talk about to each other? She probably knew everything. He swallowed hard.

Beth moved across the room and sat down on the settee. She patted the cushion beside her. 'Why don't you come and sit down next to me, Jonathan?' she invited. She licked her lips suggestively and Jonathan shivered. He sat down quickly beside her.

Ann moved over to the chair and sat down opposite him. She crossed her legs and Jonathan saw straight up her skirt. His cock stirred and he quickly crossed his own legs.

'Ann and I have been playing tennis this afternoon,' Beth explained. 'I suggested that she come back for a drink because she wanted to meet you.'

Jonathan began to sweat. This wasn't what he had expected at all. What was going on? His eyes strayed back to the crotch of Ann's panties and, in spite of his extreme embarrassment, he felt himself beginning to grow harder. He looked away again quickly and tried to cover himself again. He cursed at how unfair being a man was. It showed every time.

Beth leant forward and picked up her drink. Jonathan saw the knowing look on her lips as she watched his hands covering his bulge. He stared at the delightful way her breasts moved under her top.

'Would you like a drink, too?' she asked him. 'Ann and I are drinking gin and tonic, but I've got a lager if you would prefer?' She paused, then added, 'I think there is some Coke there as well.'

'I, um, yes. A lager would be nice.' Jonathan didn't really like lager but he wasn't going to admit it.

Beth smiled and stood up. 'I won't be a moment.' She headed out into the kitchen and Jonathan watched her avidly.

'Beth tells me that you and she work together,' Ann said.

Jonathan stared at her, unsure what to do or say. He nodded dumbly.

Ann leant forward and picked up her own drink. The neck of her top gaped and Jonathan found himself staring at the swell of her tiny breasts. Although they were smaller than Beth's, the nipples seemed larger. A pang of lust shot through him and his jeans were suddenly much too tight.

Beth returned and held out the glass of lager. He took it quickly, forced himself to take a couple of quick sips, then placed it on the table in front of him before his shaking hands could betray him.

Beth sat back down beside him and put her hand on the top of his leg. He jumped violently and Beth grinned.

'I've been telling Ann what a good swimmer you are, Jonathan. Perhaps the three of us could go swimming together sometime?' Her fingers moved gently up his leg and his thigh muscle tightened involuntarily. He squeezed his legs together more tightly.

'Would you like that?'

'Like what?' Jonathan was having trouble concentrating. Beth's hand was burning into his thigh and Ann had partly opened her legs, so that he couldn't take his eyes off the patch of white panties between the bare flesh of her thighs.

'If we all went swimming together? Pay attention, Jonathan.

You are very distant this evening. What are you thinking about?'

If it had been possible for him to grow any redder, he would have done. He was certain that she knew exactly what he was thinking about. Beth laughed. She removed her hand and leant forward to pick up a pack of cards that were lying on the table.

'Why don't we have a game of something?' she suggested as she began to shuffle the cards.

'What shall we play? Ann?' She stared across at her friend.

Ann licked her lips. 'What games do you play, Jonathan?' she asked innocently.

'I, um, I,' Jonathan floundered.

Beth laughed again. 'Let's just have a quick game of snap to warm us up a bit, shall we?' she said as she leant forward to deal the cards. Jonathan watched her breasts again.

He couldn't believe how turned on he was becoming. He started to wonder just what they had planned. Was it possible that they might end up doing more than just playing cards? He was very aware of the way Ann was looking at him. It was the same way Beth looked at him sometimes. Would she let him touch her, too? His mind went into overdrive.

A threesome! God, let it be true. He began to imagine himself lying on Beth's bed with Ann on one side and Beth on the other. As he kissed and sucked one pair of tits then the other, the two women ran their hands all over him ...

He glanced back at the tiny patch of white between Ann's parted legs. Maybe he should go to the loo and make himself more comfortable. Why hadn't he remembered to wear looser trousers? He didn't dare stand up. They would both see how turned on he was. The sweat began trickling down the back of his neck.

Beth put her hand back on his thigh and Jonathan barely

stopped himself from groaning aloud. He shifted closer and placed one arm across the back of the settee behind her. What would she do if he touched her in front of her friend? He remembered the way she had acted when he had touched her in the shop. It would be so embarrassing if she told him off like that in front of Ann.

He slipped his arm down across her shoulders. Beth moved against him so that their thighs were touching and he shivered again.

Ann picked up her cards and leant forward to play. His eyes looked down her top again and his cock jerked painfully against his zipper. Her nipples were huge. He pulled Beth closer to him so that his fingers were touching the top of her breast. He looked round at her and noticed that her nipples were now standing out quite clearly too.

Beth played her first card and both women stared at him expectantly.

'Your go, Jonathan.'

They played on for about five minutes and both women kept giggling hysterically whenever two cards of the same value were turned up and one of them yelled 'snap'.

Jonathan was losing badly. He couldn't concentrate on the cards. His eyes were too busy elsewhere. Every time one of them moved, he became more aroused. A quick flash of Ann's bra or panties, Beth's bra-less nipples rubbing against the thin fabric of her top and wobbling delightfully as she leant forward to place a card. His whole body was burning with it. Did they know what they were doing to him? Perhaps they were doing it on purpose. They must be.

What should he do? Maybe he should make a pass at Ann. How? So far, everything had been done to him. No matter what he did, Beth always took control. He knew he was being teased. He hated it, yet loved it. While there was hope, he knew that he would do whatever she told him to do, no matter how humiliating it was. He couldn't help himself.

Jonathan slid his hand behind Beth's back. She had deliberately let her skirt ride up so that, as he slipped his hand down underneath her, his fingers found her panties. She lifted her buttocks up slightly so that he could fondle her. His fingers tugged at the elastic of her panties as he gradually peeled them down her thighs.

Beth polished off her drink and stood up, giving him a clear glimpse of her now partly exposed buttocks.

'Time for a refill. Drink up, Jonathan.' She nodded towards his still half-full glass. 'Ready for another?'

Jonathan shook his head. The lager was making him feel a bit sick. Or was it just the effect the two of them were having on him?

Beth shrugged and picked up Ann's glass. When she returned from the kitchen, she placed the drinks on the table and grinned wickedly.

'You don't seem to be concentrating on the game, Jonathan,' she chided as she sat down and placed her hand back on his leg. 'Perhaps we need to up the stakes a little?' Her eyes widened. 'I know,' she continued innocently. 'Why don't we have a game of strip poker?'

Ann giggled and took a long gulp of her drink. She opened her legs wide and stretched out to put her drink back on the table. Jonathan's eyes almost popped out of his head as he gazed up her skirt. Ann shuffled forward, letting her skirt ride even higher so that he could see her tiny silk panties. He was certain that she had done it deliberately.

'Jaw closed, Jonathan,' Beth commanded, seeing his look. 'Ann, you must be more careful,' she chided.

'Sorry.' Ann did not attempt to cover herself. 'I don't know how to play poker,' she objected.

Beth grinned. 'Neither do I. It doesn't matter. We'll improvise.' She looked across at Ann and Jonathan was certain that he saw her wink.

'Ann, would you mind pulling the curtains across? It's getting a bit dark out.'

Obligingly, Ann stood up and moved over to the window. Jonathan followed her greedily with his eyes. As she stretched up to pull the curtain across, her tennis skirt lifted. Jonathan took a deep breath at the sight of her buttocks under the white lace of her panties. The material at the back had slipped up into the crease of her buttocks. Had she done that deliberately as well? His jaw dropped at the sight of her bared cheeks. His palms grew damp and his mouth dry.

He leant forward awkwardly to pick up his drink. Beth's hand slid up his leg towards his groin. His cock twitched and a shiver of longing ran down his spine. Her fingers were only inches away from touching him. He tightened his thigh muscles again. Beth smiled knowingly at him as she moved her hand away.

Ann turned round and moved across to switch the light on. Jonathan grabbed his glass and sat back quickly. Trying not to grimace at the taste, he took a long swig of the lager.

'Turn the dimmer down a bit, Ann. We don't want to be blinded.'

As soon as Ann had adjusted the lighting and settled herself back down in front of them, Beth smiled and picked up a new pack of cards she had produced from somewhere.

'Just to keep things simple, this is what we'll do,' she announced. 'We'll each take a card off the top of the pack then whoever has the lowest card has to take something off. OK?' She put a finger to her mouth and sucked its tip suggestively. Jonathan shivered.

He took another swig of his drink. In his excitement, he

missed his mouth and the liquid dripped down on to his jeans. A dark, damp stain spread just below his crotch.

Both the women immediately jumped up and began to help him mop it up. He shuddered at the touch of their hands and prayed that he wouldn't let go. The thought helped to steady him a bit. Beth probably wouldn't be too bad about it, but he wasn't sure about Ann. She looked as if she could be a bit hard. Maybe she was some kind of professional Beth had brought in to teach him not to come too quickly?

'OK, that will do.' Beth pushed Ann's hands away possessively. 'It doesn't really matter if his jeans are a bit damp. He will probably lose them before long anyway,' she added wickedly as they both sat back down.

Jonathan shivered again as the implication of her words finally sank in. He had been right! It was a threesome! His thoughts raced. I bet I'm not the first one that they have done this with, he told himself. How far would they let him go? Maybe Beth wanted to watch him with Ann? Was Ann to be his first? Oh God, if only he knew what he was meant to do.

In one of his many fantasies, Jonathan was an astronaut landing on a strange planet peopled entirely by a tribe of sex-hungry women who took him prisoner. Before he could leave he had to satisfy them all, especially their Queen. Or, he was a secret agent hiding out from the enemy in a concealed passageway inside an all girls boarding school. A passageway that just happened to lead into the girls' dormitory. When they discovered him, they insisted that he take care of all of them.

He stared at Beth then at Ann and suddenly felt a little scared. When it came right down to it, he wasn't really sure that he was man enough for both of them. In truth, he couldn't actually see how it was possible to please two women at the same time. Maybe they would satisfy each other while he watched – another fantasy. He had often wondered if girls did that so they could have sex with each other but not with boys. Girls were always kissing and hugging each other.

Beth licked her lips. 'I'll go first, shall I? Then Ann, then Jonathan. Everyone ready?'

Beth lost the first round. She giggled hysterically as she stood up to remove one of her tennis shoes. She stared around them, then frowned.

'Hang on a minute. We should have checked first to make sure that no one has an unfair advantage,' she told them.

'Let me see. I'm not wearing a bra, so it's top, one, skirt, two and panties, three. Mind you, they're so skimpy they should really only count as half,' she joked. 'Then, shoes, four and five, and socks six and seven. She scanned Jonathan quickly.

'Shirt, jeans, pants, two shoes and two socks. I make it you've got the same,' she told him. 'Unless, of course, you forgot to put any pants on tonight. Maybe I should check, just to make sure.' She grinned and turned to Ann. 'Not fair. You've got an extra piece on since you are wearing a bra,' she accused. 'You'll have to take it off.'

Ann shook her head and suddenly seemed to look a little less sure of herself.

'Yes, come on. You have to start the same as me. Quick, or I'll get Jonathan to help you.'

Ann blushed and reached round under the back of her top. She quickly undid the bra, slipped the straps down her arms, and reached into one armhole of her top to pull the garment free.

Jonathan stared in disbelief at the ease with which Ann's bra came off. His eyes locked on to her nipples, now clearly poking through the thin sports top.

Beth took the top card, placed it on the table and turned it over. It was a ten. She smiled. 'Ann.'

Ann turned over the next card to reveal six. She frowned and Beth sniggered.

Jonathan reached for his card. He turned it over slowly. It was the Ace of Spades. He looked up at Beth.

'Is Ace high or low?' he questioned anxiously.

'Low,' said Ann quickly.

Beth pursed her lips and stared at him. His heart began to pound. He was certain that she would decide he had lost the round.

'High,' she ruled. 'Ace is always high. You lose, Ann.'

Ann looked pained then suddenly grinned. She reached down, untied one of her tennis shoes, and slipped it off. Jonathan stared down her top and licked his lips again. He couldn't stop himself from looking at her breasts.

Beth took the top card. It was the Jack of Clubs.

Ann reached for the next one. It was a Queen. She smiled triumphantly as Jonathan reached for his card. It was a three. His stomach flipped as both women giggled. He removed one of his trainers.

Beth emptied her glass and left the room. When she returned, she was carrying two more drinks for herself and Ann. As she sat down again, Jonathan caught another quick flash of her panties.

The game continued.

Ten minutes later, all three had removed their shoes and socks and Jonathan's shirt had gone as well. Beth lost another round. With a broad grin, she stood up and slipped off her sports top. Jonathan's eyes bulged at the sight of her bare breasts. Still smiling, she took another card.

Two rounds later, both women were down to their skirts and panties and Jonathan found himself sitting, red-faced, in just a pair of black briefs. He crossed his legs. Ann's nipples were huge. Much larger than Beth's. He wanted to run his hands over her breasts and take her nipples into his mouth.

Beth took her next card. It was the five of diamonds.

Ann drew a seven and Jonathan a nine. Both of them breathed a sigh of relief. Jonathan stared at Beth excitedly.

Beth stood up slowly and turned her back. She leant forward and reached behind her to lift her skirt, then began to peel her panties down slowly. Jonathan drew his breath in sharply at the sight of the tiny white thong dividing her buttocks. She wriggled her hips seductively, dropped her panties to the ground, and stepped out of them.

His penis instantly surged back up to full size and began to strain against the elastic at the waistband of his pants. He felt an almost overwhelming urge to reach out and grab her. He quickly placed both hands over his groin and tried to hike his pants up higher to cover himself. Beth reached for the top card again.

It was Ann's turn to lose. Jonathan watched with delight as she pulled her panties down quickly under her skirt and pushed them under the chair with her foot. She sat back down and pulled her skirt as far down as she could before folding her arms again to cover her breasts.

Although she had not stripped in nearly such an exciting way as Beth had done, Jonathan felt a strong surge of lust as he caught a glimpse of her naked thighs and imagined her exposed mound. Would he be able to catch a glimpse of her pubes? As she moved her hands to pick up another card, he watched her like a wolf, his eyes riveted to her crotch.

Beth took the top card. It was an eight. Ann drew a three and a look of sheer terror crossed her face. Jonathan sighed with relief. He turned his own card over. It was the two of spades. His heart missed a beat.

Ann squealed with delight. Jonathan swallowed hard. He

only had his pants left to remove. He couldn't take them off in front of both women. He just couldn't.

'Pants down, Jonathan.' Beth's grin reminded him of a Cheshire cat.

'Come on. It's only fair,' she insisted. 'You lost. Or, do you want us to take them down for you?' Beth stood up and leant over him so that her naked breasts were bobbing delightfully in front of his face.

'Come on, Ann, give me a hand here.' Beth reached down and pulled his hands away. She grabbed the elastic.

'Lift up,' she commanded.

Jonathan closed his eyes and lifted his buttocks off the cushion. As his pants began slipping down his hips, he clenched his teeth. Beth caressed his bare skin softly. Her fingers felt icy cold against his burning flesh. As she let her arm brush accidentally against his penis, he jumped and opened his eyes again. He felt his erection grow even harder.

Beth slipped his pants off over his ankles and began to wave them around above her head like a trophy. Jonathan quickly moved his hands back into his lap to try to hide himself. He risked a quick glance in Ann's direction. She was sitting on the edge of her chair with her eyes riveted on him. Her face was flushed and her eyes sparkling. Her lips were slightly parted, so that he could see the tip of her pink tongue.

'Time to see who is the overall winner,' Beth announced as she turned to reach for the next card.

Jonathan lost again and Beth laughed. 'That means you have to pay a forfeit,' she told him. 'We'll decide what it's going to be later.' She took another card. It was a ten.

Ann drew an eight, Jonathan a King.

'I win,' Beth chortled. 'Skirt off, Ann.'

Ann sank back in the chair and shook her head. Jonathan thought that she looked as if she were afraid to move. Was she as embarrassed as he was? Surely not. Ann shook her head again and closed her eyes.

Beth stood up. 'You can't back out now, Ann. If Jonathan can do it, so can you.' She moved over to her friend and reached round for the zipper.

Jonathan sat forward and crossed his arms over his nakedness. He felt as if he must be dreaming. This couldn't be happening. Was Beth really going to start undressing her friend, right in front of him?

Beth had leant over Ann's chair so that her tiny tennis skirt covered nothing. Her bottom was waving in the air as she struggled to pull Ann's skirt off. Jonathan gasped and began squeezing himself tightly.

'Give me some help here, Jonathan.' Beth grabbed Ann's arms and pulled her up to her feet so that they were standing, literally, breast to breast. He didn't know where to look first.

'I'll hold her, you whip it off,' Beth instructed.

Jonathan stood up and moved round behind Ann. He crouched down. Slowly, almost reverently, he began pulling her skirt down over her narrow hips. As his hands made contact with her skin, he saw her begin clenching herself, so that the muscles of her buttocks and thighs were twitching spasmodically at his every touch. Jonathan pictured himself sinking his teeth into the soft white flesh of her bottom and his whole body quivered.

As he continued to try to pull the skirt down with fingers that were not working properly, his hands skimmed over the exposed flesh of her bum and thighs, taking full advantage of the situation. Ann didn't seem to be doing much to protect herself. He noticed that she had even opened her legs a little as if to encourage his prying fingers. Another pang of longing engulfed him and his cock throbbed.

The skirt finally dropped to the ground. Quickly, Jonathan

stood up again and put his hands back in front to cover himself.

Beth pushed her friend round towards him and Jonathan glanced down at her. He gulped and moved his hands away from his cock quickly, frightened that he might let go if he so much as touched himself. His penis was sticking straight out in front of him as if it were straining to get a better view of what was going on. He didn't blame it one bit.

He stared silently from one to the other. Ann sank back on to her chair. Her face looked quite pale and she appeared to be having trouble deciding how to sit to try and cover herself. He knew how that felt!

He looked back at Beth, dressed only in a tiny skirt that left almost nothing to the imagination. When she saw him looking at her, she ran her hands down her sides and smiled teasingly. He felt his whole body shudder and his cock began to dance and bob in response. He gritted his teeth and stared into her eyes, holding her gaze boldly.

He knew that she was trying to make him lose control. He was suddenly desperate for her to realise that he knew what she was trying to do to him. He was determined not to let her get the better of him again. Seeing the look, Beth just shrugged as if to tell him that there was nothing he could do about it. The brief spark of defiance and confidence deserted him. He turned away from her gaze and sat back down on the settee.

Beth spun round to face him. 'And now for your forfeit,' she whispered as she stared down hungrily at him.

'Since I won the game, I should choose the forfeit,' she said hoarsely. 'So I choose.' She paused, then grinned wickedly. 'I choose that Ann gets to say what you have to do.' She turned back to her friend. 'What's it to be, Ann?'

Ann was still staring silently at him. He heard her sigh softly. His eyes dropped to her golden pubes.

'Well?' Beth demanded.

'I want, I want,' she stammered, as if the words just would not come.

Beth's eyes narrowed.

Jonathan shuddered, suddenly knowing what was coming. It was written all over her face. All women must love watching men doing that to themselves. He shivered again at the thought, not sure what he wanted any more.

'Why don't you tell him to wank himself,' Beth suggested boldly, confirming his fears. He felt himself shudder again at her words. Beth was watching him avidly, her eyes glued to his bursting cock. He could feel it jerking from side to side almost uncontrollably. His balls were already pressed up tight against his body, hard and swollen. Despite his embarrassment, he kept his hands well away from himself, certain that he would lose it completely if he touched himself.

'Go on. Say what you want,' Beth commanded. Jonathan felt sure that she was enjoying the way they were both now in her power.

'Yes. I want him to,' Ann whispered, so softly that they barely heard her.

Beth grinned triumphantly. She walked over and knelt down on the floor in front of him.

'I'll get you started, shall I?' She reached out, took his erection in her hand, and slid her fingers gently and slowly down towards the base.

Jonathan gasped sharply at her soft touch and sank back against the cushions. His whole body began shaking like a man suffering from malaria. Unable to stop himself, he raised his buttocks and thrust against her hand. He twisted his head round to look at Ann.

She was sitting forward on the edge of the chair again with her mouth open. She seemed to be so engrossed in what was happening that she had completely forgotten her own naked-ness. One hand was fondling her pubes, the other playing with her right nipple. She appeared to be totally unaware of what she was doing.

Jonathan's eyes widened with shock and lust when he saw what she was doing. Jesus! She was actually playing with herself. He drew another sharp breath and the tip of his cock began to glisten damply. With a desperate groan he pushed Beth's hand away, grabbed himself, and began to pump up and down.

Beth beckoned Ann to move across and sit on the other side of him. She leant back on her heels and watched him pleasuring himself. Jonathan noticed that she was fingering herself as well, and he felt another powerful surge of lust shoot through him. He began to pump even harder, his eyes swivelling back and forth between the two women. Oh God. He couldn't take much more of this. He stopped and squeezed, then pumped again.

'Not so fast, Jonathan. Ann and I want to enjoy this, don't we, Ann?'

Ann just nodded. Beth reached for the blanket on the back of the settee and placed it on the floor in front of them.

'Kneel down there,' she demanded. 'Knees together. Then carry on.'

Powerless to resist, Jonathan settled on his heels and took himself in hand again. He watched both of them like a hawk. Ann no longer appeared to care whether anyone was looking at her or not. Her eyes were wide and her face red. Her hand was back between her legs, rubbing herself. Her earlier self-consciousness was completely gone. He groaned again.

Beth immediately reached out and pulled his hand away, as if determined to prolong his moment of release.

'Play with your buttocks. That's it. One hand on each cheek.

Good.' She watched hungrily as his cock twitched urgently from side to side.

'Don't you dare come yet,' she told him, 'or Ann will spank your bottom.'

Jonathan's stomach tied in knots. He stared excitedly at Ann, picturing himself bent over her with his cock pushed hard against her thighs.

Beth pushed him forward on to all fours. 'Start again, Jonathan,' she commanded softly.

Jonathan obediently took hold of himself and began to pump up and down again. He knew he was just seconds from letting go.

'No, not like that,' Ann whispered suddenly. 'Keep your hand still and use your hips.'

Jonathan hesitated, unsure what she wanted. Beth put her hands on his hips and began to move his body back and forth, so that he was thrusting his cock in and out of his clenched fist. Oh Christ. Did they know what that felt like? He moaned again and began pumping harder.

Suddenly, Beth grabbed him and pulled him up on to his heels again. She pushed his legs apart so that they could both get a better look at what he was doing.

Jonathan pumped harder still, thrusting his hips up and down as he pushed himself into his hand. He was so close that he barely noticed as Beth leant down and pushed his hands aside. As she grabbed his throbbing cock in her own fingers, he finally lost it, groaning loudly as he began spurting violently into her hand. He jerked again and felt another spurt, then another. Finally, he sank back, red-faced and gasping.

Beth reached for the tissues and wiped her fingers. He heard Ann sigh urgently.

'I think we could all use another drink, don't you?' Beth picked up her top and slipped it on over her head.

Ann blinked and looked around as if she wasn't sure where she was. Jonathan watched her thoughtfully. He remembered the small sigh he had heard just after he had come. Had Ann come too? He felt a shiver of excitement at the idea.

'Don't you think you had better put your clothes back on, Ann?' Beth suggested as she turned to leave the room. Her voice sounded strangely spiteful. Jonathan saw a sudden look of horror and embarrassment cross Ann's face.

He stood up, grabbed a handful of tissues to clean himself up, and then quickly slipped back into his pants. He glanced at the clock on the mantelpiece and frowned. It was getting late. It was after ten o'clock already. He would have to be going home soon or he would be in big trouble. He sighed heavily.

Ann sat as if she were made of stone. Neither of them said a word.

Out in the kitchen, Beth poured fresh drinks with shaky hands. If she sent Ann on her way now, perhaps there would still be time for her to amuse herself some more with Jonathan on her own. She found herself wondering why she had wanted to do this with Ann at all. It had seemed such a good idea at the time. In a way, it sort of alleviated the guilt she felt by forcing Ann to share some of the responsibility for her own actions.

She had to admit that it had been fun.

Still, it would have been fun without Ann, too. She didn't need Ann there. She didn't need to share Jonathan with anyone. Had he been more turned on than usual? Did he find Ann more exciting than her or was it just because there were two of them together? Was that some kind of a male fantasy? She glanced at the kitchen clock and frowned.

It was getting late. It was after ten o'clock already. Jonathan would have to be going home soon or he would be in trouble.

He hadn't actually told her that he had a curfew, of course, but she had noticed the way he watched the time.

She reluctantly abandoned her plans. Once Jonathan was gone, maybe she could have a little chat with Ann about a few things. Did her friend own a vibrator? Perhaps she could pick up a few tips. It could be an interesting discussion.

9

The next few days proved to be even more dull and frustrating than Jonathan had anticipated.

Still angry with him over his lack of schoolwork, and only half believing his explanations of how he spent his weekends, his mother had made him study every evening. His only respite had been the swimming trials he had taken part in on the Thursday evening. That and the delightful moments he spent under his duvet each night, fantasising about what he wanted to do to Beth and Ann.

His mother hadn't even allowed him to go round to Jason's house to watch the mid-week match on TV. He was certain that Mark and Jason had spent the entire evening talking about him and laughing about his claims of what he had done to Beth. They had made his life hell at school all week with their sly looks and pointed comments. By Friday, he was so incensed that he was determined to shut them up for good.

All he had to do now was to find a way to get Beth to go along with his plan.

His heart was already thumping painfully by the time he reached her house on Saturday evening.

'Why don't we go out for a walk,' he suggested, almost as soon as he was through the door. 'It's a nice evening. We could go to the park.'

Beth stared at him, clearly puzzled by the suggestion.

'There's a cold wind tonight,' she objected quickly. 'Besides, it will be dark soon. What on earth could we do in the park that we can't do here?'

As she spoke, she reached out and placed a hand on his thigh. Despite his anxiety, his muscles tightened at her touch and his eyes stared hungrily at her breasts. Beth smiled encouragingly.

'Why not go through and make yourself comfortable,' she suggested. 'I'll just make a coffee and then I'll join you.'

While Jonathan sat in the living room waiting for her, he tried to think if there was anything else he could say that would persuade her to go with him. He had always known that it had been a long shot getting her out of the house. Beth had already made it quite clear to him in the shop that she didn't want anyone to see them together. Apart from Ann, of course. Still, he had to try.

He pictured Jason and Mark shivering under the bushes in the park as they waited to spy on them. They would give him hell if he didn't turn up. He grimaced at the thought of how they would tease him the next time he saw them. After this, nothing he said would ever convince them that he had been telling them the truth about Beth.

When Beth finally walked into the room, he steeled himself to try again to convince her. Before he could say anything, she sat down beside him and began to run her fingers up his thigh. Her top was so thin that he could see her breasts through it, and her skirt was already up high enough to reveal her stocking tops.

He felt a pang of lust rush through him as he reached out and pulled her into his arms. He pushed his tongue inside her mouth and squeezed one of her nipples between his fingers. His cock began straining urgently against his clothing. All his thoughts about walking in the park mysteriously vanished. Who cared what Jason and Mark thought? What did they know about anything?

He felt Beth relaxing under his caresses and his confidence soared. He wouldn't make any mistakes this time. He would do everything just right and then maybe, just maybe ... Slowly and carefully, Jonathan moved his other hand on to her thigh. So gradually that she would barely feel it, he began to move his fingers up under her skirt.

His whole body was quivering with his impatience, yet he was terrified that she would become angry again at any moment. His fingers sought for and found the bottom edge of her panties. Beth stiffened slightly and Jonathan stopped moving. He hardly dared so much as to breathe.

He caressed her breast again and pushed his tongue even further inside her mouth. Beth whimpered softly and relaxed against him and another surge of longing raced through him. He moved his fingers again, slipping them gently under the elastic. He touched her pubes.

Beth shuddered and her own kisses became more urgent. She lifted her hand to place it over his crotch and Jonathan pushed himself against her palm, his pulse racing. She wasn't going to stop him.

Slowly, he pulled his hand out again and began to peel her panties down from the back. Beth lifted herself slightly to help him and his fingers moved round to the front. He tugged gently. He was making an awful mess of it. He hadn't realised how difficult it would be. He should have used both hands. Finally, they were down on to her thighs.

Beth squirmed underneath him and raised herself even further off the couch as if to make it easier for him. Trembling with anticipation, Jonathan slipped the panties down her thighs. His excitement at his success was almost more than he could bear. Quickly, he shifted back slightly, moving his erection away from her hand. His need was almost unbearable. He didn't trust himself to let her keep rubbing him there.

Guiding her gently, Jonathan moved her round so that she was lying full length on the couch. He pulled her skirt up her thighs and placed his hand over her exposed pubes. Beth jumped, but made no move to push him away. He knelt on the floor beside her and watched himself stroking her with his fingers.

Beth shivered again and another whimper of pleasure escaped her lips. She closed her eyes and lay back, her breathing quick and ragged. Another surge of triumph raced through him.

She really wasn't going to stop him. Finally, after all the embarrassment and humiliation he had been through for her, he was going to have her properly. His cock pulsated violently against his jeans and Jonathan fumbled to undo the button and ease his zipper down.

He stared down at her pubes. Now that he was so close, he was suddenly filled with fear. What if he couldn't hold it? What if he came before he could even get it inside her? Just the thought of what he was about to do to her was almost enough to make him lose control.

Pulling at his trousers and pants with one hand, he began kissing her neck. His fingers continued to play with her pubic hair. He was sure that if she just let him finger her there, then she would let him go the whole way. He slipped his hand further down between her legs. Beth squeezed her thighs together, but not in a threatening way. She sighed softly and his pulse quickened.

He kicked off his shoes and used his free hand to remove his socks. Although reluctant to move his other hand, he had no choice. Quickly he stood up, whipped his jeans off and stepped out of his pants, almost losing his balance in his haste. As soon as he had pulled his shirt over his head, he sat back over her and marvelled at the sight of her nakedness.

Beth barely seemed to register the fact that he had stripped. Her eyes were half-closed and she was breathing rapidly. Shakily, Jonathan raised one hand and began to undo the buttons on her blouse. As soon as he had pulled the material open, he lifted her bra and began to tease her erect nipples with his fingers. Beth pushed his hand away and arched her back, raising her breasts towards him. Following her lead, Jonathan leant down over her and placed his lips on one of her nipples.

Beth writhed with excitement; her eyes closed and her face twisted with pleasure. Jonathan sucked her nipple gently and his own excitement mounted even further at the way she was responding. Just the sound of her whimpering like that was driving him wild. She shifted slightly, presenting the other nipple. Jonathan took it into his mouth greedily.

Beth reached out and took hold of his hand to guide it downwards. Jonathan shivered and pushed his fingers back between her legs, marvelling at how wet and soft the skin felt. He could barely believe this was finally happening. What would his friends think if they could see him now? What if he lost his erection at the last minute? He bent over her and tried to suck her whole breast into his mouth. With his free hand, he played with her other breast.

Beth began to roll her body from side to side and push her buttocks up towards the feel of his caress. She shivered as his fingers began running across her clitoris. Urgently, she pulled at him until he was kneeling between her legs. She grabbed his hands and placed them under her thighs, lifting then lowering her buttocks as if to try and trap him. She raised her arms and pulled his head down towards her clit.

Jonathan realised what she wanted. He knew he had to explore her clit as he had explored her mouth. He didn't really want to do it, but he would do anything for her. Hesitantly, he moved his head down her stomach and ran his tongue across her mound.

Beth cried out and thrust herself up to meet him. Her hand pushed his head further downwards, closer and closer to her swollen clitoris. She parted her legs slightly so that, for the first time, Jonathan could see her inner lips; see the mysterious place he so longed to enter. He shuddered and shifted back slightly to ensure nothing was touching his cock. His mind willed his body to hold off.

Desperately trying to focus on something, anything, else, Jonathan pushed his tongue into the slit between her lips and ran it softly across the tiny bump of skin at the top.

Beth cried out and Jonathan tried to pull back, scared that he had done something to hurt her. She grabbed the back of his head and pushed him harder against her. Releasing his hands, she lifted her legs and curled them round his back so that her heels were digging painfully into his skin. Jonathan reached up and grabbed for her breasts. He raised his eyes to look up at her.

Her eyes were closed and her face red. Her lips were open and she was panting rapidly. As he watched, she ran her tongue over her lips and whimpered softly. He lifted his head and looked down. He had never seen her nipples so swollen and puckered. They were almost as big as Ann's. He reached out again and pinched one between his finger and thumb, delighted by the way she immediately began to shudder and writhe under him.

'Don't stop,' she begged breathlessly. 'Put your tongue there again. Move it up and down.' She pushed his head urgently back down.

Jonathan put his tongue back on the little bulge of skin he had discovered and began to lick it slowly. It tasted strange; slightly sharp, yet unlike anything he had ever tasted before.

He groaned again. Would she let him now? He didn't think he could wait any longer. He lifted his head and raised his body over her.

'No, don't stop.' Beth twisted her fingers in his hair and forced his head back down between her legs. Jonathan began flicking his tongue rapidly back and forth. Beth sobbed again.

'Yes, that's it. Like that. Oh God, don't stop.'

She twisted and turned urgently, thrusting against him. Jonathan began flicking his tongue even faster, losing himself in his task. She was bucking and gyrating under him like a mad thing. He had her under his control. He was bringing her off. He remembered his fantasy. She was desperate for him, begging for it. He felt her squirming against him helplessly as he played with her.

Suddenly, he felt a great convulsion sweep through her as if every muscle in her body had tightened then relaxed again. She sobbed loudly and fell back, exhausted. With a contented sigh, her whole body collapsed like a puppet that had lost its strings.

As he sensed the change in her, Jonathan stopped and sat back up. He stared down at her. Her face was calm and serene. Her nipples were still hard and swollen and there was a hot flush across her chest, almost like a rash. A thrill of excitement shot through him.

She had just come! He was sure of it. He had done it to her with his tongue and she had come. His bursting cock throbbed urgently. If he didn't stick it in her now, it would be too late. He just couldn't hold on any longer.

Jesus, she had just come. He had made her come. He grabbed himself and began to pump wildly, his senses reeling. He mustn't lose it now. He had to hold on. He swung his leg over her.

Beth opened her eyes and stared up at him. For once, the sight of his excitement appeared to do nothing for her. She sat up and pushed him away.

'I think that's far enough,' she told him shakily.

Jonathan sat back, thunderstruck. This couldn't be happening! Not again. Not when she had just ... When he was just about to ... He stared down at her dark opening that was beckoning him seductively.

'I was, I want to.' He groaned with despair. 'Please, Beth. Don't stop me now. I want you so much,' he was practically begging.

'No.' Beth sat up further. 'I never said you could do that. Not now.'

As soon as he released her, Beth stood up and hurried from the room. Jonathan perched on the edge of the settee with his head in his hands. Desperately, he tried to sort out his muddled thoughts and rationalise what had happened.

She had only lost interest after she had come. Before that, she had seemed to be almost as excited as he was. If he had only gone ahead earlier, she probably wouldn't have stopped him. But he couldn't do anything then because she had been holding him. His hands had been trapped under her. He hadn't realised that she was so strong.

Maybe his mates had got it wrong. The way they told it, women could come again and again, without having to wait at all in between, like men did. They just got better and better. What if that wasn't true? Beth had seemed to lose all interest afterwards. Perhaps she couldn't do that. After all, what did Mark and Jason know about it? He was certain that they had never done it. With them, it was all just talk.

Yes, that must be it. Next time he wouldn't wait too long. Just long enough to get her really turned on and then ... He wouldn't let her trap him, wouldn't allow her to wrap her legs

around him. God, his back ached where she had been kick
him with her heels. What if she had done that with him insi
her?

Bitch. Why did she take such pleasure in taunting him like
this? How he would love to get his revenge on her. One day,
he would find a way to get his own back. He would make her
parade and perform for him while he watched her.

Beth stood outside in the hallway and tried to calm herself down.
She was furious. Not so much with him as with herself. She had
almost completely lost control of the situation again. She
had certainly lost control of herself.

He must have realised what he had just done to her. Christ!
She could feel herself blushing at the memory of the way she
had screamed and writhed under him. If she didn't know
better, she would have sworn that wasn't the first time he had
done that to a woman. She pushed the thought away.

Now he thought he had her just where he wanted her. It
was exactly what she had feared earlier. If she let him have
his way, then what?

Then it would all be over, of course. She was far too old for
him to be seriously interested in her for long. He was probably
only here with her at all because she had let him do things
that the girls his own age wouldn't let him do; because she
had done things to him that they probably wouldn't even
think of.

What would happen once he had got what he wanted? He
would be gone, that's what would happen. Maybe he would
even try to move on to Ann to see if he could get his way with
her, too. If he hadn't already.

Beth went into the kitchen and picked up the kettle. She
was so upset, she knew she wasn't thinking clearly. She just
wanted to sit quietly and savour the sensations she had

experienced. She didn't need this. She abandoned the kettle, picked up the gin bottle, and poured herself a stiff drink. She took a long gulp. What was he doing now? She closed her eyes.

Immediately, she pictured the way his cock had been straining and throbbing for her. After what had just happened, he must be bursting for release. Perhaps she had been a bit hasty? She began to imagine him sliding slowly into her, his rigid cock pulsating urgently against her softness. Oh God, he was so hard, so desperate. She could sense her own desire building again. Things were getting out of hand. She had to take charge again, quickly.

Beth finished her drink and headed thoughtfully back into the living room. Jonathan hadn't moved from the settee. She walked across the room and stood in front of him.

'You've still got a lot to learn,' she told him. 'You must remember that I am the one in charge here. I say what we do and when we do it. Do you understand?'

Jonathan nodded. 'I'm sorry. I'll do anything you tell me to, Beth. Anything.'

Anything to have your way, she added for him. She realised that she wanted to see him pleasuring himself again. 'Anything?' she questioned.

Jonathan nodded again without speaking

'OK. Why don't you go out into the garden and do it for me?' she suggested, testing her control.

Jonathan gazed up at her in dismay. 'In the garden?' he repeated stupidly.

'Yes.' Beth found herself beginning to get excited at the idea. She could watch him through the window.

'I want you to go out into the back garden and do it there while I watch you.'

Jonathan shook his head in horror. 'Someone will see me.'

Beth's eyes narrowed. 'What about your promise?' she demanded. 'You just said that you would do anything I ask.'

His face filled with defeat, Jonathan stood up and reached for his clothes. He kept his head down.

'What are you doing?' she demanded, suddenly afraid that she had gone too far.

'My clothes. If I have to go into the garden, I need my clothes.'

She almost sighed with relief. For one awful moment, she had thought he was going to walk out on her. 'You won't need your pants for what you are going to do,' she told him. 'You can put your T-shirt on if you want.' She felt sure that he wouldn't.

Jonathan opened the patio door and walked slowly out into the night. He looked like a trapped animal, jumping at every sound.

'Right in the middle where I can see you,' she called after him.

Beth knew that only one house overlooked her garden and that the occupants were away on holiday. She also knew that they had one of those intermittent safety lights on their porch. She couldn't wait to see how he would jump when that came on! She closed the door so that he couldn't get back in until she let him, then turned the lights off and pressed her nose up against the glass.

It was already quite dark and a full moon was riding high in the sky. Jonathan looked like a silver statue of the god Pan. His pale skin was almost translucent in the shimmering moonlight. Beth shivered with anticipation. She placed her hands between her legs and began to move her fingers gently.

Jonathan closed his eyes and reached down to take his limp penis in his hand. He began to fondle himself gently and she saw him start to harden. He squeezed himself savagely, then began to pump himself slowly.

Beth gasped with delight at the sight of him. Until then, she had only half believed that he would actually do it, despite his promises. Her power over him was absolute! She watched, almost without breathing, as he began pumping harder and faster. She saw his lips part and she strained her ears for the sound of his desperate moans. Her own fingers caressed her tiny bud and shivers of desire raced through her.

She waited until he had totally given himself up to his approaching pleasure, then opened the door again.

'That's enough. You can come back in now,' she told him softly.

Jonathan jumped at the sound of her voice and opened his eyes. He was still squeezing himself urgently and, for a moment, she thought she had left it too late for him to stop. Almost reluctantly, he let himself go and turned towards her.

As he walked slowly back towards the house, Beth hurried across the room and curled up on the settee. Although she had replaced her panties and pulled her skirt back down, she hadn't bothered to re-button her blouse. Her nipples were still hard and swollen.

She smiled at him and patted the cushion next to her invitingly.

'Come and sit down,' she told him. Her voice was soft and friendly, with no trace of her earlier anger.

Looking a little self-conscious, Jonathan moved across the room towards her. Beth ran her eyes over his chest. She could see the beads of sweat running down his skin to pool in his navel and trickle on to his golden pubes. Her gaze lingered almost hungrily on his still half-erect penis.

Wearily, Jonathan sank down beside her. Beth noticed that he did not attempt to cover himself. For some reason, that pleased her.

'You shouldn't have tried to push me so hard earlier,' she

told him. 'As I told you, I make the rules here, not you. If you ever try anything like that again, I shall have to punish you.' She licked her lips. 'Is that what you want? Do you want me to put you over my knee and spank you again?'

Jonathan shuddered. 'If you want to,' he whispered.

'Do you want me to?' she questioned excitedly as she remembered the way he had come across her legs the last time she had threatened to spank him. What if she spanked him just at the moment he let go? Would he like that?

Jonathan shook his head and Beth frowned with disapproval. He winced. She moved closer to him and placed her hand on the top of his thigh. His cock had softened almost completely again. She liked it like that, too. Innocent, yet full of potential. She knew that it would not take much to reawaken the sleeping tiger. She knelt in front of him and pulled his legs open, then placed her hand on his limp penis.

Jonathan sighed and his penis stirred slightly under her hand. Beth smiled at the feel of him moving beneath her fingers. She began to rub him gently up and down, watching his face to judge his reaction. She saw his expression begin to change and felt him start to expand.

Would he like it if she licked him there the way he had licked her? What would it feel like in her mouth? What would it taste like? What had she tasted like to him?

Excited by her thoughts, Beth began pumping harder and felt him respond. She glanced down. He was already fully erect again! She licked her lips again. He was so huge now that she doubted if she would even be able to fit him in her mouth. Before she could lose her nerve, she leant forward and ran her tongue across the tip and down the back of the shaft.

Jonathan shuddered from head to toe. He thrust his hips up towards her and rolled his buttocks from side to side. A long, soft groan came from his lips. His eyes were tightly shut.

Beth shivered with delight at the intensity of his reaction. She licked him again.

'Suck it,' he whispered, so softly she barely heard the words. 'Please, suck it.'

Beth opened her lips and wrapped them gently round the tip, taking care not to touch him with her teeth. Very slowly, she slid him up into her mouth until over half of his penis was inside her. He trembled all over and she felt his cock jerk violently against her tongue.

'Oh God,' he sighed as he involuntarily raised his buttocks to push himself up further inside her. 'That feels so good.' He groaned again.

Gently, Beth moved her head up so that her lips slid up his shaft. Her hands began to explore his buttocks as he had explored hers, and her little finger teased the soft down on his balls. Hearing another sigh, she lowered her head again and moved back down so that she was pumping him gently with her mouth. A tingle of excitement ran down her back.

She realised that she was going to make him come as he had done to her. He couldn't help himself. She had him completely at her mercy and there was nothing he could do about it. She felt drunk with her power over him. She began to move her head more quickly.

Jonathan rolled his head from side to side, raising and lowering his buttocks as he thrust against her. His cock jumped and juddered against the roof of her mouth with every move-ment and she could feel his balls tightening, ready. She released his prick and ran her tongue over them, then gently sucked one of them into her mouth.

'Oh God,' Jonathan sobbed with delight and reached down with one hand to pump himself. Beth pushed his hand away possessively and ran her own fingers softly down the shaft, squeezing and kneading him with her fingertips. He groaned again and she felt another tremor rush through his whole body. He was almost there.

Quickly, she released his testicle and put her mouth over his prick again. As she pushed him deep inside her, she began to suck as hard as she could.

'God, no!' Jonathan groaned in desperation and reached down to pull her head away. He was too late. Even before his cock sprang free from her mouth, he was already spurting. He grabbed himself quickly, spurting again and again, as he tried to direct the flow. He slumped back, physically and emotionally drained, apparently too exhausted even to wipe the spunk off his hands.

Beth licked her lips curiously. His fluid tasted thick and salty, but not unpleasant. She wondered why he had pulled out at the last minute. Did he think she might be angry? Perhaps he still believed girls could get pregnant that way. She giggled at the idea and wiped her lips with the back of her hand.

It was something to think about, though. If she did decide to let him go all the way then she would have to do something about contraception. The way it pumped out of him, he was probably extremely virile! She wondered if he carried something with him just in case.

If she asked him about it, he would think that she was going to let him and she wasn't sure about that yet. Well, there was no hurry. She had plenty of time to do something about it.

If she decided that she was going to let him.

10

'It's Gerri's birthday soon,' Ann muttered breathlessly as she
and Beth strode along, side by side, on the treadmills. 'You
haven't forgotten it, have you? It's the big one this time.'

Beth nodded. She hadn't actually forgotten about it but she
hadn't really thought about it all that much either. She had
other things on her mind.

'Well? Are we going to arrange something special for her?'
Ann panted.

Beth pursed her lips. It was depressing to be reminded that
Gerri was about to turn forty. She was only a couple of years
away from it herself.

'Do you think she will really want us to make a fuss?'

Ann sighed with relief as the treadmill began to slow. She
reached for her towel and wiped the sweat off her neck and
brow.

'Are you kidding? Since when did Gerri not want to be the
centre of attention? She'll be devastated if we don't go the
whole hog.'

Beth's own treadmill came to a stop. She stepped down
slowly and waited for the ground to stop moving. 'I guess so.
I suppose we had better see about arranging a party. Perhaps
we could book that little room in the back of the Hare and
Hound. You know the landlady quite well, don't you? Can you
have a word with her?'

Ann nodded and moved over towards the exercise bikes. She
pulled a face. 'I suppose we had better do our penance on these

as well before we go for a dip? God, there must be an easier way to keep in shape.'

Beth laughed. Reluctantly, the two women settled down on to the bike seats, set the programmes, and began to peddle furiously.

'I bet I know what Gerri would like for her birthday,' Beth said suddenly. Ann stared at her expectantly.

'What?' Her voice was faint with exertion.

'A man,' Beth responded as she peddled even harder.

'Very funny. Where do you suggest we get one?'

'Maybe we could get her a strippergram,' Beth replied. 'You know. Can't you ring up somewhere and arrange for that sort of thing?'

Ann looked thoughtful, then nodded. 'I think so. Goodness knows where, though. Do you think she would mind?'

'Mind? She would adore it. Can you imagine how much she would revel in a chance to get her hands on some sweet young lad, instead of just lusting after one? She would be knocked out by it. It's a great idea.' Beth's enthusiasm grew.

Ann shrugged. 'If you say so. You can organise it, though. You're not dumping that one on me. It's your idea. I'll see to the room and the food and you provide the entertainment.'

'Maybe I could ask Jonathan to do it for us?' Beth suggested with a giggle. 'At least it wouldn't cost us anything.'

Ann snorted. 'You're not serious, are you? You can't be. He wouldn't do it anyway. He would never dare.'

Beth bristled. 'He would if I told him to. He'll do anything I say,' she insisted. 'Mind you we can't very well take him into a pub, can we? We'd probably all get arrested.'

She sighed with disappointment. It would have been such fun. She had really liked the idea of seeing Jonathan dressed up like that. Maybe she could get him to give her a private show. The idea appealed enormously. She imagined him dressed in a body-hugging outfit with some sort of mask over his face. Where did one get that sort of thing from?

After their swim, the two women sprawled out on a pair of sun loungers and ordered coffee and cakes.

'Although what the point is in half killing ourselves in the gym just to put it all back on again afterwards, I can't think,' Ann mumbled through a mouthful of chocolate fudge cake.

'A few calories won't exactly do you any harm,' Beth replied as she sank her teeth into a slice of the cake. 'Me neither,' she added, as soon as she could speak again. She glanced down at her slinky new green swimsuit. She wouldn't mind Jonathan seeing her in this. It was a pity that half term was over or they could all go down to the public pool again.

'When are you seeing Jonathan again?' Ann asked casually, as if reading her thoughts.

Beth shrugged. 'In the shop on Saturday, I suppose. Why?'

'I just wondered.'

Beth examined her friend closely and tried to guess what she was thinking. Was it in Ann's mind to try to steal Jonathan away from her? She would be wise to keep an eye on both of them. Perhaps she should make it clear to Ann that Jonathan always told her everything he did. That should hold Ann at bay!

Following up on her idea, Beth took a little trip up to London after work the next day. To her great delight, she had found exactly what she was looking for. Providing she had guessed his measurements properly, the things she had purchased should fit him like a second skin. She could hardly wait to see him in them.

As it turned out, Jonathan wasn't at the shop that Saturday. He had been competing in another swimming contest for his school and Beth was surprised at just how much she had missed him.

That night, while she waited for him, she once more examined the things she had purchased for him. She particularly liked the mask. It was made of some sort of soft plastic, painted silver. It reminded her of one of those ceremonial masks handed out at television awards ceremonies. She remembered the way he had looked at the pool. Like a young Greek god. She couldn't wait to see him in the mask.

It was too bad that she couldn't risk taking him to Gerri's party so all the girls could get an eyeful of him! She had managed to organise a stripping policeman instead. It would probably be all right. After all, Gerri would never know what she was missing!

She giggled as she thought about the knowing look on the shop assistant's face when she had purchased the clothes. She had never been in a shop like that before. She picked up the shirt and trousers and ran them through her fingers.

They were both made of soft grey silk. The shirt was sleeveless and had silver buttons up the front. The front of the trousers did up with silver buttons, too. Best of all was the tiny black thong with its thin strip of material to divide his tiny buttocks, and its shaped pouch at the front. She shivered.

As soon as she opened the door for him, Jonathan realised that Beth was excited about something. His stomach tightened. What was she up to now? Did she have some new game in mind? He looked around, wondering if Ann were there again too. The idea excited him.

'Hello, Jonathan.' He shivered in anticipation at the look in her eyes.

'I've got a surprise for you in my bedroom,' she told him enthusiastically as she took him by the arm.

In spite of his uneasiness, Jonathan couldn't help his own tremor of excitement at the mention of her bedroom. She had never taken him in there before. Did she know how much he had fantasised about taking her in her own bed? Maybe Ann was already there, naked and waiting for him. As Beth turned towards the stairs, he followed her quickly, his eyes all over her.

Beth led him into her bedroom and pointed to a pile of men's clothes lying on the bed. Jonathan stared down at them in astonishment. He had never seen anything quite like them. What were they for? He spotted the silver mask and picked it up curiously to examine it. Beth watched him avidly.

'Go on. Try it on.' She nodded towards the mirror.

'What's it for?' he demanded suspiciously.

'It's just for fun,' Beth replied. 'Ann and I decided to get a strippergram for our friend's birthday party and I thought it would be fun to see you dressed like that.'

'A strippergram?' He failed to disguise the note of panic in his voice. Oh God. What now? Was Ann hiding somewhere? Did Beth expect him to strip for all her friends? Would she expect him to do it in front of dozens of watching eyes? He couldn't.

'Don't worry. I don't expect you to be one. Well, not so that anyone else can see, anyway. I'm sure you won't mind giving me a little thrill, will you? Go on. Try it.'

Jonathan felt himself relax slightly at her words. It wasn't what he had feared. He examined the mask again, wondering why she seemed so excited by it. Slowly, he moved over to the mirror and pulled it over his face. It fitted perfectly. He peered at himself through the eye slits. His face was unrecognisable. He heard Beth sigh gently.

'Now put the clothes on,' she commanded softly.

Jonathan walked back across to the bed. He unbuttoned his own shirt and pulled it off, then picked up the silk one and slipped his arms into the holes. His fingers fumbled over the buttons and Beth moved closer to help him.

'Now the rest.' She took a deep breath and he felt her hands running down his chest; sliding effortlessly over the slippery silk.

Jonathan undid his jeans and pulled them down quickly, then picked up the silk trousers. His eyes widened when he saw that they had button-through flies. He lifted one leg to pull them on.

'Wait. Don't forget this.' Beth was holding up a tiny thong. Before he could react, she moved closer to him and began to pull his pants down. He shivered at the feel of her hands on his skin as she slipped them slowly down his legs. His limp penis sprang free and he stiffened with shock as she reached up to cup his balls in her hand.

'I hope it will fit,' she flattered him. 'It's the largest size they had.'

Jonathan stepped into the elastic of the pouch and pulled it up. The tight satin clung to him, moulding round him like a second skin and perfectly outlining the shape of his prick. He heard Beth sigh and felt her hand running down his thigh again.

He bent over to stick one leg into the trousers, jumping as Beth gave him a quick pat on his left buttock. He pushed his bottom up in the air to give her better access. Beth removed her hand and stepped back. With a sigh of disappointment, he pushed his other leg in and began wriggling to pull the tight silk up over his hips.

Beth moved forward to help him do up the buttons at the front. She seemed to be deliberately taking her time. Long before she was finished the pouch was already fitting him much more snugly. He heard her breath catch as she stepped back and eyed him up and down.

'Turn around,' she commanded huskily.

Jonathan swivelled round slowly until he was facing the mirror. He found that he was having trouble breathing. The way she was watching him like that was sending goosebumps up and down his whole body. He stared silently at his reflection. He looked as if he had been sprayed all over with silver-grey paint. Every swell and curve of his body stood out clearly.

Just then, the doorbell rang, making them both jump.

He turned to stare at her. Now what? Oh God. Was that Ann at the door? She had told him that he wouldn't have to strip for all her friends. She hadn't specifically said anything about Ann. He remembered how Ann had looked naked.

The bell rang again.

'Wait for me here,' Beth whispered. 'I'll just get rid of whoever it is. I'll be back in a minute.'

While he was waiting for her, Jonathan turned back and stared at his image in the mirror again. He didn't recognise himself. He had seen the way Beth had been looking at him. The expression on her face had told him exactly what she thought. A thrill of excitement ran down his spine. He liked the idea of turning her on. It made him feel strong and commanding.

He ran his hands down his sides and over his buttocks, pleased to see how hard his body was from all his swimming. He shivered again at the memory of Beth's hands touching him. It was as if her fingers had been charged with electricity. He twisted his head round to look over his shoulder and examined the back. The trousers were so tight that he could see the strip of the thong disappearing into his crease. He smiled.

Jonathan turned back and moved closer to the mirror. He felt different. Strange and distant, as if he were floating above his own body, watching himself. The mask gave him confidence, like Jim Carrey's character Stanley Ipkiss in the film, *The Mask*. He felt as if he could do or say things that he normally wouldn't dare. He wanted her. Now, tonight. On her bed. No more of her games. He was going to have her.

What was she doing? Was it Ann at the door? Beth had seemed surprised by the doorbell but perhaps she was just playing more of her games? He was excited at the idea of seeing Ann again, yet scared that it would spoil his plans for Beth. Could he take care of both of them?

He turned round anxiously as Beth walked back into the room.

'It's all right. It was just someone collecting for charity,' she told him softly.

As she spoke, her eyes examined his body hungrily and the husky note in her voice drove him mad with longing.

Jonathan walked over to her and pulled her into his arms. His lips found hers. He could feel her trembling and his feeling of power grew stronger. The buttons of his new trousers were pushing urgently against his erection.

Beth leant against him, her body swaying. Her hands slid down his hips and over his groin. She ran her fingers down his cock, lingering on each button. The silk caressed every inch of his body. It felt as if there were hands running all over him.

She opened the top two buttons and reached into the pouch to expose him. Jonathan groaned and thrust against her. Beth lowered her head and opened her lips. Slowly, she took him inside her mouth.

Jonathan strained forward and placed his hand on the back of her head to stop her escaping. He closed his eyes and thrust gently against her lips. He imagined he was inside her properly and his excitement grew. He began to thrust harder and deeper.

Beth gagged and pulled her head back slightly. She tightened her lips around his tip and began sucking him, gently at first, then harder. She moved her hands so that one was groping his bum and the other was fondling the soft hair surrounding his balls. His face tightened with pleasure.

'I can't hold it if you do that,' he whispered as he tried to pull back against the suction. Beth immediately tightened her lips even more.

Jonathan began twisting from side to side, unsure what to do. He knew that he was about to come. Part of him wanted to pull back and part of him wanted to thrust forward. Beth's mouth held him like a vice so that he couldn't move in or out. She sucked again.

'Oh Jesus, I can't hold on.' He closed his eyes and surrendered to the inevitable.

Beth opened her lips and released him. She moved back and stared down at his throbbing penis, then lifted her hands and began to rub them over her own breasts.

Jonathan swayed, almost falling. His breath was coming in little pants. She had taken him so close to the edge that he still didn't know how he had held on. His whole body was on fire. He opened his eyes and saw the way she was playing with herself. He sobbed. The bitch was teasing him again, taunting him with her lips and her body. She was revelling in her power over him. Oh Christ, how he wanted her. He had to have her.

Jonathan pushed her hands away, grabbed the top of her blouse and ripped it open. He heard one of the buttons pop off and fly across the bed. The sound inflamed him. He pushed her bra up roughly and sank his mouth over her nipple, sucking hungrily. He manoeuvred her to the side of the bed so that she lost her balance and fell backwards. Now. He was going to take her.

Quick as a flash, Jonathan leant over and pushed her skirt up. He grabbed her panties and pulled them down so smoothly that Beth couldn't have stopped him if she had wanted to. The material caught on one of her heels and Jonathan ripped the shoe off too.

Beth half turned and tried to crawl up on to the bed. Her bra was still pushed up above her breasts. He grabbed it with his right hand and pulled it up over her head so that her arms were tangled with bra and gaping blouse, restricting her movements. As she struggled, Jonathan pulled her round on to her back and knelt over her. His mouth sought her nipples while his hands pulled her skirt roughly over her hips. He pushed his hand between her clenched thighs and Beth groaned aloud as his fingers began to caress her swollen clit.

Jonathan was almost beside himself. The feel of her struggling against him was overpowering. He was in charge now. All the longing, all the pent-up frustration of the past few weeks was boiling up inside him. He was going to take her properly this time; thrust himself deep inside her hot, moist cunt and pump himself into her until she screamed for mercy. His erection throbbed desperately against the tight clothing. Dear God, don't let him lose it yet. He had to get these clothes off.

Jonathan stood up quickly and ripped at the remaining buttons of the trousers with fingers that were trembling too much to work properly. He peeled the tight silk down his body, cursing as it stuck to his damp, sweaty skin. Frantically, he ripped the pouch off. His erection bounced free, swollen to bursting point with its desperate need for release. Please God, he thought again. Not yet! He turned back to face her, his whole body stiff with anticipation.

Beth had struggled free of the tangled bra and blouse and rolled on to her stomach. As he reached for her again, she tried to crawl across the bed away from him.

Jonathan slumped down on top of her again. One hand began groping her breasts while the other slipped under her hips to fondle her pubes. She moaned again and tried to wriggle out from under him.

Jonathan leant forward across her bottom and thrust against her. He heard her cry out with shock as his hard cock pushed against her buttocks. He thrust again and felt himself slip in between her crease. Beth whimpered and lifted her hips to push herself up against him. She slipped her own hand underneath her hipbones and ran her finger over her clit. He felt a shiver of desire race through her body as he thrust again.

As if suddenly realising what he was trying to do, Beth pushed herself back down against the bed and tried to slide out from under him.

'No. You mustn't,' she sobbed.

Jonathan barely heard her. He no longer cared that she had turned over. It didn't matter that he wasn't properly inside her. Her buttocks were still closed tightly around his cock and her legs were holding him like a vice. The sight and feel of himself impaled like that was driving him insane. The feel of her skin wrapped around him was more than he could bear. He knew he couldn't last much longer.

He reached under her and grabbed her breasts in his hands. He squeezed them between his fingers and felt her pushing her buttocks up against him again. Jesus, he couldn't hold on. It felt so good.

He began to thrust harder and faster, savouring the relentless pressure building up inside him. He gritted his teeth to stop himself yelling aloud. Her buttocks tightened against him and every muscle in his own body constricted. He groaned in ecstasy and despair as the semen shot out of him with a violence he had never experienced before. He groaned again, still pumping desperately. Another spurt tore from him. It splattered across her buttocks and began to drip down her thighs.

Beth gasped. As he slumped against her, she began to wriggle frantically underneath him. Jonathan rolled off her and lay beside her, totally spent.

Beth stood up and left the room without a word. He heard the sound of the shower running in the bathroom. He removed the mask and placed it on the bed beside him.

When she finally returned to the bedroom, wrapped in a bath towel, he still hadn't even bothered to dress himself. He looked up silently, trying to gauge her mood. He could feel his penis shrivelled up against him as if it were trying to hide from her expected wrath.

'I think perhaps you had better leave,' she told him. Her face gave nothing away.

Jonathan stood up quickly and began to pull on his clothes. When he was ready, she led him silently down the stairs. As she opened the front door, she put a hand on his arm and scanned his face thoughtfully.

'Just remember to stop and think a bit next time, Jonathan,' she told him with a slight grin. 'You weren't even wearing any protection, you know.'

Jonathan felt relief washing over him at her words.

'You mean, you'll let me come round again?' His conflicting emotions choked his voice.

'Yes. If you do as you're told.'

Jonathan took a deep breath. He knew he was pushing his luck, but after what had so nearly happened, he couldn't stop himself. To his eager mind, her words seemed full of almost unbelievable potential.

'When I do,' he began. 'Then ...' His voice trailed off.

'Then what?'

He was certain from the look on her face that she knew exactly what he was trying to say.

'Then, will you? I mean, can I?' He hesitated again.

'We'll just have to see, won't we?'

Hearing the tremor in her voice, Jonathan smiled triumphantly.

Beth made her way slowly back upstairs. Although she was feeling completely drained, her body was still tingling. She spied his silk clothes in a heap on the floor where he had thrown them. She picked them up and ran them through her fingers, then lifted them closer to her face. She could smell his body scent, harsh and musky. Beth closed her eyes and remembered how he had looked wearing them. She could feel herself growing damp again.

She moved over to her dressing table and opened the top drawer. She lifted out a long, thin box and opened it. The vibrator felt cold and hard in her hands. She flicked the switch at the end and jumped at the loud buzzing sound it made. It sounded like a swarm of angry bees.

Beth slipped the bath towel off and lay down on the bed. The vibrator hummed impatiently in her fingers. It was so hard. Even harder than Jonathan had been. Her fingers trembled as she lowered her hand and slipped the vibrating plastic between her legs.

She gasped. It felt almost as good as his tongue. Maybe even better. She closed her eyes and shifted it slightly, then gasped again as she placed it directly over her clit. The waves of pleasure began to build up inside her. She wriggled her hips and used her other hand to play softly with one nipple. The pressure increased, intensified.

Beth waited until she felt as if she were going to explode

then moved the vibrator away. She rolled her hips from side to side, unable to lie still. As she thrust herself up into the air, she imagined Jonathan was lying on top of her and a small whimper escaped her lips. She moved the vibrator back into her slit and whimpered again.

She was about to come. She could feel her muscles beginning to contract. She moved the vibrator away again and moaned with desperation for release. This was what she enjoyed doing to him. Teasing him, leading him up to the edge and then making him hold off. Jesus, how he must have suffered.

She squeezed her thighs together tightly and whimpered again. She couldn't wait any longer. She just couldn't. Crying out at the intensity of the sensation, Beth placed the vibrator back against her now throbbing clit and moved it up and down gently.

Oh Jesus! She couldn't stand it. Her muscles contracted again. She felt as if her insides were on fire. The back of her thighs prickled and a long, sharp tingle raced down her spine. She tensed and flexed the muscles in her buttocks and thighs and thrust herself up against the vibrator. She ran her other hand rapidly all over her body, then began to squeeze and knead her breasts roughly as she writhed from side to side. Her breathing deepened until she was panting with desire.

Her clit throbbed and burned, growing increasingly sensitive by the second. She held her breath and eased off on the pressure so that the vibrator was barely touching her. She groaned loudly, arching her back and thrusting upward as her orgasm exploded inside her. Spasms of pleasure rushed along every nerve of her body and she groaned again.

Her muscles relaxed and she slumped back on to the bed, utterly exhausted. The vibrator hummed on relentlessly. Beth flicked the switch and dropped it weakly at her side. She closed her eyes and shuddered all over.

She had never imagined it could feel that good. Her whole body was drenched with perspiration. Her clit was tingling as if the vibrator was still massaging it. She felt as if she had just run twenty miles. She felt utterly exhausted, as if she would never be able to move again. She felt good all over. She sighed contentedly.

She remembered her parting words to Jonathan. She had more or less agreed to let him have her properly. Is that what it would feel like? She shivered at the idea.

11

Beth stood completely still as her heart began to thump violently in her chest. She stared across the store, unable to think straight. It was definitely Tony. She would know that profile anywhere.

How long since she had last seen him? A year? Longer? He hadn't changed much. Hardly at all, really. The same couldn't be said for her.

Beth glanced down appreciatively at her trim figure in its above-the-knee, tailored dress and matching jacket. He probably wouldn't even recognise her. The temptation was almost too great to resist. She glanced around again to make sure that his new wife was definitely nowhere in sight, then she glided across the store towards him.

Tony was standing at the tie rack. He had never been any good at choosing ties. He had never liked the ones she chose for him, either. He glanced up and looked straight past her. She had been right. He didn't know her.

His eyes swivelled back towards her and a strange look crossed his face. He examined her slowly, his eyes taking in her high heels and long shapely legs before they moved on up to her breasts. Still, he said nothing. Was he going to cut her dead?

Suddenly, she realised that he still hadn't recognised her. He was eyeing her up because of the way she looked, not because of who she was. A shiver ran down her spine at the look on his face. She had seen other men looking at her like that lately too. Was she really so changed?

'Hello, Tony. How are you?' Her voice was different too. Deeper and more confident.

Tony started guiltily, as if his wife had caught him ogling another woman. He stared into her face and his eyes widened as recognition finally dawned.

'Beth! I didn't know you. I, that is ... You're looking well.'

She revelled in his obvious confusion.

'Thank you.' She smiled knowingly as he ran his eyes hungrily over her body again. Get a good look, she thought spitefully. This is what you threw away. She licked her lips.

'Janet not with you?' She made a pretence of looking round the store.

He flushed slightly and shook his head. 'No, no. I'm on my own. You really are looking very well,' he said again. Beth continued to smile.

'So, how have you been keeping?' she asked. 'Is work going well?' Tony was in finance. Once, they had both worked for the same company. It was how they had met. He made good money, which was fortunate for Beth as far as the divorce settlement was concerned, but he worked long hours. It left him little time for other pursuits.

'Fine. Good. I'm well. We're both well ...' He broke off, as if he had suddenly realised that Beth would not be interested in how Janet was. His eyes examined her again lustfully.

Now what? Beth wondered, as she watched him watching her. She couldn't think of anything else to say to him. It was funny how they were like two polite strangers. Once they had shared everything together, even their bodies. Not very well, perhaps. She smiled as she imagined how he would react if she tried to do to him what she did to Jonathan.

What had they once talked about together? Whatever it was, it wouldn't be appropriate now. Maybe she should just say goodbye and get on with her shopping. She liked the way he was looking at her. Was he comparing her with his new wife? She examined him more closely in return.

Now that she was standing right next to him, she could see that he had changed a bit. There was more silver-grey in his dark hair for a start. Actually, it suited him. Why was it that grey hair just aged women, while it seemed to make men look more distinguished? His face had a few more worry lines and he seemed a little plumper round the waistline. All in all, he had worn well. His eyes were the same as ever. Twin pools of darkest brown, like liquid chocolate. She used to tell herself she had married him for those eyes.

They were still watching her avidly and Beth felt a little of the old love and tenderness sweeping through her. Love, tenderness, and something else. She pushed in front of him so that her body rubbed against him, ever so accidentally.

'You never could choose ties, Tony,' she murmured softly. With a smile, she picked out a tie of wine-red silk and held it against him. 'This would look great on you. Especially with a white shirt and dark grey suit.'

Tony smiled in return as his hand reached into his jacket to find his wallet. His eyes continued to devour her body.

It was only a small victory, but it made her feel ten feet tall.

He handed both tie and cash to a hovering sales assistant, then waited silently while she wrapped it. Beth wandered over to examine a rack of shirts. Would Tony think she was shopping for another man?

Tony pocketed the package with a nod of thanks and turned back to her.

'Actually, I was just thinking about getting something to eat,' he told her as he moved over beside her. 'I don't suppose you would care to join me? My way of saying thank you for finding the tie.'

Beth smiled. 'Yes. Why not? I can't afford to turn down a free meal.' Why had she said that? True, she had spent rather a lot on new clothes lately. Even so ... She was enjoying her shameless taunting and the obvious effect it was having on him. She didn't want to let him go. Tony sighed with what sounded like relief. She wondered if he was anxious not to let her go again yet either.

Hesitantly, Tony held out his arm for her. His eyes continued to feast on her firm breasts. She glanced down and almost giggled with surprise. Although she could hardly believe it, she realised that Tony was actually becoming physically aroused. When had she last had that effect on him? She glanced down again, marvelling surreptitiously at the telltale bulge. Would he realise that she had noticed?

As they left the store, Tony held the door and stood back for her. Beth found herself basking in the attention. She had to admit she had missed his manners. They might be a bit old-fashioned, but it was nice to be cosseted and taken care of sometimes. As long as it didn't go too far, of course. All men should be taught that there were times to be gentle and protective, and times to ... She broke the thought off. Why dwell on what was over and done with?

Tony took her arm and tucked it through his as they walked out into the sunshine.

To her amusement, he selected one of their old favourite restaurants. It was also one of the most expensive in the area. Beth was certain that his wife would be very angry if she ever found out. They talked little while they ate and Beth noticed that, for once, Tony hardly touched his food.

Beth chose the most expensive items on the menu and ate heartily. When she had finished her meal, she pushed the chair back from the table slightly and smiled contentedly at him.

'That was delicious. Thank you, Tony.' She crossed her legs

and turned her body so that he got a good look at her legs. She smiled to herself as he watched her skirt ride slowly up her thighs. She had never used to wear stockings when they were married.

Beth uncrossed and then re-crossed her legs and leant forward so that he could see straight down the top of her dress. His eyes seemed almost to home in on her tiny lace bra.

'So. Tell me about yourself. What have you been doing lately?' she questioned.

Tony didn't answer. He was still staring, mesmerised, down her front. He had also crossed his own legs. As if that hid anything.

Beth stared blatantly at his crotch. 'I do believe you've put on a little weight,' she told him. 'You seem, well, more filled out than I remember. It suits you.'

'You certainly haven't,' he replied. His voice was squeaky and he cleared his throat quickly. 'Put on weight, I mean. I've never seen you looking better, Beth.' She could see the perspiration forming on his brow.

'Thank you, again,' she responded. 'I've never known you to be so free with the compliments, Tony. Perhaps we've both changed?'

'Coffee?' Tony spluttered.

Beth nodded.

'Unless you would prefer to come back to the house?' she suggested with a smile. 'I've finished my shopping anyway.'

Tony looked startled. Beth remembered that it was not so long ago when she had told him never to so much as cross her doorstep again. No wonder he looked bewildered. Did he realise that she was enjoying what she was doing to him? That she was deliberately toying with him? Did he mind?

'Why, yes, thank you. I'd like that.' Tony beckoned the waiter.

He used his gold card at the table and added a much bigger tip than usual. The waiter gave him a knowing look. Beth noticed several men staring at them and she realised with a small thrill that she must look more like his mistress than his ex-wife. The thought delighted her.

As soon as he had paid the bill, Tony stood up and held the back of her chair. He stretched his arm out to help her rise and Beth smiled with pleasure.

Tony held out his arm again. 'Shall we?'

She took it, still smiling.

As he helped her into his car, he made the most of his opportunity to get a good look up her skirt. Beth moved as slowly as she could, deliberately encouraging his stares. She let her skirt ride up when she had sat down and did nothing to correct the situation.

As he drove, Tony kept darting little glances at her thighs out of the corner of his eye, as if he still could not believe the changes in her. She loved every moment and was almost sorry when they reached the end of her road.

It seemed strange to be arriving back at her house sitting beside her ex-husband. It was almost as if someone had turned the clock back five years.

As soon as he had switched the engine off, Tony leapt out of the car and ran round to hold the door for her. She smiled at his prying eyes. He must have seen practically all the way up to her navel that time!

She unlocked the front door, stepped inside and removed her jacket. As she did so, she dropped her keys and bent down slowly to retrieve them. Posing was becoming second nature to her now. She straightened slowly and ran her eyes over his crotch. She was certain that the bulge was not due to poor tailoring. Smirking, she moved into the kitchen to put the kettle on and make the coffee. Tony wandered through into the living room.

'I see you've been decorating,' he called. Beth grinned. She had always hated the wallpaper he had chosen for the living room. It was one of the first things she had got rid of after he left.

'That old lamp of mine would still go well in here,' he continued and Beth snorted.

The hell it would, she thought to herself and grinned wickedly as she remembered her own use for the hook in the ceiling. She poured the coffee and grinned again at the thought of how much he would hate it. He had always insisted on real coffee beans, claiming that instant wasn't fit for human consumption. Tough. She walked through to join him.

Tony was sitting on the settee. He watched her hungrily as she moved across the room and leant from the waist to place the mugs on the table. She felt her skirt lifting up above her stocking tops and saw his eyes widen.

'I'm afraid it's only instant. I wasn't expecting you,' she apologised as she sat down beside him and smoothed out her skirt. She leant forward to pick up her mug. His eyes dived down the front of her dress.

'I've got used to instant,' he explained sheepishly. 'Janet can't be bothered with the real thing.'

Beth smirked again. Good for Janet. She wondered what other changes her successor had brought about, or what other things she couldn't be bothered with. She crossed her legs and heard his quick intake of breath. He had swivelled round on the settee so that he could see her better.

She wondered how far she dared to go. This wasn't a young, naïve boy. This was Tony, her ex-husband. She couldn't play with him the way she played with Jonathan. Or could she?

She examined his groin curiously. He was definitely aroused. She remembered that she had never actually seen his cock properly in all their years together. Was he bigger than

Jonathan? What would he do if she whipped his zipper open and took him in her mouth?

She almost laughed aloud at the idea. He would be so shocked he would either come straight away or shrivel up like a prune. She was surprised to realise that her thoughts were not exciting her. Amusing her, yes. Exciting her, no. She felt nothing for him any more. Not love, not even lust.

Only revenge. On him and on Janet. Every look he gave her was one less for that marriage wrecker he now called his wife. Perhaps he would go home that night and see his mistake.

'Why don't you take your jacket off?' she suggested. 'You must be sweltering.'

He looked startled. She fought to stop another giggle bubbling up inside her. He looked as though she had suggested that he strip naked. She had always thought that it was she who had been the prude. Perhaps it was him? She almost felt sorry for Janet.

She put her hand on his thigh and patted him gently. 'I really am glad we bumped into each other like this,' she told him truthfully. She was learning a lot about Tony that she hadn't known before.

Tony jumped at the touch as if she had scalded him.

Beth removed her hand from his thigh and reached forward to take another sip of her coffee. She realised that she was growing bored with her little game. She might not love Jonathan but at least she lusted after him. It wasn't all that much fun prick-teasing a cock you didn't really fancy anyway. The idea of Tony touching her left her completely cold. This had been a stupid idea.

Mind you, the satisfaction of knowing what she was doing to him was revenge enough. She imagined him lying frustrated in his bed that night thinking of her, and then pictured him getting up to creep off to the bathroom the way he always used to.

She glanced at her watch. It was only a few more hours until Jonathan arrived. It had been a good idea to take a holiday from work this morning. It was more frustrating than fun being at the shop with him these days, trying to act normally and pretend that there was nothing between them. Maybe she would talk with Mr Bailey about giving up her Saturday shift for good.

She glanced back at Tony. His face was flushed and his breathing shallow. His eyes were greedily devouring her body. How often had she seen Jonathan looking at her like that? Despite her disinterest, she felt an overwhelming surge of power. She was enjoying teasing him and loved picturing his frustration. Why hadn't she discovered this skill years ago? How different might their marriage have been?

She needed a bath. She wanted to take lots of time to get ready for Jonathan's visit. She wasn't sure yet where the evening might lead. Jonathan was probably already hard just thinking about her half-promise. It was up to her. Whatever happened or didn't happen, she was in charge. Beth shivered in anticipation and finished her coffee.

'Look. I don't mean to be rude Tony, but I've got someone coming round this evening. I really should be getting on.' She almost laughed at the expression on his face. She had seen that look before, too.

'It really was great to see you,' she added. 'Thank you again for lunch. Perhaps we could do it again some time? If you'd like to, of course.' She smiled sweetly.

Tony moved over and slipped his arm round her shoulders.

'Look. Are you all right financially? I mean, if you're a bit short of cash, ever . . .' He shrugged. 'I could always let you have a bit more to help you out.'

Beth looked thoughtful. 'What did you have in mind?' she

questioned. Did he mean what she thought he meant? The idea was almost too delicious.

'Oh, well. Maybe a hundred or so, now and again.'

Beth pursed her lips. She put her hand on his knee and ran her fingers gently up his thigh. She felt him shudder.

'I'm not sure a hundred would make all that much difference one way or the other,' she began. 'After all, you already give me a fair sum and then, there's my own earnings.' She couldn't remember whether he knew about her job in the shop or not.

'Well, a hundred and fifty then. Would that do?' He lowered his own arm and grabbed a handful of her buttocks.

Beth shrugged. 'Perhaps. If I ever need it.' She smiled again and moved smoothly out of his clasp. 'Look. I really have got things to do now, Tony.' She stood up.

'I'll think about it. If I ever find myself desperate for some extra cash, I'll know where to come.' She enjoyed the way he winced at her choice of words. How high would he go? She stared innocently at his crotch. She could see his trousers were still too tight. Janet might be in for a treat!

She could almost feel the disappointment coursing through him as he stood up beside her.

'Well, just don't forget my offer,' he told her stiffly as he left.

Beth closed the door behind him thankfully. She was still feeling vaguely nauseous at the thought of sex with him. Had he really been offering her money to sleep with him? She could hardly believe it. Not of Tony. She giggled. And to think he had once been in a position to have it for free whenever he had wanted it. The irony of the situation appealed to her sense of humour.

She ought to be insulted. Although, in a way, it was kind of flattering to think he wanted her that much. She wondered what it would be like to sell herself to a man as his plaything. Only someone she knew, of course. Someone she already fancied anyway. Definitely not Tony.

She shrugged and dismissed him from her mind. Some things were better left where they belonged. Tony was part of her past. She didn't want him any more. She didn't even need him any more. The realisation startled her. Not so long ago, she would probably have got down on her hands and knees and begged if she had thought it would have brought him back to her. It was a good moment. She felt the last shackles of her old life fall away from her.

The evening ahead with Jonathan was beckoning to her. She felt a small shiver of anticipation running down her back. It was time to go and make herself irresistible for him. Whatever happened that evening, she wanted it to be special; something they would both never forget.

She pictured herself slipping a condom down over Jonathan's erect cock before she lowered herself slowly down on to his waiting manhood.

Tony drove home to his wife slowly, his mind going round in circles. Jesus! What was wrong with him? His palms felt damp and sticky and he could swear that his cock was still slightly stiffer than it should be. He hadn't undressed a woman with his eyes like that for years. Fancied one or two, maybe, but not like that.

What the hell had happened to her? Perhaps she had found another man. Tony was surprised at the rush of jealousy he experienced. Why not? She was a free woman. He had no hold over her any more.

Had she meant her remarks to sound like they had? Surely not. Beth was far too straight-laced even to think something like that, let alone say it. Wasn't she? She couldn't have been leading him on. She didn't have it in her. She was practically frigid. She always had been. That was one of the reasons he had left her for Janet.

Not that it had done him a lot of good. Janet wasn't all that much to write home about in the sack, either. At least, not any more. Maybe at first. He could feel the sweat under his collar and he shifted uncomfortably. God, she had looked fantastic.

He couldn't think of that beautiful and desirable creature as his ex-wife. She seemed more like one of those women at the massage parlour he sometimes visited with a work mate. Sensual and sure of herself, yet, at the same time, cold and matter-of-fact. But they were nothing but brassy tramps. Beth put them to shame. He shivered again. He hadn't even felt like visiting a place like that lately. How long had it been since he and Janet had last had sex? A month, two?

He had practically offered her money to sleep with him. He was certain she had understood. Would she take him up on the offer? She couldn't be like them now, could she? Not Beth. No one could change that much. He forced his eyes back on to the road, scared that if he allowed himself to become too distracted, he would end up in a ditch.

Maybe he wouldn't go straight home after all. Maybe he would stop off at that place his mates had shown him. His cock throbbed as images of Beth, naked and ready, flooded back into his mind.

11

Jonathan slid inside the door and pushed it closed behind him with his bottom. Beth never ceased to be amazed at how fast his hands could move when he wanted. He seemed to cover all the important areas in the first few seconds!

As he pulled her hard against himself, she could feel his excitement. His whole body was tense with anticipation. Had he been thinking about their last conversation, turning her words over and over in his mind until he had convinced himself that she had agreed?

Beth disentangled herself from his clasp and moved away slightly. Whatever happened, it was going to be her decision, not his. She turned to lead the way along the hall towards the living room. She could feel her own excitement building inside her in response to his obvious enthusiasm. Jonathan followed her like a shadow, his fingers still fondling whatever he could reach.

As they reached the stairs, Jonathan hesitated. Beth noticed the way his eyes were staring hopefully upwards. She knew that he wanted her in the bedroom. After what had happened there last time, he was probably even more turned on by the idea of taking her on her own bed.

'Why don't you go up and put on your special clothes,' she suggested. 'They're on the bed. You can give me another private little show.' Her whole body began to tremble at the idea of seeing him dressed in all that tight silk again.

Jonathan immediately began to unbutton his shirt. Beth moved closer and put her hand on his to stop him.

'Not here. Go and change upstairs and then wait for me in the bedroom.' She smiled at the way his eyes lit up. She would never tire of the thrill his almost desperate desire for her body gave her. Teasing him was so much more fun than teasing Tony.

Would he still react like that once he had had what he most wanted? Supposing she did let him have his way with her tonight – would that be the end of everything? Maybe she should string him along a bit longer.

Almost tripping over his own feet in his eagerness to obey her, Jonathan scurried up the stairs. As he moved, Beth could see that he was already ripping his shirt off and trying to undo his jeans with shaking fingers. She walked slowly into the kitchen and poured herself a large drink. If ever she had needed a little Dutch courage, it was now.

She sighed longingly as she pictured him dressed in all that tight silk, with his face obscured by the mask. She remembered the young man she had booked for Gerri's party. He hadn't looked anywhere near as desirable as Jonathan did. Mind you, Gerri had seemed to be more than satisfied.

Beth smiled as she remembered the way Gerri had drooled all over her surprise present from the moment he had arrived at her party. How would she have felt if she had had the chance to do to him what Beth was now intending to do with her plaything?

She took another sip of her gin and tonic and tried to sort out her muddled thoughts. She could picture Jonathan already lying on her bed with his cock hard and twitching for her. It made her feel weak at the knees just to imagine it. Her unexpected encounter with Tony had reminded her just how long it had been since she had had full intercourse. In a way, she was looking forward to it almost as much as Jonathan was.

Could she still keep his attention afterwards? Would he still lust after her the way he did now, or would it all be spoilt by his loss of virginity? She would have to let him sooner or later, or she would lose him anyway. What if he was already using what he had learnt with her to experiment with girls his own age? She pictured the little blonde at the pool. Supposing he didn't wait for her? Supposing he lost his virginity to someone else? The idea was unthinkable. She felt almost possessive about his virginity. It was hers to take. After all that they had been through together, no one else had the right.

Did he see it like that? Probably not. He just wanted to lose it. He wouldn't be all that particular with whom, just so long as it happened. If she didn't take care of him soon ... She almost had a duty to finish his education, to protect the innocence of his little blonde friend. If the little tramp was innocent. Beth put her glass down and headed slowly and thoughtfully up the stairs.

As she had anticipated, Jonathan was already dressed and in the bedroom, waiting for her. He wasn't actually lying on the bed. He was lurking by the doorway as if unsure whether to wait or to go down looking for her.

Her breath caught at the sight of him in the skin-tight clothing. She hadn't been wrong about the hard cock either. The buttons at his crotch already looked as if they were strained beyond endurance. She realised that she was looking forward to putting those buttons out of their misery.

As soon as she walked into the room, he was all over her again. Even before his tongue had prised her lips apart, his hands were up under her top and bra fondling her breasts and nipples. She could feel him pushed hard against her stomach and hear the urgency in his breathing. If he didn't calm down a bit, it would all be over before she had to make any decisions. She pushed him away.

'Take it easy, Jonathan. There's no hurry. We've got all evening.'

Jonathan grabbed for her again. He groaned softly at her words and began to run his hands all over her again. She could see the passion burning in his eyes.

Beth pushed him away again and moved over to sit on the edge of the bed.

'Come over here and stand in front of me,' she commanded. He obeyed her without question and Beth smiled to herself. She was still in control for now. She had better make the most of it, just in case.

She reached up and pushed her hands between his legs, delighting in the feel of the soft slippery material covering the swell of his balls.

Jonathan shuffled closer and shifted his feet so that his legs were parted. He reached out for her head and pulled it towards his groin. As she ran her tongue up his bulge, her lips played with each of the buttons in turn. Jonathan closed his eyes and sighed deeply. Beth began worrying the top button with her teeth. She used her thumb to slip it through the buttonhole, all the while squeezing and rubbing his cock through the silk.

Jonathan bent over her and began to pull her blouse out of the back of her skirt. As soon as the first button sprang open, Beth moved on down to the next one.

It wasn't the easiest way to undo buttons, but his reaction more than made up for it. As each one came open to expose his cock further, Jonathan's face became more flushed and his breathing heavier. She noticed that he was having trouble keeping still. His weight was shifting from one foot to the other as he gyrated his hips and pushed his pelvis forward to seek her tongue's soft caress.

As she undid the final button, his cock seemed to leap out at her like a snake uncoiling. She marvelled at how hard he was. She didn't remember ever seeing him so stiff. She felt the lubrication between her own legs starting to flow. The deep burning, tingling sensation she had grown to know and love intensified, twisting her insides in knots. Her nipples hardened.

Beth ran her fingertips down his back and slid them into the top of his waistband. She peeled the trousers slowly over his hips and let her fingers caress the thin material of the thong. His buttocks felt as tight and hard as if they were made of stone.

As she pulled the back of the trousers down, his prick began to move up and down in response to her movements. Beth leant forward and began to tease its tip with her tongue. She squeezed his buttocks with her hands as if testing the ripeness of a melon, then slid her hands round to the front. Slowly, she pulled the gaping material free from his balls and slipped it down to his thighs.

Jonathan unfastened her bra and leant back, sliding his hands round her front to grab her breasts. He pulled her blouse and bra away roughly and bent his knees so that he could cup her breasts in his hands.

As he strained forward to push his cock into her mouth, he moaned softly and his hips began gyrating faster. Beth heard his breath catch and noticed the way he was drawing it in and out, slowly and deliberately, like an athlete preparing for a race.

She stroked the skin under his balls gently, almost as if she were petting a dog under the chin. Jonathan squeezed her breasts and sighed desperately. His breath whooshed out of him in a violent gasp. So much for his breathing techniques! She grinned wickedly and increased the pressure of her caresses.

Jonathan pinched her nipples and then began to flick them gently with his fingers, pushing them like the buttons on a vending machine. She noticed with amusement that he was concentrating on his breathing again.

Beth finished removing his trousers and began on his shirt. As she stood up to reach the top button, she lost her balance and swayed into him. His cock pushed against her and she heard him cry out.

His obvious excitement inflamed her and she felt a powerful surge of desire deep inside. For a moment, she almost thought she was going to come just thinking about it. Quickly, she pulled the shirt down his arms and stepped back. Her panties were dripping. She needed to find a way to calm herself down a bit. Would his controlled breathing techniques work for her?

'Lie down on the bed and spread your arms and legs out at the sides,' she instructed huskily.

While he was obeying her, Beth quickly slipped out of her remaining clothes. They suddenly felt much too hot and constricting and she wanted to feel the cool air on her burning flesh. When she turned back, she almost gasped aloud.

Jonathan was lying as instructed. His face was intense with concentration as if he were trying to think about something very important. His arms and legs were spread-eagled and his cock was sticking up like a giant tent pole. She pictured lowering herself down on to him and her stomach flipped over. She was tempted to kneel over him and suck it, but she was certain that the feel of her hands and mouth would be too much for him to resist.

Beth walked unsteadily over to her dressing table and opened the drawer. She took out four pieces of cord and a small foil-wrapped package. She moved back to the bed and slipped the condom under a pillow, then reached for one of his hands.

Jonathan opened his eyes and turned his head towards her.

He examined her breasts and cunt hungrily, then reached out with his free hand to squeeze her left breast.

Beth dodged back out of his way and tied one of the pieces of cord to his wrist. She turned round and attached the other end to the headboard of the bed.

'What are you doing?' Jonathan strained his wrist against the cord. It held fast.

'Just making sure I know where you are,' she replied.

Beth raised herself up and climbed across him to reach his other wrist. Her pubes brushed lightly over his cock and Jonathan instinctively arched his back to push himself against her. He was following her every movement like a hawk and his eyes seemed mesmerised by the way her breasts were swinging gently from side to side. She lingered over him a moment, teasing him, then secured his second wrist swiftly and deftly. Slowly, she moved down the bed towards his feet.

As if suddenly realising what she was doing and what it would mean, Jonathan began to struggle more fiercely against his bonds. Beth turned round over his legs so that her bottom was high in the air in front of him, and her breasts were resting lightly on his shins.

'Lie still before you kick me,' she commanded as she grabbed one foot and bound his ankle. She tied the other end of the cord around one bedpost and grabbed his other foot.

'What are you doing?' he demanded again. His voice was beginning to sound angry.

Beth ignored him and finished securing his final limb. She turned back towards him again and lifted her right leg over his as if mounting a horse. Sitting astride his legs, she admired her handiwork.

Although his cock was still sticking up in the air, it was definitely not quite as stiff as it had been. She would have to do something about that. Whatever she did to him, he was powerless to stop her. He was completely secured by his hands and feet so that all he could do was raise his buttocks in the air. She didn't mind the idea of him doing that!

Jonathan regarded her silently. She could see that he was angry. As usual, things were not going the way he had undoubtedly planned them! She suppressed a giggle and climbed back off him. She moved up the bed until she was kneeling beside him with her knees just touching the bare flesh of his chest.

'Don't look like that,' she told him. 'I'm not going to run away and leave you like this.' She leant over his chest and smoothed the bed cover back into place. Her breasts dangled tantalisingly in front of his face. She pushed herself back until she was resting her buttocks on her heels. With one hand on his chest to steady herself, she moved her leg round in a circle, exposing herself totally to his eager gaze. A quick glance told her that it had done the trick. He was as hard as ever.

'In fact,' she added conversationally, as she settled back on her heels and moved in towards him, 'I was thinking about us getting a lot more cosy.'

She leant across him again and lowered her head until her lips had enclosed his rigid cock. She bobbed her head, allowing her mouth to slide down its length to the base. Her tongue and teeth alternately gripped then released him.

Jonathan raised his hips to meet her so that his arms and legs were straining against his bindings. His mouth opened in a wide expression of surprise and pleasure. Beth lifted her head again, slipping back upward. She began to flick her tongue back and forth rapidly across the tip, delighting in the dribble of lubrication bubbling out of the top to mingle with her saliva. With her lips open wide, she ran her tongue down the outside then sucked one of his balls into her mouth. She could feel his soft down tickling her tongue.

Jonathan's cock bobbed excitedly from side to side as his

muscles alternately contracted and relaxed. He gritted his teeth and his buttocks tightened.

Beth released his testicle and ran her tongue slowly back up his length to the tip. She reached out one hand and took hold of him, thrilling at the way he was throbbing and pulsating against her. She remembered the way she had held and squeezed him until he had begged her to stop. She began pumping him gently.

Jonathan closed his eyes again and lay back, still attempting to control his breathing. Beth increased her pace and watched his face carefully. Jonathan gritted his teeth and his breathing became more ragged. She tightened her grip, pumping urgently.

Suddenly, he pulled down against her hand and pushed his buttocks hard into the bed in an effort to escape her grasp. Desperately, he began rolling his body from side to side. Beth ignored him, lost in her own pleasure and in the excitement of knowing that if she didn't stop soon, he would lose it.

Jonathan clenched his fists until his fingernails were biting into his hands. She noticed the look of intense concentration on his face and wondered what he was thinking. To her surprise, she felt him begin to relax slightly.

Beth stopped pumping and released him. She leant back, admiring the view. His cock was still twitching slightly from side to side as if invisible hands were fondling it, and his body was covered in a fine sheen of perspiration. She looked back at his face.

His eyes were screwed tightly shut and his face was filled with concentration. She could see his lips moving as if he were muttering to himself. Instinctively, she sensed what he was doing. She had discovered for herself when she was playing with her vibrator that she could last longer if she allowed her mind to wander. It wasn't foolproof and it didn't help for very long. She wondered if men were better at it. She decided that they probably were. After all, if he could lose or partly lose his erection then he would be safe, wouldn't he? Could men do that? There was so much she still didn't know.

She glanced back at his cock and tried to decide if it was still as hard as it had been. It certainly wasn't twitching as much as before.

A strange feeling came over her. It was almost as if he were setting her a challenge. Could he think his excitement away in spite of whatever she did to him? Could she so inflame him by her actions that he would be totally unable to keep his mind off what she was doing to him?

Beth ran her hands up his spread thighs, loving the way his face changed and darkened. She lowered her head and took him into her mouth again. He shuddered and twisted his hips from side to side and a thrill of triumph ran through her. She took him in deeper. He was definitely softer than he had been. She frowned and sucked harder. The softness vanished.

Beth sat up again. She reached over him and slipped her hand under the pillow. Holding the little packet in her hand, she put it to her lips and ripped the top off with her teeth. She peeled back the foil and took the condom out carefully. She realised that her hands were shaking. It had seemed so easy when she had practised it. She looked up at his face again.

His eyes were still closed. His whole body was tense, as if he expected her to touch him again at any moment and was determined to be ready to withstand her. She smiled, took his cock firmly in one hand, and placed the condom over the tip. She began rolling it slowly down him, careful to ensure she did not trap any air.

Jonathan opened his eyes and lifted his head. His arms automatically began pulling against the constraints at his wrists. When he saw what she was doing, a shudder of excitement raced through him. His fists clenched harder and his nails sank into his palms. She noticed that he was gritting his teeth again, almost biting his tongue as he struggled to control himself. His breathing sounded harsh and uneven.

Beth finished unrolling the condom and examined her handiwork. She thought his cock looked quite sweet in its new skin. She took hold of him in her hand again and was surprised to find that he was not nearly as hard as he had been. It was the last thing she had been expecting. She had thought that the idea of her getting ready to straddle him would have driven him crazy. She felt a tinge of disappointment. Was he having second thoughts?

She ran her hand down the outside of the condom and was surprised by the ease with which her hand slipped over it. She gripped it harder and ran her hand back up. She felt him returning to full size and her disappointment vanished. She slid back down again, then up, increasing the speed.

Jonathan moaned softly, his buttocks rising and lowering in time with her movements. She saw his look of panic as his urgency increased again.

'Untie me,' he begged, tugging so violently at the cords that they bit into his flesh. 'Please Beth, I want to –' He groaned again.

'If you don't stop what you're doing, I can't help myself. Please.' He tugged again and began twisting his ankles from side to side to try to get his legs free.

His words inflamed her. Beth let go and stared at him nervously. She realised that she was trembling all over with a mixture of excitement and fear. She had never even contemplated what she was about to do when she had been married to Tony. She wasn't sure that she had even known there were any other positions in those days, apart from flat on her back with the man on top.

Beth raised herself up on her knees and swung her left leg over his stomach so that she was balanced above him with her pubes just inches above his rubber-covered tip. Still shaking, she put her hands between her legs and opened her sex-lips. They felt damp and sticky. She took his cock in her other hand, drew a deep breath, and started to lower herself slowly down on to him.

Jonathan shuddered from tip to toe and his face grew flushed and swollen with desire. With his head raised up as far as it would go, he watched open-mouthed as Beth sank down on to his waiting cock. She felt him make contact with her, then start to slip slowly into her welcoming darkness. Deeper and deeper, she felt him sliding into her until her lips made contact with the base of his erection. Then, as she raised her body, he began to slide slowly, so slowly, back out again. Her breasts danced and bobbed in front of her. Her nipples were tight and puckered, her face flushed and her breathing shallow.

Jonathan bit his lip and gasped in anticipation. She could tell that he was already at bursting point. It was just sheer willpower holding back the inevitable.

Beth began lowering herself back down, squeezing him inside her as she moved.

'Oh Christ!' He groaned aloud as his pleasure and excitement finally overwhelmed him. With a small thrill, she felt him erupting, spurting like a Roman candle. His head fell back against the pillow, rolling from side to side with the ecstasy and elation of the moment.

Beth sat quietly across his thighs. She had seen his face and heard his cry. Already, she could feel him shrinking away inside her, as if recoiling in distaste. She remembered reading that the man should withdraw soon afterwards, but she didn't want to let him go.

She examined her feelings. Her whole body was still on fire.

The longing that had rushed through her as she had impaled herself on him was still gnawing away at her. She was more aroused than she had ever been in her life. She was aching with the need for her own release. She had wanted to know what it would feel like to come with him inside her. It had been too quick. Much too quick. She felt a rush of anger at him for satisfying himself yet leaving her burning and frustrated.

She glanced back up at his face. He was lying back peacefully and his face looked relaxed and sated. A slight smile of triumph played across his lips. That had been his greatest moment. Victory. No more virginity. Bully for him. I suppose he thinks he's God's gift to women now, does he?

Beth raised herself up slowly and used her hand to help slip his now flaccid penis out of her. It lay curled up against his body like a sated slug. Her eyes narrowed. He wasn't finished yet. She still needed satisfying. She swung her leg over him and crouched down by his side. She took him in her hands, pulled the condom off, and dropped it over the side of the bed.

His cock felt wet and sticky as she rubbed it between her fingers. Using his sperm as a lubricant, she began to run her hand up and down. Nothing. Not so much as a twitch. For the first time ever, Jonathan wasn't responsive to her.

She could almost have wept with frustration and sorrow. She had been afraid that this would happen. Now that he had had what he wanted, he had lost interest in her and become immune to her touch. Her sorrow turned to anger. If his prick wouldn't play, so be it. There was more than one way he could satisfy her.

Quickly, Beth straddled him again and moved up his body until she was kneeling over his head with her vagina exposed to his mouth.

Jonathan opened his eyes and stared up blankly at her, his

eyes glazed. She could see from his expression that he was still floating on some magical cloud of his own imagination, lost in the pleasure and the triumph of his achievement. The inane, self-satisfied grin on his face almost made her want to hit him! Angrily, she thrust herself down on to his mouth.

Jonathan's eyes widened as the realisation of what she wanted dawned on him. He turned his head away from her. Beth reached forward and pulled his head back round.

'Lick me,' she demanded gruffly.

Jonathan just lay there, staring at her. She could see that for the first time ever, he didn't find the sight of her nakedness exciting. He obviously had no desire to do what she wanted. Beth's eyes flared with anger.

Little sod. Just because he had had what he wanted, he didn't care that she was panting with her own need and desperate to feel the same joy she had just given him. Furious, Beth leant back and reached behind her for his genitals. She grabbed his limp penis and loose balls in her hand and tightened her grip.

'Lick me,' she demanded again as she thrust herself towards him so that she was within easy reach of his tongue.

Jonathan's eyes widened with shock and fear at her rough grip. Beth knew she wasn't actually hurting him, yet. It wouldn't take much more pressure before it started to become painful. She could feel him squirming beneath her as he struggled to get his dazed mind in focus. Beth squeezed slightly harder and heard him gasp.

Jonathan stared silently at her angry face, then raised his head and ran his tongue along her slit and over her swollen clitoris. Beth sighed with pleasure and loosened her grip on his genitals. She pushed against his tongue and savoured the shivers of longing that were already racing through every nerve of her body.

He moved his tongue back and forth gently, teasing her clit with his lips. Beth shuddered again as he began flicking his tongue more quickly. She could feel her climax building up inside her and she whimpered softly as her muscles tightened. Her fingers continued to fondle his limp penis and she felt him gradually beginning to respond. As he sucked her lips between his own, she cried out.

Jonathan closed his eyes and sucked harder. His cock continued to expand between her fingers. Beth cried out again and pushed herself even harder against his mouth. She put her other hand behind his head to pull him against her as her thighs began to roll rhythmically with his tongue.

Jonathan's cock reached full size again. He raised his hips and thrust himself against her hand. Beth gasped at the feel of his erection pushing urgently into her fingers. She was almost there. She let go of his cock and ran her hands over her breasts. Dear God, his tongue felt so good. She was so ready. She shuddered violently as the delightful waves of fulfilment washed over her and set every nerve of her body jangling.

'Jesus.' She pulled back and slumped down wearily on his chest.

Jonathan began straining impatiently against the cords.

'Let me go,' he demanded hoarsely. 'Untie me, Beth. Please. My wrists hurt.'

Beth sat up wearily and climbed off his chest. She was so tired that she was having trouble moving. Her whole body was still tingling with the intensity of her orgasm. She wanted to take a hot bath and curl up in bed.

As she moved to untie his feet, she noticed how hard and ready he was again. She marvelled at his powers of recovery and a thrill of hope ran through her. If he already wanted her again so soon, then maybe she wouldn't lose him just yet. She still wanted to know how it would feel to come with him inside her. Eventually. Not now. After so long, even the few seconds he had pumped into her had made her vagina feel bruised and sore. She couldn't wait for that hot bath. She moved round the bed to release his hands.

Jonathan sat up and rubbed his chafed wrists. He reached out and pulled her on to the bed beside him so that his hand was cupping one of her breasts. He took her hand and placed it on his cock.

Beth's eyes widened in amazement. Surely, he didn't expect any more now? She felt his cock push against her hand and instinctively tightened her fist around it, loving the feel of its hardness. He was like a sex robot. Tireless and insatiable. She pulled her hand away and pushed his hands off her breasts.

'I think it's time you put your clothes back on,' she told him. 'It's getting quite late.'

Jonathan sat back, looking stunned. Beth stood up.

'I mean it, Jonathan. That's enough for now.' She was delighted to see that the implied promise in her words had the anticipated effect. His eyes narrowed hungrily.

She picked up her robe and pulled it round her, doing her best not to let her eyes linger on his still stiff and hopeful penis. She was too weary to allow herself to weaken to the temptation. Much too weary.

She couldn't help reflecting that it seemed a shame to waste it.

13

Jonathan floated home in a euphoric haze, his feet scarcely making contact with the pavement.

He had actually done it. Screwed her. He had had Beth. All the way. He was invincible, a super hero, ten feet tall, unstoppable. He wasn't a virgin any more. His elation knew no bounds. He leapt into the air, grabbed a twig from an overhanging branch, then continued to hop, skip and jump along, whistling and dodging cracks like an overactive four-year-old.

Of course, if he was being totally honest, she had actually taken him, rather than the other way round. Still, why worry about technicalities? Just wait until next time!

His mother was sitting in the living room watching a rented video. She looked up from the TV and smiled lovingly at him as he danced into the room.

'Hello, love. Have you had a good time?'

Had he had a good time? Did mice like cheese? 'Er, yes thanks, Mum. Are there any biscuits or cakes?' He wondered why she seemed in such a good mood. He had been expecting another lecture.

Madge smiled again. 'You've got hollow legs, that's your trouble. Go on, there's some of your favourites in the tin.'

Jonathan hurried across the room towards the kitchen. He hoped his mother wasn't going to ask too many more questions. He was frightened he might say something to give himself away.

'Where have you been?' she called after him. Jonathan shrugged. 'Just out. Around. You know.' He wanted to escape to his room, to lose himself in his dreams. 'With Mark,' he added quickly, before she grew angry again at his evasiveness.

'I bet you'll never guess what happened today,' she told him as he returned, munching happily. 'It's the best thing that's ever happened to you.'

Jonathan flushed. Jesus! How the hell?

'Your swimming coach called,' his mother continued excitedly. 'He says that you have been selected to represent the south-east in the county championships. Isn't that marvellous? I'm so proud of you, love.'

Jonathan sighed with relief. Then, as the implication of her words sank in, he grinned with delight and impulsively threw his arms around his mother's neck, hugging her fiercely.

'Of course, it'll mean extra practice sessions,' Madge continued, as she returned the hug. 'And, with your exams coming up too, you're going to be pretty busy for the next few weeks. Not quite so many evenings off out enjoying yourself for a while, my lad.'

That brought him back down to earth with a crash. He opened his mouth to argue, then closed it again quickly.

'I think I'll just go on up to bed,' he mumbled, as he disentangled himself from her and headed for the door. 'I'm really tired this evening.'

Upstairs, Jonathan stood in front of the basin in the bathroom and stared at himself in the mirror. What a day! First Beth and now this. He pictured himself bending forward to receive an Olympic gold medal and imagined Beth standing in the crowd watching him, her face filled with pride and desire.

His mother's words swam back into his mind. Surely she wasn't talking about his weekends? She couldn't stop him going out on Saturdays. She just couldn't. She hadn't actually said anything about weekends. Not specifically. He wouldn't worry about it until it happened. He was too excited to worry now. He just wanted to lie back and dream about the Olympics and Beth.

Jonathan brushed his teeth quickly and sniffed under his armpits. He needed a shower but decided that it would have to wait. He went into his bedroom and stripped off. Lying back under the duvet, he finally allowed his mind free rein.

The county championships! If he won those, he might very well go on to the Olympics one day. First, he had to win the championship. The team would have to stay away from home that weekend. Would Beth come with them? He imagined her waiting for him at the hotel afterwards.

'Not a virgin any more.' He savoured the words aloud, his chest almost bursting with pride. Wait until Jason and Mark heard that! They would be green with envy.

If they believed him. It was a pity that there wasn't some way to prove it, something that would make them believe it. Maybe he could get his hands on a video camera from somewhere and film himself with her. He grimaced. As if Beth would allow that!

He closed his eyes and conjured up the image of her as she had lowered herself down over him. He could almost see her hand parting her lips and feel her fingers guiding him inside her. His cock sprang back to attention and he reached down to begin kneading himself softly.

Next time, she would be begging for it. He pictured her down on her knees, grovelling.

'Oh Jonathan. You're such a man. All those others never prepared me for you. No one can do to me what you do.' Her imaginary pleading faded away to be replaced by a less pleasant thought.

Why did he have to go and lose it so quickly? He writhed in shame. In and out once and he had let go. Oh God. He remembered how angry she had been and how she had forced him to satisfy her with his tongue afterwards. Why hadn't he held off long enough to satisfy her, too? It was his first time. It was just so ... He felt the pleasure again. There was no comparison. He would never do it by hand again.

'That's enough for now.' His mind latched on to her words in desperation. 'For now.' Perhaps she would give him another chance. It could be his last chance. She might make an exception for his failure just this once. He was certain that she knew it had been the first time. She wouldn't forgive him twice. Next time, he had to hold off until she was satisfied too. He just had to.

Already forgetting his vow, he began pumping himself slowly, enjoying the gradual build up of his pleasure. Next time, he would make her beg for it. She would be so hot that she would come as soon as he entered her. Maybe he could use his tongue on her first until she was just about to come. Yeah, that was it. That way, he wouldn't have to last so long himself. She would be so desperate she would ... His mind filled with visions of her in various erotic positions, begging him to take her.

How long were men normally expected to last? To listen to Jason and Mark, you would think that they ought to be able to keep going all night! Fat chance. He stopped pumping and his face grew thoughtful.

It usually took him longer to come the second time. What if he masturbated before he went round to her? If he had already come once he might be able to last long enough, providing she didn't tease him too much first. He began moving his hand up and down again.

If only he could keep his mind on other things. He remembered the struggle he had had practising his breathing and trying to keep his thoughts elsewhere. Thinking about his swimming had helped a bit. Thinking about her in the shop hadn't helped at all. Oh God, the sight of her lowering herself on to him like that. He pumped harder and felt the pressure intensifying.

He took his hand away and bit his lip to help control his excitement. Only when he was quite sure that the danger had passed did he take himself in hand again. Eagerly, he pumped as fast as he could, then began to knead and squeeze his whole length as he raced back towards his climax. He slowed down and slid his hand up and down as softly and gently as possible.

Gradually, cautiously, he increased his speed again, then slowed and stopped. His whole body was alight, every nerve on edge, waiting. He took his hand away again and rolled his hips back and forth. Even the touch of the duvet was too much to bear. He pushed it off quickly and waited again.

After a while, the intensity of his need abated. He reached out and squeezed himself. He moved his hand slowly up and down and felt himself start to harden again. He increased the pace, then slowed it again. He was still holding off. He turned his head and looked at the luminous dial on his alarm clock. He had been at it for nearly three minutes. He took his hand away again.

He pictured Beth bending over him naked with her pubes shaved. He would love to see her shaved and posing like the girls in the magazines. He reached under the mattress and pulled a couple of them out. The girls seemed dull compared to her. He imagined her spread-eagled on the bed like he had been, and pictured himself allowing his friends to creep in and watch her. Maybe he could tell her to give them oral to demonstrate his power over her.

Jesus, his cock was bursting. It was worse than when she had held him. No, he mustn't even think about that! He moved his hand down and fondled his balls, almost sobbing aloud at the intensity of the sensation. He ran his hand back up his swollen cock then gripped it and began to pump again. The pressure built up quickly until he was almost at the point of coming. He pulled his hand away and twisted from side to side. His cock twitched and bucked like a wild horse. Had he left it too late?

He gritted his teeth and started to recite the twelve times table under his breath. He had to learn to hold back. He had to. 'Five twelves are sixty, six twelves are seventy-two.' The urgency diminished fractionally. 'Seven twelves are eighty-four.' He moved his hand back cautiously and began to fondle himself again.

Changing speed seemed to help a bit and stopping completely helped more. What if he did that with her? He could speed up and slow down, even withdraw completely whenever it got too much. Would that help him last until she was satisfied?

He could see himself lying on top of her, pumping in and out. He imagined himself pulling away and then pushing back inside her again. Treacherous mind! He shouldn't have allowed himself to think about it.

Even as he stopped pumping, he knew that he had lost it this time. He could feel that he had now passed that point when there was anything else he could do to stop himself. Before he could even reach down for his box of tissues, he was spurting wildly into the air. He groaned with pleasure. It certainly felt better the longer he held back. Jesus, it felt as if his balls were being pulled up inside his prick. He groaned again and fell back, utterly exhausted. So much for no more wanking!

He glanced at the clock again. Six minutes, nearly seven. It had felt like seven hours! Would seven minutes be long enough to please her? How long did women normally take? What if she tried to hold back as long as possible too? Could women do that? Could they do it better than men could? God, he would have no chance.

He cleaned himself up. Maybe he could manage nine minutes next time or even ten. He would keep practising. He had all week. By next Saturday, he would be ready for her. He had to be the one in control.

Jonathan had a pleasant but sleepless night and arose drained and listless.

Beth didn't like the way he looked at her in the shop the following Saturday. His face was too cocky; he was too sure of himself by half. He grabbed and groped her at every opportunity and she almost felt as if she didn't know him any more.

She wondered how he was feeling about everything. He must be over the moon now that he had finally achieved his heart's desire. She had seen the way he had skipped and bounced down the road the previous week. He would believe himself to be a man now. A real man. She smiled. He wasn't wrong there. He was certainly more than man enough for her, boy or not.

Had she damaged his pride with her obvious dissatisfaction? She hoped not. What if she had given him a complex or something? But he had been hard and ready for her again before he left. The randy little sod. He couldn't have too much of a complex, could he? Anyway, it was probably all for the best if he did feel a bit of a failure. She had so little left to hold over him now as it was.

Beth sighed. What a shame he had to grow up. He would never again be that shy, desperate little boy panting after her with his legs reduced to wobbly jelly just by a glimpse of her stocking tops. He would never sneak down the passageway to snatch a precious peek of her through the keyhole. Why should he? He had already seen more of her body than any other living person had, her ex-husband included. If only she could turn the clock back a couple of months.

'Don't do that,' she hissed, as he gave her rump an affectionate pat on his way through to the stockroom. Jesus, why did men seem to have so many pairs of hands!

'I've told you before about touching me in public.'

Jonathan just grinned cheekily and pushed the door open with his foot.

'Cocky little sod,' she muttered to herself under her breath. She was half tempted to tell him not to bother coming round that evening because she was going out on a date. That would wipe the grin off his face.

She pictured herself curled up on the settee, alone, watching the TV with the long, lonely evening stretching out endlessly before her. Worse, she pictured him off with that little tart from the swimming pool instead.

Her jealousy burned. Stopping him from visiting her would be cutting off her own nose to spite her face. Did she need him that much? When had the tables been turned on her? At what moment had she come to need his visits as much, if not more, than he did? How could she ever get him back under her thumb again?

As she remembered how exciting it was when he took charge and how intense her own response had been, she wasn't sure if she even wanted to.

As soon as he was through her door that night, Jonathan pulled her into his arms. He was feeling keyed up and excited yet, at the same time, sure and in control. There had been another bad moment at home when his mother had tried to stop him going out at all. It had taken some fast talking and rash promises on his part to bring her round. Next week would be even more dull than last week had been.

He kissed Beth hungrily and was pleased to note that it was having little serious effect on him. He had already taken care of the worst of his passion in the loo before he had left home. Twice, in fact, just to make sure. With luck and careful concentration, he should be able to keep himself under control. At least for a while.

Beth was wearing another new dress that he hadn't seen before. It was made of a thin, lacy sort of material with buttons down the front. It was short, tight fitting and practically seethrough. The tiny black bra and matching thong underneath were clearly visible, as were the black stockings.

Jonathan devoured her image greedily and wondered just what it was about stocking tops that drove him to distraction. As Beth turned to lead him through to the living room, Jonathan grabbed her from behind.

'I'd prefer to go upstairs,' he informed her boldly as he began to kiss the back of her neck.

Beth's eyes flashed and she began to shake her head.

Jonathan put his hands round on to her breasts and fondled them lustfully. He was feeling aroused but not so desperate as sometimes. His precautions seemed to have worked. That desperate urgency wasn't there yet. He ran his hands down her hips and thighs, then lifted the bottom of the dress. He slipped one hand inside the thong and began to rub her pubes. Beth moaned and pushed herself eagerly against his groping fingers.

Jonathan began fumbling with the buttons of her dress. They were the wrong way round for him and he had to use both hands to open them. As the dress gaped apart, he pushed her bra up over her breasts and pulled the front of the thong down to expose her mound.

Beth swayed against him as he began to guide her to the bottom of the stairs. As she mounted the first step he pushed his hand up the back of her skirt and fondled her buttocks. She stopped and leant back against him.

Jonathan whipped the thong down to her ankles with one hand and pushed the other one between her slightly parted thighs. Beth stepped out of the thong and mounted the next step.

Before she was halfway up the stairs, he had peeled the dress from her shoulders and unhooked the catch of her bra. The dress fell in a heap behind them. She took another step as he fondled her body again. Her bra fell to the floor as they stepped on to the landing.

When they reached the bedroom door, Jonathan stopped her again and grabbed her from behind, taking full advantage of her exposure. As she leant forward and tried to pull free, Jonathan pushed her down further so that her naked bottom stuck up in the air.

He heard her gasp as his teeth sank into the flesh of her left buttock, then gasp again as he slipped several fingers into her moist opening. She reached up and fumbled with the door handle. As the door opened, she stumbled into the bedroom.

Jonathan had been crouching on one knee, fingering her. As she fell forward, escaping his caress, he stood up. He stepped into the room, pushed the door closed, and ran his eyes over her. He could almost see the excitement radiating from her. It fed and drove his own need. He could feel his cock beginning to push against his clothing as he reached for her again.

Beth turned towards him and began to kiss him as she struggled to undo his shirt. She wound her left leg around the back of his and rubbed herself urgently against the front of his trousers. His final button came undone. She tugged the shirt free from his trousers and ripped it back off his shoulders. She leant forward and took one of his nipples with her teeth.

Jonathan jumped but didn't pull away. Beth moved her lips across his chest and bit the other one.

'Your nipples get hard too,' she whispered huskily.

Jonathan pushed his hand back between her legs and began to finger her again. His middle finger slipped effortlessly up inside her dampness and Beth squirmed.

'Yes, oh yes,' she whispered.

He pressed the palm of his hand hard against the bulge of her clit and she squirmed again, pulling him against her with her leg as though trying to crush him into her. Her face darkened and her whole body stiffened.

'Jesus!' He felt her tremble as her climax raced through her body. Her left leg was holding him like a vice and her nails were digging into his back. Sobs wracked her entire body as if she were crying and her head was bobbing up and down like a nodding dog in the back of a car. She went limp and would have collapsed if he had not held her against him.

'Was that OK? Are you all right?' His concern made his voice sound small and anxious.

Beth nodded feebly.

Encouraged by his success, Jonathan half pushed, half carried her to the bed. The blood was pounding in his veins. He'd brought her off again! Beth sank back, surrendering her control.

Jonathan pulled the rest of his clothes off quickly and dropped them on the floor beside the bed. He bent down, rummaged in his trouser pocket, and extracted the condom he had put there before leaving home. He shuddered at the memory of the effort and embarrassment it had caused him to buy them. He had had to go into the supermarket on the other side of town. Well, he couldn't risk the local chemist – his mother knew everyone who worked there and everyone knew him.

With the little foil package clutched in his left hand, Jonathan knelt down on the bed beside her and ran his right hand up her stomach and over her breasts. Beth's body shivered at his touch. She stared at him silently, saying nothing. As he continued to caress her, she began to roll her hips slowly from side to side and clench her thighs together tightly.

The action excited him. He could see that she was rubbing her thighs against each other and guessed that it was turning her on again. He squeezed one of her nipples in his hand and smiled at the way she flinched from him.

His own excitement was mounting rapidly. When he was on his own, it was easy to convince himself that he could resist her. It was quite different when she was lying back, naked and exposed, in front of him. His erection was hard and urgent.

Jonathan opened his left hand and ripped the condom wrapper with his teeth. Beth watched as he very carefully held the tip to squeeze out the air and then rolled it slowly down his shaft. The look he gave her when he saw her watching him was all animal.

Jonathan leant over and reached for a pillow. He pushed it under her buttocks and guided her on to it with his fingers. Beth was trembling underneath him like a trapped moth.

He put his hands inside her thighs and pushed them gently apart. Although she jumped at his touch, Beth did nothing to resist his demands. She watched without comment as he knelt between her parted legs with one hand on his prick and the other prising open her lips. As he began to slide into her, he reached round and pulled her legs up behind his buttocks.

Beth gasped and tightened her legs, forcing him in deeper.

With one foot hooked over the other, she pulled against him, trapping him inside her. Jonathan struggled against her. As soon as he felt the immediate spasm of her legs relaxing, he started to slide out slowly. Beth sighed gently and closed her eyes.

Jonathan began to thrust in and out. He moved slowly. He could feel her vagina contracting with muscle spasms. He had to be careful of those; they could easily take him over the edge. It was as if she had another hand inside her cunt, squeezing and massaging him. He tried to slow down further. 'Nine twelves are one hundred and . . .' As the urgency increased, he pulled right back and began to tease her with just the tip of his cock inside her lips.

He put his hands on her breasts and held them while his tongue played with her nipples. His fingers slipped round under her back and slid down to her buttocks. He lifted his body up and pressed his erection against her clit, teasing it. His fingers groped between her legs and stroked her outer lips. He pushed himself harder against her breasts and forced his tongue into her mouth. As she started to squirm beneath him, Jonathan moved back down and began to push himself slowly back inside her.

Her nipples were huge and swollen with her passion, and Jonathan used one hand to knead her breasts. He grunted urgently and his movements grew faster as he thrust himself as deep inside her as he could get and began to pump in and out like a piston.

Beth arched her back and squeezed her thighs. She wrapped her legs around him again. As he thrust into her, she forced him deeper, pushing with her hips and pulling with her legs until it felt as if he were halfway up to her stomach. The motion was unbelievable. He quickly got into the rhythm.

A numbing sensation crept up his body as if he were being

cocooned in silk. He could feel Beth tightening and struggling against his movements. He increased the pace even more, sensing the urgency of her climax building within her.

Beth whimpered softly, her fingernails raking down his back. His own urgency increased, almost taking him over the edge. Please God, not yet. He gritted his teeth, stopped thrusting and tried to pull out. Beth immediately tightened the pressure of her legs, squeezing him with her thighs and continuing to caress him with her muscles. She whimpered again and her fingers pushed even harder into his flesh.

He could feel his own orgasm welling up, ready to burst. He struggled against her again, slipping out until he was just teasing her clit with the tip of his throbbing cock. He was panting hard, fighting not to lose it. Fighting her.

'Oh yes, Jonathan, fight me. That's it. Don't give in.' Her words inflamed him further and he groaned in desperation. She arched her back again, grinding her hips against his in a rough circular movement and caressing him with her hands. Unable to resist, he thrust back deep inside her again.

Jonathan clenched his teeth, his breathing fast and ragged. Droplets of sweat ran down his temples and his face was flushed scarlet. Sweet Jesus, he couldn't hold it much longer if she kept doing that to him with her muscles!

'Oh Jonathan, yes. I'm coming,' she whispered urgently. Her words were the final straw. He was almost sure that they both came at the same moment. He felt himself let go a second time and shuddered as another wave of ecstasy engulfed him. Spent and exhausted, he collapsed on top of her with his penis still buried deep within her. Beth continued to squeeze him gently with her muscles. He could feel himself shrinking inside her, feel her muscles contracting, pushing him out. With a small sigh of loss, he drew back and rolled off her.

He stared down at her lying beside him and felt an almost overwhelming rush of pleasure. Pleasure and something else – pride. He was bursting with pride for what he had just done. She wouldn't think him an inexperienced little boy now. Not after that.

Beth turned her head and smiled at him. He noticed that she was looking almost as pleased and proud as he was. She reached out to run her fingers through his tousled hair.

Jonathan shook his head irritably at her touch and pulled back out of reach. He slid down the bed and rested his head against her legs. He was delighted to notice that she was still trembling from the after-effects of their lovemaking. Beth smiled at him again, then, with a small sigh of contentment, she fell back and closed her eyes.

Jonathan stood up and headed for the bathroom to clean himself up.

When he finally returned he stood, naked, in the doorway and stared down at her. Beth sat up and returned his gaze. His penis lay quietly against his body.

'I'd better get on my way.' Jonathan picked up his clothes.

Beth looked at him in surprise. 'There's no hurry, is there?' She glanced at the clock. 'It's only just after nine.'

He shrugged. 'Even so. I should be getting home.' His mother was losing patience with his feeble excuses.

'Why don't you come round a little earlier next week?' she suggested. 'Then, we'll have more time together and you can still get away before it's too late.'

Jonathan frowned, wondering how to tell her.

'I, um, I won't be able to make it next week,' he mumbled as he finished dressing. 'I've got this important swimming competition coming up soon and the coach has called an extra training session.'

Beth stared at him without comment. He thought she looked

worried or maybe angry. He didn't want to spoil everything. Not after what had just happened.

'It won't go on much past eight o'clock,' he added quickly. 'The training session, I mean.' He hesitated, undecided, then decided it was worth a try. 'Why don't you pick me up in your car afterwards?'

Beth suddenly looked much happier. She picked up her robe and slipped it on.

'OK,' she agreed quickly. 'If you want. Where is it? The local pool?'

Jonathan nodded, stunned and delighted by her agreement.

They left the bedroom and headed downstairs. As she opened the front door for him, he turned towards her, his face expressionless. Was he about to go too far?

'When you come to fetch me I want you to wear a warm coat,' he told her. 'Your red one will do.'

Beth stared, at him, confused.

'Oh, and nothing else,' he added firmly, before she could argue. 'Just the coat. I want you completely naked under it. Naked and shaved.'

He turned his back and walked away swiftly, before she could comment.

Beth closed the door slowly behind him. Her hands were suddenly shaking. She realised with a shudder that it was Jonathan who was playing the games now. The thought thrilled yet scared her. She savoured his commands in her mind.

Shaved, just like the women in the magazines! Despite her shock and fear, she already knew that she was going to do it. Just the thought of it was enough to send a thrill of excitement and anticipation running down her spine.

14

Beth slipped her arms into her red coat, pulled it closed around her, and did up the buttons. She felt utterly ridiculous. The fact that no one could possibly guess she was naked underneath it was neither here nor there. She knew.

Her hands were shaking. He would know. The thought thrilled yet scared her. She stared down at her naked toes. She would have to put some shoes on. She couldn't possibly drive with bare feet. Did his instructions exclude stockings? She knew they didn't. With a small sigh, she slipped her feet into a pair of slingback sandals. As she moved, she could feel the material of the coat sliding freely across her newly shaved mound and her face burned. The lack of pubic hair made her feel even more naked than the lack of clothing.

Why was she doing this? What possible reason could Jonathan have for wanting her to collect him with nothing on? Would it give him some kind of a cheap thrill to know that she was driving like this? She pursed her lips thoughtfully.

If the idea of it got him really hot and excited, then it might not be so bad. He would be the one with a hard on. What would she have to be embarrassed about?

She checked the clock again. It was time she left. Although, to be honest, it wouldn't do him any harm to have to wait around for her, wondering whether she was going to show or not. She picked up the keys and headed out for the garage.

By the time she arrived at the pool, it was just gone eight. Although the drive had been short, Beth felt as if she had been travelling for hours. Her senses seemed to have been mysteriously heightened by her lack of clothing.

She could feel little flutters of air circling round the car in previously undetected ways. They caressed her bare shins and thighs, sneaked up under her coat, and ran icy fingers across her clit. It reminded her of when Jonathan blew gently across her flesh. It was as if a dozen Jonathans were exploring her nakedness. It had taken all her concentration just to keep the car on the road.

She parked the car on the far side of the pool car park, as far away from the doors and floodlights as she could get. Shakily, she turned the engine off and leant back. Her breathing was shallow and her skin felt electric. She adjusted the mirror so that she had a clear view of the exit. Her fingers kept straying to the keys and a part of her felt desperate just to start the car and flee. She glanced in the mirror again.

Jonathan was standing outside the main entrance talking to a couple of lads about his own age. He wasn't planning to introduce her to his friends, was he? She couldn't meet anyone, not like this. She glanced down quickly and her fingers checked each button to ensure that they were still secure.

Jonathan looked round and spotted her car. He said something else to his companions and then began to walk towards her. She drew a sharp breath. It was too late now. Thank God that the others weren't following him. She watched with relief as they collected their bicycles and rode off.

Jonathan drew closer and Beth watched him in the mirror as he walked around to the driver's side. As he opened the door, she felt herself jump. She was surprised to find that she was feeling almost as nervous as the first time he had come round to her house. Her eyes were wide and the colour on her cheeks was due to more than the touch of blusher. She watched without comment as his eyes ran slowly up her legs to the spot where her coat had fallen open to expose her upper thighs.

She looked down at his groin. She could see he was beginning to harden. She almost laughed aloud when she saw him reach down into his jeans and adjust himself. She took her left hand off the steering wheel and pulled the coat back over her thighs.

'Get in,' she whispered. She hadn't meant to whisper.

'I intend to.' Jonathan gave her a knowing smile as he continued his examination. He hooked his finger into the front of her coat and pulled it forward so that he could look down it. He couldn't have seen much but he seemed happy. Beth glanced quickly in the mirror again to ensure no one was watching them.

Like Beth, Jonathan looked around carefully and then crouched down beside the car. He placed his right hand on her knee and began to slide the coat gently up her thigh. Almost involuntarily, Beth opened her legs to allow him access to her naked mound. Her breathing quickened, so that it was coming in short, noisy little gulps. She stared unblinking out of the front windscreen.

His hand stopped, its progress hindered by her coat. He began withdrawing it slowly and Beth let out a long sigh, more of disappointment than relief. She felt his fingers begin undoing the bottom button and she tried to cover his hand with hers.

'No. Not here.'

'Yes. Here,' he cried out with success as the button flipped undone. 'Put your hand back on the steering wheel,' he commanded as he started his slow journey back up her thighs.

As she obeyed him, Beth noticed that the bottom of the coat had fallen open. There was only one more button between him and what his fingers were searching for. Her breathing quickened again and she checked the mirror once more.

His fingers found the button and began worrying at it. He was so close to her lips that she could almost feel the heat radiating from his hands. He seemed to have grasped the technique now; the second button opened easily.

Beth could feel the coat sliding off her thigh, exposing her further. His hand started to move on up. She could feel the breeze rippling across her naked mound and noticed the way Jonathan's face had changed to a smile.

She glanced around again, terrified someone would see them. If only she could catch her breath properly. She knew that she was panting again. Panting like a dog. She had read a letter in *Mayfair* about a woman panting for it like this. She hadn't believed a word of it. Women didn't pant!

Every move Jonathan made just seemed to make things worse. He was being so deliberate about everything. First, he pushed the left side of the coat away, then slid his fingers underneath the material until it slipped off his hand. He did the same thing the other side, all the while caressing her flesh with his fingertips. He raised his other hand and pushed her thighs as far apart as he could.

Beth closed her eyes. She could feel him staring at her hairless mound and her utterly exposed outer lips. Her flesh burned under his piercing gaze. Her body started to twitch and she felt little spasms of excitement running down her legs, up her spine and between her thighs.

Jonathan reached under the seat and released the catch. Beth immediately slid forward, pulling herself along with the steering wheel.

'Not that way,' he reprimanded.

'Sorry.' Beth pushed against the wheel and used her legs to slide the seat back as far as it would go.

Jonathan let go of the lever and there was a sharp click as the seat locked into place. Beth jumped at the sound and stared around fearfully like a deer starting at the click of a hunter's rifle as the bullet slid into the barrel.

Jonathan climbed into the car and crouched in front of the seat between her legs. At first, she assumed he was just trying to get a better look but, as he began to push her legs even wider apart, she felt her heart race. Jesus! He was going to go down on her, right there, in the car park! She shivered all over as he blew softly across her lips and mound.

'Yes. Do it!' Suddenly, she seemed to lose all sense of fear of discovery. She lifted her buttocks and pushed herself up towards him. Her coat dropped away completely. Jonathan continued to blow gently, his lips not quite touching her. Beth sighed with frustration and tried to raise herself further.

Jonathan moved his head back and climbed out of the car, leaving her raised up in the air like a beached whale. Beth flushed and lowered herself quickly back on to the seat. He reached into the car and began to undo the belt of her coat. Beth realised that he was also having trouble breathing and she began to relax.

She twisted her body and reached out towards him. She wanted to see his erection, to watch the way he was pulsing and throbbing for her. Jonathan wriggled back out of reach and his hand pulled the loop of her belt undone as he moved. Beth fought her instinctive urge to close her thighs.

She realised that the bulk of the coat had rucked up underneath her, exposing most of her buttocks. Now, she was sitting on it and the tension on the next button was enough to cause it to slip open.

Jonathan stood back to admire his handiwork and his left hand involuntarily slipped down inside his jeans again.

Why don't you just unzip it, Beth thought impatiently. That would solve his problem and give her what she wanted. He looked around again and Beth was sharply reminded just how exposed she was. She snapped her legs together and used her hands to try to release the coat from under her.

Jonathan obviously wasn't having any of that. He bent forward, knelt on the doorsill, and reached inside to try to push as much of the coat under her as he could. Beth remained perfectly still, neither stopping him nor doing anything to help.

In the distance a car door slammed. To Beth's heightened senses it sounded dangerously close. She jumped and stared around fearfully. How could this be happening? She thought about all the people in the nearby building. What on earth would they think if they knew what was happening right outside in the car park? Please God, don't let anyone see them.

Jonathan reached up and began to undo the remaining buttons. Beth glanced down at herself. She saw the swell of her breasts as the coat gaped wider. One nipple poked out, then the other. Her terror increased, overcoming her passion. They had to get out of here.

'No.' She reached up to try to stop him from pulling the top of the coat off over her shoulders.

'Just for a minute.'

'No,' Beth repeated. 'I did what you asked. Now, let's go to my house where we can be in private.'

'Just for a minute.' He was still trying to force the coat off her shoulders. 'Then we can go.'

'You promise?'

'Yes,' Jonathan agreed quickly.

'Just for a second.' Beth scanned the area rapidly. There was no one in sight. Shaking, she slipped the coat off her shoulders as Jonathan helped her pull her arms clear. Suddenly, she was totally naked. Another shiver ran through her. Jonathan reached in and pinched her nipple.

'Ow!' Beth squirmed with shock and pain. He smiled and pinched the other one. Ready this time, Beth remained silent as they both watched her nipples harden. Jonathan smiled again.

'OK. Let's go.'

As he stood up and began to walk around to the passenger seat, Beth quickly pulled the coat from underneath her and slipped her arms back in the sleeves. As she tried to pull it round her and do it up, she glanced around again.

Did she dare get out of the car? It would be so much easier to straighten the material out if she weren't sitting on it.

Jonathan slammed the passenger door closed and reached across to stop her.

'Leave it open.'

'I can't. If anyone were to see, there would be trouble. I could be arrested.'

Jonathan seemed to think about this for a moment. 'Just the belt then.'

He helped her pull the rest of the material from underneath her and Beth tried to cover herself as best she could. It was only slightly better than leaving it gaping open. She could feel the rough material of the seat on her bare buttocks and thighs. It excited her.

She glanced round at him. The way he was still looking at her made her feel weak and dizzy. She lowered her eyes and stared between his thighs. She could see his erection straining at his zipper. She felt an almost irresistible urge to lean down and undo it. To expose him as he had exposed her.

'Let's drive out into the country. I know a good place. I'll direct you.' Beth didn't fail to notice the longing in his voice.

The sound of it drove her wild. She reached up and started the engine, then put the car in gear.

She drove slowly and carefully, following his directions and taking great care to keep her eyes on the road. If they had an accident then she would have a hell of a lot of explaining to do.

She could feel his eyes burning into her as she drove. She did her best not to picture what he might be thinking. She completely avoided thinking about his arousal or the way his zipper was straining. She prayed he would keep his hands to himself, knowing that she would never be able to drive if he began to touch her again. The seat continued to rub urgently against her buttocks.

Every time they passed another car, Beth sank down in her seat as far as she could. What if they passed a police car? What if they passed someone she knew? Thank goodness that it was beginning to get dark.

They drove for about three miles before Jonathan instructed her to turn right down a narrow lane. She knew about this place, although she had never been here. It had a bit of a reputation as a local Lover's Lane. How did he know about it? He didn't have a car. He wasn't even old enough to drive. Had he been here with another woman? Impossible. So, how did he know about it?

She reached the end of the lane and pulled over to the grass verge, grateful that no one else seemed to be about. She turned the ignition off. Now what? Was he going to try to make love to her here in the car? She almost laughed. The idea of doing it on the back seat didn't really appeal to her at all. Apart from being cramped and uncomfortable, she would be terrified of being discovered. Was it some kind of special fantasy of his?

'Let's go for a walk.' Jonathan appeared to be shaking with

excitement. He eyed her exposed thighs again and she shivered with anticipation.

Beth nodded silently. She didn't know what he had in mind, exactly, but a walk would be good. Her head was still spinning. The fresh air might calm her and clear her head. She still had to drive them both home safely.

Jonathan jumped out of the car and rushed around to open her door. Beth grinned as she thought of Tony. She was certain that Jonathan was not trying to be a gentleman. He just wanted a quick flash. So had Tony for that matter!

She looked around to make quite sure no one was nearby, then slid her legs out carefully and pulled her coat down as she stood up. He didn't even have a fraction of a glimpse.

Beth locked the car and checked the coat belt was still secure. Jonathan slipped his hand around her waist, stretching his fingers out to try to grope inside the front of her coat. Unable to reach, he was forced to settle for fondling her buttocks from behind. They began walking down a narrow, yet obviously well-used, pathway. Beth prayed they would meet no one else.

It was a beautiful late spring evening. There had been some rain the night before and the ground smelt damp and fresh. Beth could hear a few evening birds chirping in the trees and feel the gentle breeze playing across the bare flesh of her legs and swirling up under her coat.

She began to feel awkward. She had no idea what they should talk about. At home, things were so simple. They just got on with enjoying themselves. This was different. It was more like being at work with him. Worse really. At least they had customers to serve or work issues to discuss at the shop.

'How did your practice go?' she asked finally.

'All right.' Jonathan obviously wasn't in the mood for talking.

He kept looking around anxiously and she wondered if he was also afraid that they would be seen.

'Are you practising for anything special? I mean, why the extra session this evening?' Beth tried again.

Without answering, Jonathan took her arm and steered her towards a particular oak tree.

As soon as she was out of sight behind the bushes, he pushed her back against the solid, broad trunk of the tree and pulled her belt undone. Her coat fell open and he feasted his eyes on her body again. Beth shivered as the breeze caressed her exposed flesh. Her nipples puckered. She could feel the gnarled bark digging into her back and smell its musty, woody aroma.

She raised her hands to pull the coat back round her. Jonathan immediately grabbed her arms and pinned them back against the trunk. She struggled against him. He was far stronger than she was.

'Don't. Stop it. Someone might come along.' Beth's voice sounded almost girlish. Part of her didn't want him to stop. She had never felt more exposed, more vulnerable. It terrified yet, at the same time, inflamed her.

Jonathan leant forward and ran his tongue over her breasts. He sucked one of her nipples into his mouth and Beth gasped. Her struggles became weaker. She sagged forward against him, her legs like jelly. Jonathan let go of one of her arms and put his hand between her thighs. Beth gasped again.

Jonathan slid his other hand down her back and under her legs, so that he was fondling her from both sides. He dropped to his knees, pulled her towards him, and ran his tongue over her shaven mound.

Beth sighed. His breath and tongue felt almost hot against her flesh in the cool of the night air. He moved one hand away and she heard the sound of his zipper opening. She sighed again.

Jonathan ran his tongue slowly up over her stomach and navel. He pulled her coat further and further open as he moved until she was totally exposed from the waist down. His tongue continued to explore her and his teeth toyed gently with her nipples. Finally, he stood back up and pushed against her with his groin as he began to kiss her neck.

Beth could feel the rough bark of the tree rubbing against her naked buttocks. She thrust herself forward against his erection and jumped at the feel of his cold zip on her bare skin. His lips moved round to her mouth and his tongue began to probe. Her coat was pushed right up behind her back, trapped against the tree.

Jonathan ran his hands all over her body. Beth could feel his jeans against her legs as he thrust against her mound and rubbed his penis over her burning skin. She slid her hands down his back and started to pull his pants down from behind.

Jonathan grabbed her hands and pulled them around to the small of her back. He flipped the bottom of her coat over her arms so that she was holding it open for him, then stepped back to look at her. She could see the smile on his face. Like a naughty child that had got its own way. His eyes examined her from top to toe, then scanned the bushes behind them. His hand reached down to take hold of his cock and he began to rub himself slowly as he watched her. She could see the condom, ready, between his fingers.

Beth nibbled her bottom lip. Her fear and excitement had combined into a burning need for release. His teasing looks were driving her mad. She wanted to beg him to get on with it, to take her, now. She sensed that this was exactly what he wanted. She was determined not to give in to him.

Still smiling, Jonathan stepped forward and pushed the sides of her coat under her arms, exposing her even more. Starting at her neck, he began to move his tongue back down her body. Beth felt her excitement growing. She shuddered violently as his tongue reached her inner thighs.

Behind them, there was a small rustling noise in the undergrowth and two pairs of eyes stared out at them greedily.

Jonathan placed his hands on her hips and started to pull her down so that she was forced to bend her knees. He pushed them apart, opened her sex with his tongue, and pushed the tip of it inside her. Beth leant back against the tree as his hands continued to explore her inner thighs and his tongue devoured her.

'For God's sake, take me.' The words came out much louder than she had intended.

Jonathan pulled his head back and looked up at her. His smile of triumph stretched from ear to ear. She was tempted to slap it off, but that would mean releasing the coat. She gritted her teeth and held his gaze.

Jonathan reached up and grabbed one of her arms, using his other hand to push the material of the coat behind her. He placed her fingers on her own trembling thigh and pushed them up towards her exposed vagina.

'All the way, Beth,' he demanded confidently. She saw him turn his head and grin, almost triumphantly, at a thick clump of bushes. There was a slight rustling noise, quickly stilled.

As she started to fondle herself, he leant forward to get a better look. He was so close that Beth could feel his breath on her skin.

'Tell me when you're almost there,' he whispered.

'I am, I am,' she sobbed.

Jonathan stood up and ripped open the condom. Beth watched silently as he rolled it down his cock and then rubbed himself gently up and down, as if to test the fit. Her own fingers continued to play with her clit.

'Hurry,' she pleaded.

Vaguely, through the haze of her mounting passion, Beth became aware of distant voices. Someone was walking along the same pathway that they had used. She stiffened and strained her ears as the voices grew louder. She was sure someone was coming this way. Jonathan had moved closer and was rubbing her clit with his fingers. A thrill of longing coursed through her body. She was burning with desire. She had to have him. Voices. Sweet Jesus! Someone was coming.

'For God's sake, cover yourself,' she snarled as she tried to pull her coat back around her. 'Someone's coming.' Beth grabbed his cock and began to push it back into his jeans. There was another rustle in the bushes and the eyes disappeared.

Jonathan shoved her hands away and grabbed her again, using all his strength to push her down on her back in the grass. He sprawled on top of her and pushed his tongue into her mouth. Her protests died away. Beth reached down and guided the tip of his cock between her legs. She whimpered as she felt him slide up inside her. The footsteps drew closer, then stopped.

'I'm sure he's around here somewhere, I thought I heard a noise.' It was a man's voice, only feet from where they were lying.

'Skipper. Come on, good boy. Where are you?' A second voice, female, so close Beth was certain she could reach through the bushes and touch the woman's leg.

'Damned dog. It's always running off. I told you to keep him on the lead.' Beth could hear the man moving closer, rummaging in the undergrowth beside the path.

Jonathan pulled back, then thrust again, pushing himself even deeper inside her. Beth bit her lips to stifle a moan. Unable to help herself, she arched her back to meet his thrust. She heard him sigh with pleasure as her muscles tightened around him. She could feel her climax gathering, feel the terror of imminent discovery pushing her excitement over the top. She wanted to scream. She couldn't hold it.

Jonathan groaned softly and began to pump even harder. Beth could feel him throbbing inside her and knew he was almost there too. She moaned again.

'I know he's in there. I can hear him scrabbling about.' The bushes rustled as the man poked a stick into the leaves. The branches began to part.

Further down the path, a dog began to yap excitedly.

'There he is. With those two lads. Bad dog. Come here.' The woman's voice began to move away.

The man withdrew his stick and the branches fell back into place. Jonathan thrust into her again, hard and fast. Beth felt him stiffen and heard his sigh of pleasure just before she, too, climaxed. She gasped with terror, with pleasure, with relief. Jonathan collapsed silently on top of her. The voices faded, disappeared.

Jonathan said nothing on the return journey. Beth wondered if he was feeling guilty. What if they had been caught? She shivered again as she remembered how close they had come to being discovered. She had never climaxed like that before. She was still having trouble catching her breath. It took all her concentration to keep the car on the road.

As soon as they reached the safety of the house, Beth headed into the kitchen and poured herself a strong gin and tonic. Her hands were shaking. Jonathan went into the living room.

Now what? she wondered. Maybe she should just tell him to leave, so that he would know that he had gone too far.

She reminded herself that she didn't have to go along with it. She didn't have to go out to meet him with nothing on, drive him out to the woods, let him play about with her. She was as much to blame as he was. Perhaps more. She had been so excited by what he had done to her that she had actually begged him to take her.

Beth finished her drink and poured another. Why was everything getting so complicated? She headed into the living room, half expecting to find him upset and repentant. Maybe she would comfort him a little.

Jonathan was leaning over the table, rummaging in the sports bag he had brought in with him from the car. Beth stood by the door and admired his taut little buttocks. She was already feeling much calmer. After all, no real harm had been done. It was quite funny, in a way.

He turned round. She saw he was holding a Polaroid camera in his hands.

'What's that for?' As if she couldn't guess.

Jonathan smiled and stared at her meaningfully.

Beth stared back at him thoughtfully. She would be mad to let him take any photos of her. Supposing someone else got hold of them? She thought about the pictures of the models in the girlie magazines. She would love to see herself in some of those poses. The idea was just too tempting.

'They stay here,' she told him firmly. 'Any pictures I let you take of me do not leave this house, ever. Is that clear?'

Jonathan nodded.

Beth smiled, excited at the idea of posing for him. She could take her revenge for what he had just done to her. By the time she was finished with him, he would be a nervous wreck.

'Give me a few minutes,' she told him as she left the room to change.

When she returned, she was wearing the new lace dress again. Well, it was expensive and she wasn't likely to wear it anywhere else.

'Kneel down in front of the settee,' he instructed. 'Pull your skirt up above your stockings.'

Beth did as she was told and then put her hands on her left suspender as if undoing it. The camera flashed and Beth grinned. This was fun.

'Open the top of the dress.'

Beth undid the first four buttons and exposed her skimpy red bra. She parted her knees slightly, still keeping the lacy hem up almost to her crotch. The camera flashed again.

'Stand up.' His voice was gruff and deep. She glanced at his crotch. The bulge was clearly outlined. She wondered if he would let her take a few pictures of her own! She shivered at the idea.

'Turn round with your back to me and bend over the couch as if you were trying to find something.'

Beth obeyed. Her buttocks were just covered by the skirt hem and the black straps of the suspender belt were fully revealed. Jonathan knelt down behind her to take a shot up her skirt. She heard him draw his breath in sharply. The camera flashed.

Where was he getting all his ideas for poses from? She wondered if he had a bigger collection of girlie magazines than she did. Did he play with himself, looking at them? Is that what he wanted these pictures for? It was almost a pity she couldn't allow him to take any away with him. She liked the idea of him staring at photos of her under his bed sheets while he wanked away. Maybe she would let him have just one. One where she couldn't possibly be recognised.

Without changing her position, Beth raised her hands and pulled her dress up to her waist. She began to peel her panties slowly down her legs.

'Yeah, that's great. Now bury your head and shoulders in the couch. No. Keep your legs straight. That's it. Move them slightly apart.'

As she parted her legs as far as she could, Beth saw several more flashes. She hoped he had plenty of film. She wiggled her buttocks from side to side and heard him sigh again.

Jonathan walked over to her, pulled her panties roughly down to her ankles, and pushed her down to her knees. He ran his hands down her sides and fondled her buttocks. 'Lie forward over the cushions,' he whispered.

Beth obliged, keeping her ankles together and pulling her knees apart. She twisted her head round and peered at him over her shoulder, pouting seductively. Quickly, he snapped off a few more shots then moved over and pulled her to her feet. He spun her round towards him, finished unbuttoning the dress, and pulled it off. He pushed her back on to the floor so that one elbow was resting on the seat of the couch.

'Raise your left leg and rest your other arm on your knee,' he commanded. He bent down to pull her thighs apart, and then curled her right leg in front of her so that her cunt was fully exposed. He crouched in front of her and pointed the camera at her mound.

Beth wondered if he was close enough for the camera to catch the dampness of her outer lips. She slipped her hand down between her legs to see if she was as wet as she suspected. Jonathan sighed loudly and the camera flashed again.

'Play with yourself,' he commanded softly, his words not much more than a whisper. She looked up and saw that he was rubbing himself gently through his jeans. Beth lifted her other hand and undid her bra. She slipped the straps off and allowed her breasts to bounce free. As she put her hand back down between her thighs, she saw another flash.

'Put your other hand on your tits.' She could see how his cock was already straining against his clothing again. His face was flushed and he had begun to rub himself harder.

Beth smiled. Shouldn't the photographer be a bit more detached than this? She stood up and kicked her panties away.

She sat herself on the settee and curled up in the corner with one foot underneath so that her whole body was exposed for him. She reached under the cushion and rummaged around for the vibrator she had been using there the previous evening.

His eyes widened when he saw what she was holding. She could almost swear his bulge grew even larger. Did the manufacturers of men's jeans realise the strain their zippers were put under?

Feeling slightly self-conscious, Beth switched the vibrator on and slipped it down between her parted thighs. The buzzing seemed even louder than usual. She pushed the sound out of her mind and concentrated on the delightful waves of pleasure already coursing through her. It seemed even better than usual, knowing that he was watching her. She closed her eyes and leant back.

She sensed the flash of the camera again and heard the sound of his rapid breathing. She moved the vibrator away from her clit and pushed it further down between her legs. She was afraid she would come if she left it where it was. She wondered what he would do if she impaled herself with it.

Beth turned the head of the vibrator inwards. She lowered her other hand and parted her moist lips. As if moving in slow motion, she began to slide the tip inside herself.

She heard him gasp. The sound excited her further. What was he doing? Was he still taking photos or was he now totally engrossed in watching her? She began to pull the vibrator back out, then in again, pumping slowly and rhythmically back and forth. Her muscles contracted.

She opened her eyes. Jonathan had unzipped himself and taken his hard cock out. He was fondling the swollen tip between his fingers. His eyes were riveted on her, almost as if he were unaware of what he was doing to himself. Beth shuddered all over. She had never suspected that mutual masturbation could be so thrilling. She pumped harder and her eyes feasted greedily on what he was doing. Another shiver ran down her spine as he wrapped his hand around himself and began to pump in time with her own movements.

Still fondling himself, Jonathan put the camera down and began to edge towards her. He stood above her with his eyes glued to the vibrator. She could see the tip of his penis already glistening with his lubrication.

Jonathan moaned softly and reached out with one hand to play with her breasts. A shock of desire rushed through her. She thrust harder and felt her climax approaching. She licked one of her fingers and placed it over her clit. As she rubbed the sensitive little bud, she began to whimper at the strength of the sensations rushing through her body. She couldn't hold out much longer.

Jonathan, too, looked as if he was about to burst. His hand was flying up and down his straining cock, his mouth was open, and his eyes were glazed and bulging. Beth thought it was one of the most erotic moments she had ever experienced.

She pulled the vibrator out of her and ran the tip of it up over her swollen clit. Oh God, she couldn't stand much of that. She gritted her teeth and did it again. She was within seconds of letting go.

Jonathan leant over her so that his cock was almost touching her nipples. She realised that he was going to come all over her breasts. She would feel him splashing against her. The idea pushed her over the edge. She whimpered and cried out, then clenched her thighs as she climaxed.

Jonathan groaned. He took his hand away, so that his tortured prick was throbbing and waving in the air. He leant even further forward and pushed the tip against her right breast. As soon as it made contact with her bare skin, he let go. His semen engulfed her, splashing and spurting across her right breast and running down her chest on to her stomach. Jonathan grabbed himself again and directed the second spurt at her other breast. He groaned again, releasing another spurt, then another.

She thought he was never going to stop. She felt as if she were under a waterfall of spunk. She dropped the vibrator and ran her hands over her breasts and stomach, smearing the creamy fluid all over her bare skin and delighting in its velvety softness and its unique texture and scent.

Jonathan put his hand on the arm of the settee, as if to steady himself. His spent penis began to soften and shrink back against its little nest of curls. Beth raised her head and leant forward to lick him there, loving the taste, the smell and the warmth of him. She strained her neck and pulled him right inside her mouth. It was one of the very few times when he was small enough for that. Reluctantly, she released him again and watched his penis flop back helplessly against his groin.

Beth sighed contentedly and glanced down at her sticky body.

'I think you could do with a shower, don't you?' he suggested cheekily.

Beth smiled.

'I think we both could,' she agreed.

Jonathan took her hand and began to lead her towards the stairs. She followed happily, savouring the idea of washing him all over. He slipped his hand under her buttocks and squeezed her gently. She looked down at his sleepy cock, loving its deceptive tranquillity. She was almost sure that he was already beginning to stir again.

After he had finally gone home, Beth curled up on the settee and examined the pile of photos. She felt herself start to blush. Had she really done that in front of him? And that? Sweet Jesus, next to these shots, the pictures in the girlie magazines seemed tame enough for her mother to look at!

Thank heavens that she had had the sense to make it quite clear that they must stay here. The best thing to do would be to burn them. It was rather a shame though. Some of them were really rather good. Maybe she had missed her calling in life. It was a pity that she didn't have any of him.

Jonathan walked along the road slowly with his heart pounding. He fingered the top pocket of his shirt where three of her photos were carefully secreted. Surreptitiously, he pulled them out and eyed them excitedly. This one was definitely the best.

He examined the way she was sitting with her legs apart. One hand was squeezing her nipple while the other was fondling the exposed lips of her sex. Her face was flushed and intent. She looked as if she were about to come. Jesus!

He could feel himself beginning to swell again just looking at it. He would enjoy practising his self-control looking at this. If he could hold off for five or six minutes with this in front of his eyes, he would be invincible!

He put the photos back in his pocket. When he reached the park gate, he slipped inside and looked around. Mark and Jason were already waiting for him, leaning on their bikes with their faces red from exertion. It was a long ride from the woods. Jonathan could see the lust and envy etched in their features. He grinned.

'Well?' He challenged them. 'Do you believe me now?'

The boys nodded silently and Jonathan grinned again as he imagined what must have been going through their minds as they had lain in the bushes watching him with Beth.

'Jesus, Jonathan,' Mark whispered. 'She's so hot, I could almost taste it. Do you think she'd put out for us, too?'

Jonathan fingered the photos in his pocket again and his face grew thoughtful. Jason and Mark continued to stare at him wordlessly, their eyes filled with pleading.

15

It was the sort of day when it was hard to believe that summer was only just around the corner: cold and grey and with the threat of rain never far away.

Beth shivered as she started the car. She reached forward and turned the heater full on, then cursed as the windscreen began to mist up. She rubbed it impatiently with the back of her hand. She was almost tempted not to bother. She wasn't very keen on the gym anyway and it wasn't as if she really needed the exercise.

Her mind returned to her most recent escapade with Jonathan. Who would ever have suspected that sex in the woods could be so stimulating? What if they had been caught? It had felt as though there were hidden eyes everywhere, watching them.

Beth turned the car out of the end of her road and set off slowly along the main road. Soon, she had left the outskirts of the town behind and the houses and office blocks began to give way to fields and hedges. A steady drizzle set in and Beth switched on her wipers and lights.

Up ahead, she spotted a car stopped at the side of the road with its bonnet open. A lorry was coming in the opposite direction and Beth slowed to wait for it. What a place to break down, especially in this weather. As she began indicating to pull round the car, a man stood up from the bonnet and wiped his hands down his damp trousers. His face seemed familiar.

The man looked around angrily, then raised his right foot

and kicked the tyre. Beth grinned sympathetically. Suddenly, she recognised him. He came into the newsagent's sometimes. He must be a local then. Should she stop and see if he needed a lift or something? As she hesitated, undecided, the rain began to fall more heavily.

Beth switched off her indicator and pulled in behind him. She rolled down the window and leant out.

'Is there anything I can do? Do you want a lift or something?'

The man turned round in surprise and then began to walk towards her. He was tall, taller even than Jonathan, with broad shoulders and an athletic build. His hair was brown and darkened by the rain. Droplets of water were running down his brow and dripping off the end of his long, straight nose. Beth hadn't noticed how attractive he was in the shop. He reached the window and bent down towards her.

'I don't know what's wrong with the damn thing. It just conked out on me.' His voice was deep and strong, his teeth white and even. His eyes were as dark as Tony's. 'Don't I know you from somewhere?' He grinned awkwardly at the words. The oldest line in the book.

Beth smiled. 'I work at Bailey's the newsagent's in the High Street,' she told him. 'Why don't you get in before you drown?'

The man smiled ruefully. 'If you could give me a lift to a garage, that would be great. I can't fix the damn thing. I've never been very good with mechanical things. I'll just lock up and grab my jacket.'

Beth watched him through the windscreen as he hurried back to his car. She liked the way he walked. He looked like someone who was sure of himself and who knew what he wanted. She had learnt to appreciate how that felt.

'My name is Alec,' he told her as he climbed into the

passenger seat and reached for the seatbelt. 'Alec Conners. This is very kind of you.'

'Beth Bradley,' Beth replied as she put the car in gear. 'It's really no trouble.'

She could feel his eyes watching her. She was glad she had changed before she left. She knew she looked good in her tight-fitting gym outfit. She wondered what he was doing here in the middle of the day. He didn't look like a salesman. He didn't look like he was dressed for business at all actually.

'I hope you're not late for an appointment or anything?' Beth finally broke the silence.

Alec shook his head. 'No. I've just about finished for the summer now. I'm a college lecturer,' he explained. 'You're not working in the shop today?'

'I only work mornings. I was just on my way to the gym,' she added unnecessarily. He must realise that she didn't normally drive around dressed like this. She noticed that he was examining her body again.

'I think there's a garage up here on the left in a minute.' As she spoke, the garage came into view and Beth slowed the car. 'Here it is.'

'This really is very good of you,' he said again. 'Most people would have just driven by without so much as a backward glance. Is there something I can do to repay you? Perhaps I could take you out to dinner? Once I've got the car fixed, of course.'

It was tempting. Very tempting. It had been a long time since an attractive man had taken her out for dinner. There was something about Alec that she found very appealing. She stopped the car.

'There's no need,' she began. Alec put his hand on her thigh.

'Then just come because I'd like you to,' he told her.

'Well.' Her heart began thumping. He was still touching her thigh. She could feel the warmth of his fingers through the flimsy fabric of her leggings. His hands were large and strong. She could almost imagine them caressing her body.

'I'd like that very much,' she replied softly.

Alec smiled and his eyes lit up. She felt a slight shiver of anticipation. She could see his desire for her smouldering within those eyes. She wondered if he could see the same in hers.

Alec moved his hand away and took a pen and scrap of paper out of his jacket pocket. 'Give me your phone number and I'll call you as soon as the car's fixed.'

His call came two days later. Beth had just got in from work when the phone rang.

'Hello.' She was expecting it to be Ann or Gerri.

'Beth? It's Alec. Alec Conners.'

Beth immediately perked up. 'Alec. How are you? Is the car OK now?'

'It seems to be,' he replied with a small chuckle. 'It should be. The damned garage charged me enough. Anyway, I was wondering – would you be free for dinner this evening? I thought we might go to this little restaurant I know.'

Beth felt herself grinning with delight. He wasn't wasting any time, was he? 'Yes. Thank you. I'd love to.'

'Wonderful. Shall we say eight o'clock then? How do I find you?'

Beth gave him her address and a few directions. As she replaced the receiver, she was already searching through her wardrobe in her mind, planning what she would wear. For the first time since she had picked him up by the roadside, she allowed herself to admit what was in the back of her mind.

She liked what she had seen so far of Alec Conners. Liked it very much. Could she excite a man like Alec as easily as she excited Jonathan? She remembered the effect she had had on Tony. Could she do that to Alec, too? She was very much looking forward to finding out.

She was ready and waiting in the hall when she heard the sound of his car drawing up outside. She took her time opening the door.

'Alec. Hello again. I hope you didn't have any trouble finding the house?'

'Hello, Beth. No trouble at all. I drove straight here.' Alec was examining her closely as he spoke.

Beth noticed how his eyes brightened at the way the soft flimsy material of her dress clung to every curve of her body. She had been saving this dress to tease Jonathan. It was white and so thin that the outline of her body was plainly visible. When she stood with the light behind her, as she was now, it was practically transparent. Underneath, she was wearing only a white thong and stay up stockings. Her breasts were bare.

'You look absolutely ravishing,' he whispered.

'Thank you,' Beth responded. She resisted the urge to look down to see if her appearance was having any physical effect on him. She didn't want to appear too obvious. Not yet, anyway. 'Shall we go?'

Alec held the door of the car for her and his eyes took advantage of the view as she climbed in. Beth's confidence soared.

'Where did you say you're taking me?' she questioned, as he started the engine and backed out of her driveway.

Alec glanced down at her still partly exposed thigh, then quickly returned his eyes to the road ahead. 'Oh, just a little country restaurant I know. Very small, very quiet and very pretty. I think you'll like it. Possibly, you already know it. It's called the Penny-Farthing. It's about three miles out of town.' He turned briefly to smile at her and his dark eyes twinkled in the reflection of the setting sun.

He really is extremely good-looking when he smiles, Beth decided as she admired his craggy face and noticed the way the flecks of silver hairs in his sideburns emphasised the darkness of the rest of his hair. She guessed he must be in his early forties.

'No. I don't believe I do,' she murmured. 'I don't go out to eat much.'

'Well, that's something I would be very glad to rectify,' Alec replied softly. 'I'm really looking forward to this evening,' he continued quickly, as if embarrassed by the presumption of his remark. 'I'm absolutely famished.' He laughed awkwardly. 'Oh dear. That sounds terrible doesn't it? Makes me seem a total pig.'

'Not at all.' Beth flashed him a quick smile. 'I've got a healthy appetite myself.' She almost laughed at the expression on his face as he digested that remark.

They continued the journey in silence, both lost in their own thoughts.

'Well, here we are.' Twenty minutes later, Alec turned the car slowly into the small car park beside the restaurant and pulled in next to the only other car there. 'It tends to be a bit quiet and lonely here, I'm afraid. If they have more than three guests of an evening, they believe themselves to be crowded out. Goodness knows how they stay in business.'

Alec got out of the car and moved around to open her door for her. As she stepped out, he took her arm and guided her gently to stand beside him. Beth felt a slight tingle of excitement run down her back at the touch of his hand.

The restaurant was in the converted front room of an old cottage and was cosy, snug and quite delightful. Despite the fact that it was early summer, a cheerful fire blazed in the central fireplace and the reflection of its flames created intricate patterns on the uneven, whitewashed walls.

Apart from the fire, there was very little other lighting, with the exception of large candles dancing merrily in the centre of each of the small tables. The furnishings were sparse – just a few dark wooden tables and chairs, each covered in a peach-coloured linen cloth. The huge, dark beams in the walls and ceiling were richly decorated with numerous horse-brasses and each one twinkled brilliantly in the flickering candle and firelight.

Only one table was occupied, presumably by the owners of the other vehicle in the car park. They were an elderly couple, seated comfortably at a small table near the fire, supping mulled wine and gazing aimlessly into the flames. They almost looked as if they were part of the decor, as if the room would, somehow, be unfinished without their presence

In the far corner of the room, furthest away from the fire, was a semicircular bar that was also made of dark wood and brass. A small, plump woman was fiddling with a pile of menus behind the counter. She looked up expectantly as they entered and a huge smile animated her otherwise plain face.

'Good evening, sir, madam. Welcome to the 'Penny-Farthing'. Do you have a reservation?'

As Alec nodded and gave his name, Beth smiled with amusement. As Alec had said, they were hardly in danger of being overbooked.

Alec began to guide her towards a table by the fireside. He took the opportunity to put his hand on her back, then slipped it down to her waist as he steered her round an empty chair. She could feel her hip bone rubbing against his upper thigh. She felt another tingle of anticipation and excitement at his touch.

Beth glanced at him out of the corner of her eye and tried to gauge what he was feeling. She was encouraged to see that he was watching her as he had before. His eyes were devouring the outline of her body through the thin dress. She grinned, knowing how the firelight was revealing her to his gaze.

'Something amuses you?' His question was light-hearted, but Beth could sense his underlying tension. He was as wound up and nervous as Jonathan used to be.

'No, not amuses. Just delights,' she replied. 'This little place is absolutely wonderful, Alec. If the food is anything like as good as the atmosphere, I can't wait to try it.'

Apparently taking her words as a hint, Alec called for the menu and they selected their meal in silence. Beth chose prawn cocktail followed by steak and salad. Alec opted for the soup of the day and chicken breast marinated in wine. After they had ordered, Alec filled their glasses from the carafe of house wine he had requested and sat back comfortably. He raised his glass in the air.

'To my angel of mercy,' he toasted her. 'Once again, my thanks for coming to my rescue.'

'It was my pleasure,' Beth responded as she raised her own glass. She noticed with amusement that his eyes were locked on her breasts. She wondered if he could see her nipples. He soon would if she kept thinking about it.

The food arrived and they both began to tuck in greedily. As they ate, they chatted casually about themselves. Beth was pleased to find that they seemed to have a lot in common and relieved to learn that Alec, too, was a divorcee. She didn't need the complication of a jealous wife in the background.

'Those prawns were delicious, Alec,' she commented to cover an awkward break in the conversation while they waited for the main course to arrive. 'How was the soup?'

'Perfect. A friend of mine recommended it. Apparently, it's their own secret recipe.'

They fell silent again while the plates were cleared and the main dishes served up. After the waiter had gone, they resumed eating and their conversation darted randomly from topic to topic.

Beth felt herself relaxing. Alec was an easy person to be with. He asked questions and she just talked. Every time she paused, he asked something else or made an interesting or witty observation. She enjoyed his remarks and his sense of humour. In fact, she liked everything about him.

An hour or so later, after a heavenly serving of lemon soufflé, light and fluffy and cooked to perfection, Alec pushed back his chair and sighed contentedly.

'Would you care for a liqueur to finish?'

Beth was already slightly light-headed from several glasses of wine. She shook her head. 'No, thank you. I'm completely full. It was a delightful meal. Thank you.' As she spoke, she pushed her own chair back and crossed her legs. Alec's eyes narrowed and she heard him catch his breath as he caught a glimpse of lace stocking top.

'Well, in that case, if you're quite sure you don't want anything else, perhaps you would enjoy a short drive?' he suggested. 'It's a lovely evening.'

'Yes, all right. Why not?' Beth smiled warmly. She drained the last of her wine in an effort to wet her suddenly dry mouth and struggled to control the hammering of her heart. This was the moment she had been waiting for.

Alec paid the bill and, amidst farewells and promises to visit again soon, they headed outside.

Beth allowed Alec to help her into the car. She also allowed her dress to ride up over her stocking tops and was delighted with the way his eyes widened. She raised her arm to smooth back her hair and allowed her elbow to brush lightly against the crotch of his trousers. She heard him sigh gently.

She leant back so that the flimsy material of her dress tightened across her breasts. She could feel her nipples rising with more than just the feel of the cool night breeze. Another sigh told her that Alec had noticed them too. She licked her lips with the tip of her tongue and was surprised at how dry her mouth felt.

Alec closed the door and walked round behind the car. He climbed into the driver's seat and started the engine. As he reached down for the gear stick, his hand made contact with her thigh and Beth shivered. Alec turned and smiled at her, his eyes back on her nipples.

'Cold? I'll put the heater on. It will warm up in a minute or two.' He let out the clutch and moved off, picking up speed quickly as they left the restaurant behind.

As they sped along the dark deserted lanes, Beth stared out of the window at the full moon. Gradually, as she watched, it disappeared behind a cloud. She glanced at the treetops and noticed that they were beginning to sway as the wind picked up.

'So much for a lovely evening,' she muttered. 'It looks like we're in for a storm.'

Hardly were the words out of her mouth, when there was a flash of lightning in the distance and the first drops of rain splattered against the windscreen.

'Maybe we'd better get back home in the warm and dry before it gets any worse,' she suggested.

Alec leant forward and scanned the darkening sky anxiously.

'Besides, it is getting late,' Beth added. 'And I do have to be up early for work tomorrow.' She had trouble stopping herself from laughing at the expression on his face. She was hoping that he wanted her to ask him in. His look of disappointment at her words confirmed it.

Alec slowed the car and took the next turning on the left, back towards her home. The rain had begun falling harder now and was running in great sheets down the windows. Alec cursed and turned the windscreen wipers on full.

'It's been such a delightful evening, Beth,' he told her carefully. 'It's a pity it has to end so soon. Perhaps we could do it again some time?' He fished for the invitation she knew he wanted.

As she opened her mouth to suggest he come in for coffee, the engine misfired and stalled. Alec swore and steered over to the side of the road. He switched the ignition off and then turned the key again. Nothing happened. The engine did not even turn over. He tried again. Still nothing happened. Outside, the wind howled angrily and rattled the windows. The rain began to fall even harder and another brilliant flash of lightning was followed almost immediately by a violent clap of thunder.

'I don't believe it.' Alec's face was as black as the storm. 'This is exactly what happened the last time.' He thumped the steering wheel furiously.

'I hope you're not trying to tell me that you have run out of petrol?' Beth giggled. 'I didn't think anyone tried that on any more?'

Alec glanced at her in dismay and his face coloured. 'Oh God, you don't think – It's not the petrol. I filled up this morning. It's the same thing that happened the other day in the rain. The engine's just died on me. I'm really sorry about this, Beth.' Alec was crimson with embarrassment.

'We can't be all that far from a phone,' he continued desperately. 'If you want to stay here in the dry, I'll go and call for help.'

Beth frowned. 'I'm not staying here on my own in this storm. Look, it's not all that far to my house if we cut through the park. Why don't we just make a dash for it? You can phone a garage from there.' She wondered if it would occur to him that the garage would be closed at this time of night.

'But you'll get soaked.' Alec began shrugging his jacket off to put round her shoulders.

'A little water never hurt anyone.' Beth knew exactly what would happen to her dress if it got wet.

It took nearly fifteen minutes to reach her house. Before they had gone a hundred yards, they were both soaked to the skin.

Alec had draped his jacket around their shoulders and was using it as an excuse to hug her close. He had also found an old umbrella in the boot of the car and they huddled together under its meagre protection. The wind was so strong that the rain was lashing them from all angles and threatening to turn the umbrella inside out. Eventually, they gave up on it. Beth was pleased that Alec continued to hug her to him anyway.

'Here we are.' Beth slipped the key into the front door and reached for the light switch. Alec hurried in behind her. As she slipped his wet jacket from her shoulders and turned to close the door, she heard him gasp. She glanced down.

Her dress was stuck to her body like a second skin. The material had turned completely transparent, so that every curve of her body was clearly outlined. The tiny white thong at her groin was also wet and clinging to her mound.

Beth glanced at the front of his trousers. The wet material was plastered against him. His partial arousal was as obvious as the puckering of her own nipples. She noticed him follow her gaze then run his eyes hungrily over her body again. She saw his erection grow harder.

'We seem to be a bit damp.' Beth stated the obvious.

She realised that her voice was trembling slightly. This wasn't quite as she had imagined. Playing with Jonathan was uplifting and exhilarating. Taunting Tony had been satisfying in a vengeful kind of way, even though she had discovered that she no longer desired him. Alec was another matter altogether. He wasn't a desperate inexperienced boy like Jonathan. He was a man. A strong, experienced man who knew what he was doing. Yet, unlike Tony, she wanted Alec. Really wanted him. Her knees were practically knocking together in her excitement.

Beth stepped towards him and raised her hands. 'Why don't we get you out of these wet things,' she murmured. 'I'll pop them in the dryer and lend you a robe. They won't take very long to dry.'

As she spoke, she began to unbutton his shirt. She shivered at the feel of his curly dark chest hairs. Neither Tony nor Jonathan had any hair there. The final button came free and Beth slowly peeled the sleeves down his arms. Her body swayed against him and the shirt dropped to the floor.

Alec was still staring at her body. She could hear his harsh, rapid breathing. She looked up at his face and noticed the way his pupils had dilated, making his eyes appear even darker and more alluring. He raised his bare arms and placed his hands on her buttocks.

Beth moved her hands to his waistband and undid the button. She heard him sigh. As slowly and gently as she could, she began to open his zipper.

His briefs were dark green and as skimpy as Jonathan's swimming trunks. Before the zipper was fully open Alec's penis was pushing up out of the top of the waistband, its tip dark and swollen. Her fingers brushed it softly as she drew the trousers back and lowered them over his hips and buttocks. Alec gasped and thrust himself against her. The trousers fell to his ankles.

Beth pulled back slightly from his clasp and ran her eyes down his body. He was hard and firm all over and his skin looked damp and shiny. His cock was still straining against the restriction of the briefs and its tip was wet and glistening with more than the effects of the rain.

'I'll get you a towel,' Beth whispered. Her tongue seemed too large for her mouth and her lips were swollen with desire.

'My turn first.' Alec took his hands off her buttocks and reached for the buttons on the front of her dress. So slowly that she wanted to scream at him to get on with it, he began to open them and reveal her naked breasts.

Beth didn't have to look down to know how hard her nipples were. She could feel her arousal searing through every fibre of her body, almost painful in its intensity. As her breasts fell free of the sopping dress, his hands cupped them gently and his fingers began to massage her puckered nipples. Unable to help herself, Beth cried out. She yearned for him to suck them more than she had ever wanted anything in her life. Shamelessly, she pushed her chest forward and willed him to respond. She cried out again as his mouth made contact with her left breast and his tongue began to circle the nipple.

'Oh God.' Nothing she had ever experienced before had ever felt so exciting. Her body was tingling from head to foot as if she had been suddenly electrified. She was certain that she would come at any second. As he released her breast and moved back slightly, she whimpered again, a desperate cry of despair and longing. He couldn't stop now.

'I think you'd better fetch those towels,' he told her, his voice thick with want. 'You'll catch cold if we don't get you dry.'

Beth stepped out of her wet dress and stooped to pick it up. Without speaking, she turned her back and started up the stairs. She could almost feel his eyes boring a hole in her buttocks as she moved. She put one hand on the banister to steady herself. Her legs seemed barely strong enough to carry her.

When she returned to the kitchen, Alec had already removed his shoes and socks. She found him bent over the dryer trying to select a programme. His buttocks were tight and hard and she wanted to grab them.

'Here.' Beth held out a large white bath towel.

Alec stood up and spun round. Beth had slipped into a short cotton wraparound with a tie waist. The top gaped open to reveal the curve of her breasts and the bottom just covered her buttocks. Alec smiled appreciatively and reached for the towel.

'Thank you.'

Beth glanced down. He was still aroused, though perhaps not quite as hard as he had seemed earlier. With a slight twinge of disappointment, she realised that he had, somehow, rearranged himself so that his tip was no longer exposed to her eager gaze.

'I'll make us some coffee.' Beth moved past him and switched the kettle on. She was glad of the familiar task. It gave her something else to focus on. She was very aware of him rubbing the towel over his damp body. She longed to take it away and do it herself.

As soon as she had made the coffee, Beth led him through into the living room. Alec perched awkwardly on the settee.

'I should get you a robe or something,' Beth muttered, as if only just realising that he was naked but for his briefs. 'I must have something that will fit you.'

As she spoke, she leant over him to place the mugs of steaming coffee on the table in front of him. She took her time, enjoying his eyes watching her body under the thin gown. The end of her belt fell down across his thighs.

With a slight smile, Alec took hold of the belt and tugged it. The bow came undone and her gown fell open to expose her completely. With one smooth movement, Alec reached up and pulled her down on to his lap. He pushed the gown aside roughly so that her bare skin was against his, and then slipped the robe off her shoulders. Swiftly, he pulled her head round towards his.

His lips were hard and demanding. Beth opened her own lips and sucked his tongue hungrily into her mouth. She felt his hands playing with her breasts again and she whimpered softly as his fingers moved down between her legs. She felt him lift the silk of her skimpy panties and slip his hands underneath. As his searching fingers discovered her hairless mound, she heard a small sigh of pleasure escape his lips. Another surge of animal lust raced through her.

She placed one hand behind his head and ran her fingers roughly though his damp hair, pulling his lips harder against her own so that she could feel the sharpness of his teeth against her mouth. Boldly, she lowered her other hand and slipped it between his clenched thighs until it made contact with his swollen penis.

Alec groaned and lifted his buttocks off the settee to thrust against her. She tightened her fingers round him and marvelled at how big and hard he was. Even through the material of his briefs, she could feel the veins standing out on the shaft. Desperate to feel him properly, she tugged at the waistband and sighed with satisfaction as the tip sprang free again. She ran her fingers over its silky top and felt him tremble at her touch. She closed her hand over him.

Alec moaned and pushed her off. He lifted her easily into his arms as he stood and turned, then lowered her on to the settee and sank down over her. She felt his lips running down between her breasts. His tongue found her navel and teased it gently. Beth cried out and pushed her hips up high in the air. Alec grabbed the waistband of her panties and whipped them down to expose her totally. His eyes examined her shaven mound hungrily.

Without taking his eyes off her, Alec stood up and removed

his own pants. Beth turned her head to watch as his cock thrust out towards her. His pubic hairs were dark and thick. She reached out and cupped his balls in her palm, delighted at the way his cock began to bob up and down at her touch. She realised that he was bigger than Jonathan was. He was thicker as well as longer. And so stiff. Stiff as a ramrod. She smiled at the word and tentatively began to run her fingers up its length.

Alec closed his eyes. As she tightened her grip, he instinctively began to thrust against her, pumping himself into her clenched fist. His whole cock seemed to be throbbing now, swollen and engorged with his lust. Beth shuddered. She could feel her own lubrication flowing from her. She was so ready.

'I want you inside me,' she whispered. 'I want to feel you thrusting deep and hard.' She reached under the cushion and felt around for a condom. She was much too far gone in her own passion to worry about what he would make of her foresight.

Beth watched hungrily as Alec rolled the condom down his penis and lowered himself over her. He slipped inside her so slowly she wanted to scream again. Oh God, he was torturing her. She wanted him deep and hard. She thrust herself up against him and groaned with satisfaction as he sank further and further inside her.

She heard his grunt as he achieved full penetration and, for one awful moment, she thought he was going to come. 'Please, not yet,' she whispered. She wasn't ready for it to end, not yet. She tensed as she felt him begin to slip back out and then almost sighed with relief as he thrust slowly but strongly into her again.

As Alec continued to maintain his steady, controlled rhythm, Beth realised that she had nothing to worry about. Alec wasn't going to lose it. He knew exactly what he was doing. She had a feeling that he could control himself for as long as he wanted to. The idea both excited and challenged her. She gritted her teeth and began to squeeze him with her muscles. Gradually, she felt her orgasm approaching.

'Harder.' Beth raised her legs and wrapped them round his buttocks, trying to force him even deeper inside her. Tingles of pleasure raced up her thighs, down her spine and across her breasts. She was only seconds from exploding. 'Yes.'

As she climaxed, she gasped aloud and raked her fingers down his back. Through her ecstasy, she felt him responding to her excitement, pumping harder and faster as he built up towards his own moment of release. She tightened her thighs and urged him on.

'I want to feel you come,' she whispered. 'That's it. Thrust inside me until you can't bear it any more. Yes, harder, deeper. You can't hold on any longer.' She sensed her words were inflaming him and pushing him to the limit. The power of it fed her own desire. She felt herself building to a climax again.

Alec stiffened. She saw his face tighten and felt his muscles contract. Another spasm of pleasure raced through her, shaking her from head to toe. Alec pushed inside her as deep as he could. Even through the protection, she could feel the power of his explosion as spurt after spurt pumped from him. She felt him relax and collapse upon her, totally spent. With a small sigh of contentment, she closed her eyes and hugged him to her.

'I suppose I had better call a taxi. I can't do much about the car until tomorrow.' The sound of his voice brought her back to reality. She opened her eyes and sighed with disappointment as she felt him slip from inside her.

Alec smiled down at her. 'You're a very beautiful and desirable woman, Beth Bradley,' he told her. 'I never expected to be so happy about my car breaking down on me.'

Beth preened at his words. 'I hope it's not going to make a habit of it,' she responded. 'It could become a bit tiresome if we have to get soaked every time we go out in it.'

'The view was more than worth it,' Alec replied and Beth smiled again.

'I'll make us some more coffee first, shall I?' she suggested as she stood up and slipped her robe around her shoulders. 'The first ones seem to have gone a bit cold.'

16

She saw Alec twice more during the next two weeks. Once when they went up to London to take in a show and the second time when he came round to her house for a home-cooked meal.

'It's wonderful to have someone else to do the cooking for a change,' he confided. 'Since the divorce, I've become quite good in the kitchen, but I can't really say I enjoy it very much. During term time I usually just eat in the refectory with the students.' He helped himself to some more salad.

Beth remembered that he had told her he was a lecturer. The word made her smile.

'What do you teach?' It couldn't be any of the sciences or he probably would have known how to fix his own car. She served him another helping of lasagne.

'I'm a professor of English,' he replied as he began to tuck into his food again.

Beth was surprised. It sounded rather dull and stuffy. He didn't look the part of a boring old professor.

'It's not as bad as it sounds,' he added with a smile, as if reading her thoughts. 'Young minds can be very stimulating. Besides, I also do a bit of sports coaching at the local school, just to keep in shape.'

Beth ran her eyes over his hard, muscular frame and tried to picture him in shorts and a T-shirt, running up the soccer field.

'Actually, I think I enjoy that more than the college work,'

Alec continued between mouthfuls. 'There's something very appealing about working with teenagers. They're just on the verge of adulthood and trying to discover themselves. I find it very satisfying.'

Beth felt herself colouring. What on earth would he think of her own endeavours in helping a teenager to discover himself? Something would have to be done about Jonathan, and soon.

'What sports do you coach?' An uncomfortable thought was beginning to form in her mind. She tried to push it away.

'Swimming. Actually, I'm the county swimming coach,' he told her proudly, flexing his muscles.

Beth's fear intensified. There must be lots of swimming coaches, she told herself.

'One of the boys from The Grove has a Saturday job at the newsagents,' she commented casually. Her heart was pounding. 'He's a bit of a swimmer. Maybe you know him.'

Alec smiled and nodded. 'Oh yes. Young Jonathan Evans. He's one of my star pupils. A brilliant swimmer. He could even go to the Olympics one day if he keeps focused.' He frowned.

'He's a bit of a tearaway though. Very mature for his age and with an eye for the girls. You should hear some of the stories that circulate about him. Makes you wish you were young again!' Alec leered suggestively.

The fork Beth was holding fell out of her hand and landed on the floor with a loud clatter. She could feel herself trembling with shock and horror. Jonathan was one of Alec's pupils! Alec had heard stories about Jonathan and his escapades. Dear God in heaven. It was like some dreadful nightmare. What sort of stories had he heard? Surely not that he was seeing an older woman? Had Jonathan been bragging about her? She would wring his neck.

'Is something wrong?' Alec was staring at her. 'You're as white as a ghost.'

255

Beth shook her head, not trusting herself to speak. She could almost imagine Alec chiding Jonathan for his lack of focus and hear his cheeky voice saying, 'Sorry, sir. I had a hard night with the woman from the shop where I work. She keeps me busy, sir, but she has improved my performance.'

She reached down and retrieved her fork. Alec jumped up. 'Here. Let me have it. I'll give it a quick rinse.'

Beth shook her head again. 'Don't worry. I'm not really all that hungry any more.' She placed the fork over her half-eaten meal and rested her head in her hands.

'Are you sure you're not ill?' Alec persisted.

'No. I'm fine. I'm just not hungry.'

The rest of their evening was a total washout. Beth knew that Alec wanted her and she sensed that he was hurt and bewildered by her lack of response. She couldn't help it. How could she make love to Alec while she was filled with terror at the idea of him finding out that she had been shamelessly seducing his prize student?

She had visions of Jonathan making love to her while Alec stood behind giving instructions. 'That's it, slow down. Long powerful strokes, lad. It's a long race. Take your time.' If only someone would pinch her so she could wake up and find it was all some horrible dream.

She told herself that Alec obviously didn't know or suspect anything yet. If he had even the slightest inkling about what had been going on between her and Jonathan, he wouldn't be there with her at all. Christ, from the sound of it, Jonathan was almost like a son to him. How did a man react to the knowledge that his woman was also sleeping with his adopted son? God, it sounded so sordid and depraved.

Beth pleaded a bad headache and sent Alec home early with a promise that she would call him the next day. She was too horrified even to notice the disappointment and longing in his face. She didn't even want to think about sex.

After he had gone, Beth poured herself a stiff drink and curled up on the settee to try to sort herself out. Alec was becoming very important to her. It was early days yet, but she had a feeling that their relationship was destined to be very special. Where did that leave Jonathan?

Obviously, she would have to stop seeing him. Even if she hadn't met Alec, she had known for a while now that it was more than time to end things between them. He was getting increasingly demanding and hard to control. Now it seemed he was even beginning to boast about her publicly. She shuddered again, remembering the photos he had taken of her.

What she and Jonathan had been doing might not be illegal but it was certainly suspect. She would be seen as the guilty party. Everyone would point the finger at her. The woman who had sampled the forbidden fruit. Next to her, Eve was a saint. Alec would never look at her again.

How could she finish with Jonathan without hurting him? Whatever happened, she didn't want to do that. How could she finish with him in a way that ensured he never told anyone about her? How could she make certain that Alec never found out what she had done?

The questions buzzed around her head and made her feel dizzy. Somehow, before she saw Jonathan again, she had to find the answers. She just had to. Anything else was simply too horrible to contemplate.

Beth swore. Her fingers wouldn't do up the fiddly catches on her suspenders. Damn! She cursed again as she broke a nail. The final suspender snapped closed.

She peered at herself in the mirror and admired the black all in one bra, bodice and suspenders. It made her waist seem even slimmer and enhanced the curve of her hips and breasts. She twirled round to examine the back and was more than satisfied with what she saw. She really shouldn't be dressing up for him like this at all. She wanted him to remember her at her best. He had deliberately left a magazine open on a page where a woman was dressed just like this. She knew it was meant as a hint.

She glanced nervously at the clock again. It seemed ages since she had last seen him. He hadn't been round to her house for three weeks because of his swimming and he no longer worked at the newsagent's on Saturdays. This was it. Somehow, tonight, she must find a way to put an end to their relationship for good. She grimaced at the word. Relationship. She could only imagine what Alec would call it if he ever found out.

She finished dressing and hurried downstairs. She was as nervous as a kitten. Would she be able to make him understand? She must. Everything depended on it. She was surprised to realise just how much she would miss him.

When the doorbell finally rang, Beth jumped as if she were not expecting it. As she passed the hall mirror, she checked her appearance quickly and smiled at the tiny skirt and even tinier top that barely concealed the bodice underneath.

She peered through the opaque glass of the front door and felt a brief pang of disappointment. It wasn't Jonathan after all. There were three people on the doorstep. Perhaps it was Jehovah's Witnesses. She would have to get rid of them quickly, before he arrived. She fixed a polite yet determined smile on her face and turned the catch.

'Hello, Beth.' Jonathan was smiling at her innocently. His big blue eyes and soft golden hair made him as irresistible as ever. In spite of her tangled emotions, her heart flipped.

'I've brought some friends I want you to meet,' he added, as he put his foot through the doorway, making it impossible for her to close the door. Beth stepped back silently, totally confused. What was going on? Why had he brought anyone around here? Especially now.

Jonathan entered the hallway and turned round to beckon his friends. Jason and Mark followed him inside, their faces red and their lips smirking. The truth began to sink in.

Dear God! He had told them about her! Told them what the two of them did together. Alec had been right. He had been discussing her and boasting about what he had done to her. How could he? She felt utterly betrayed and totally devastated. Who else had he told? Was his whole school talking about her? Oh Jesus, maybe Alec already knew.

Before she could say anything, Jonathan indicated to his friends that they should go through into the front room. He turned back to her, pushed the door closed, and stared down into her face.

'It's all right,' he told her. 'Trust me.' He pulled her towards him and kissed her gently. She felt his hands running down her sides to fondle her bum.

Maybe this was just more of his games, she wondered hopefully. Perhaps he had asked them here so that he could watch her, watch them watching her, imagine what he would do to her once they had gone? Yes, that must be it. What should she do? If she made a fuss, he would be humiliated. If she gave him a reason to want to take revenge and then he found out about Alec . . .

Despite her shock, Beth couldn't help briefly contemplating the fun she could have teasing these lads. What would it be like to make all three of them strip for her, to watch the way they looked at her and know how crazy she was making them all? Were they both virgins? She was certain that they were. Enough, she reprimanded herself.

Jonathan released her and followed his mates. Beth took a

deep breath and smoothed her skirt down. She began to walk after him, enjoying the view in spite of her fears.

The two boys were sitting awkwardly, side by side, on the settee. They looked like a pair of hungry sparrows perched on a fence. Beth almost giggled. She stood by the doorway and examined them more closely, doing her best to ignore the way they were eyeing her in return.

The one on the left looked as though he was nearly as tall as Jonathan was. He had darkish brown hair that was somewhat longer and less tidy than his friend's. His face was round and babyish and his eyes wide-set and very dark. Tony might have looked a little bit like that thirty years ago.

The other boy was shorter and thicker set. His hair was almost as red as Gerri's. His eyes were blue-green and he had a smattering of freckles over his snub nose. The two were dressed alike in jeans and T-shirts. They both looked very young and very innocent.

Jonathan perched on the arm of the chair opposite them. He looked so much more confident and adult. He had been just like them a few short weeks ago.

'This is Mark.' Jonathan pointed to the dark-haired boy. 'And this is Jason.' Both lads reddened even more. Neither said anything.

'They have been wanting to meet you.' He echoed the words she had once used when introducing him to Ann. Cheeky young devil! She was determined that he wasn't going to intimidate her.

'That's nice,' she replied as she walked over and sat herself on the chair beside him. 'I'm pleased to meet you, too.'

Deliberately, she crossed her legs and almost laughed aloud at the way their eyes bulged. It had been a while since such a small act had had quite that effect on Jonathan.

'Are you both swimmers, too?' she enquired anxiously as she prayed that Alec did not coach them as well.

Both boys shook their heads and Beth heaved a sigh of relief. When she saw where their eyes were, she couldn't resist leaning forward slightly so that they could see down the top of her blouse.

Jonathan was obviously thoroughly enjoying himself. He had twisted slightly so that he could see her better, and he smiled down at her encouragingly before he slipped his hand around her shoulder to fondle the top of her right breast.

Beth jumped. She hadn't been expecting that. Trying not to be too obvious about it, she raised her own hand and pushed his fingers away. Jonathan immediately put them back again.

Beth glanced across at Mark and Jason. They were both sitting forward on the edge of the settee, their eyes wide. She thought that it must be a bit like watching a dirty movie. Perhaps she and Jonathan should give them a bit of a peep show before she kicked them out? The idea excited her. What prestige Jonathan would have. She could still remember how important it was to look big in front of your friends. That was the last thing needed now.

She left his hand where it was and placed her own hand on his thigh, close to his groin. She was pleased at the way he responded to her touch. The thought of entertaining his friends was probably turning him on too. She turned her head to look at his crotch. It was definitely expanding.

Jonathan leant over and began to kiss her. His tongue pushed urgently into her mouth and she could sense his heightened excitement at the idea of having an audience. She could imagine just how he felt. Despite herself, she responded eagerly, surprised at how aroused she was becoming. She wanted to take his cock and suck it until he was crying for mercy. She wanted to feel him thrusting deep inside her. It was the last time. She wanted it to be perfect. It was more than time for Mark and Jason to be on their way. She pushed away her tinge of disappointment at the lost opportunity.

Jonathan took his mouth away from hers and moved his lips round her neck. He nibbled her ear lobe and Beth shivered all over at the feel of his breath.

'Why don't you go upstairs to the bedroom,' he whispered, as if reading her thoughts. 'Slip out of your top and skirt and lie on the bed. I'll just see to my friends and then I'll join you.' He blew softly into her ear and Beth shuddered again. She nodded silently.

As she left the room, she avoided looking at the two boys.

Jonathan turned towards his friends. 'Give me a few minutes and then sneak up. It's the first door on the right.'

He left the room and walked down the hallway. Mark and Jason followed. 'See you then,' he yelled loudly as he opened then slammed the front door.

As soon as she heard the door slam, Beth removed her outer clothing and shoes and lay back on the bed, waiting. After a few seconds, she heard him coming up the stairs. She sighed with anticipation and turned her head towards him as he walked in.

Jonathan stood at the end of the bed and eyed her hungrily. She watched the way his eyes examined her lacy bodice. She knew she must look like something out of *Mayfair*. He took a deep breath and began to walk towards her.

Jonathan peeled off his clothes quickly. He lay down on the bed beside her, rolled over on to his side and put his hands on her breasts. His mouth found hers again and she felt him shiver as she thrust her tongue into him.

The stairs creaked and stealthy footsteps approached the

door. Jonathan kissed her harder and ran his hands through her long hair.

'You're so beautiful,' he whispered as he put his hand on the top of her panties. He began pulling them down slowly, gradually exposing her naked mound. She moaned and arched her back. He ran his hand over the soft skin and his fingers teased her clit. Someone gasped.

Beth stiffened. 'What was that?'

'Nothing.' Jonathan pushed her back down on to the bed and began to untie the little ribbons holding her bodice closed. As her breasts sprang free, he leant across and licked her nipples hungrily. There was another soft gasp from the doorway.

Beth pushed herself up on her elbows and stared towards the door. Mark and Jason were standing just inside the doorway with their mouths gaping. One of them had already opened his jeans and was rubbing his erection. The other looked as if he was about to come in his pants.

'What the hell?' She began to struggle. Jonathan put his hand over her chest and pinned her back on to the bed. He pushed his tongue into her mouth and his fingers slipped back between her thighs. Her struggles lessened and she closed her eyes.

'Forget about them,' he whispered. 'Just concentrate on me.' He pushed his middle finger up into her sex. Beth gasped with surprise and pleasure. She could feel his erection burning against her thigh, throbbing and pulsing in its eagerness to pleasure her.

She arched her back against his probing finger and a small whimper of desire escaped from her lips. She pushed her hand under his legs and fondled his balls. She heard him moan with a mixture of pleasure and longing.

His hand began to play with her breast again and his fingers felt as soft as a feather brushing across her nipple. Both nipples. She sighed. An octopus was a very good description for him. Hands everywhere.

He wasn't the only one touching her! The realisation was like a slap across the face. Dear heaven, his friends were touching her. This couldn't be happening! She must be dreaming.

Beth twisted her head to one side. She saw a swollen penis only inches from her face. Its base was covered with red curls. It wasn't Jonathan's! She felt unfamiliar hands on her breasts and thighs. She was going to be raped. Gang banged. To think she had trusted him. She began to struggle again.

'Just relax. I won't let them hurt you.' Jonathan started to kiss and nibble her ear lobe again. Sweet Jesus! Did he have any idea what that did to her? She could feel the goose bumps springing up all over her body at the touch of his teeth and the feel of his breath. Beth stopped struggling and closed her eyes again.

She could feel hands running all over her body, touching her and caressing her everywhere. She felt someone – Jonathan? – open her thighs and start to finger her clit. She was so turned on that she didn't know what to do with herself. Her head was spinning and she couldn't think straight. She should put a stop to this. She must put a stop to it. She groaned loudly with a mixture of fear, confusion and almost uncontrollable passion.

Jonathan sat up and took hold of Beth's wrists. He guided her hands on to Mark and Jason's cocks and held her there until she began to fondle them gently with her fingers. Both boys gasped and their faces glazed with lust. Beth looked up at Jonathan and saw the knowing grin on his face. Despite herself, Beth grinned back and squeezed both cocks even harder.

Jonathan reached for a condom, ripped it open, and rolled it expertly down his erection. He positioned himself over Beth, parted her thighs, and guided himself inside her. His breath sighed from him as he slipped effortlessly into her waiting warmth and dampness. He began to thrust powerfully.

Beth stopped fondling his friends and grabbed Jonathan's buttocks. She arched her back against him and whimpered urgently. She no longer cared what was happening to her or who was touching her. His cock felt so good. He knew her body so well. He knew just how to drive her wild. She whimpered again and instinctively tightened her vaginal muscles around his hardness. She heard him moan in response and begin pumping harder. She felt her climax gathering like a storm cloud. Jonathan deliberately slowed his pace, prolonging his own pleasure.

She heard Jason moan softly as he lost control. As soon as he saw Jason lose it, Mark's own excitement seemed to get the better of him. He moaned in desperation and she felt him fondle her left breast again. She realised that it was probably the first time he had ever seen a woman so totally exposed.

She noticed Mark staring down at where Jonathan was pumping in and out of her shaven mound. It was obviously too much for him. With another shudder, he began spurting urgently into his hand.

Beth cried out and raised her buttocks high into the air, then stiffened as her own climax enveloped her. Jonathan lifted his head and stared at the flush of red forming across her puckered nipples. She felt his balls drawing up tightly against him as his orgasm approached. He slowed the pace again, obviously still trying to prolong the moment, and she tightened her grip on him and closed her eyes.

With a shout of triumph, he pushed deep inside her and began to pump his seed into the protective rubber casing.

He groaned loudly and she felt the waves of pleasure washing over him before he slumped down almost protectively over her stomach.

Beth opened her eyes as if she were awakening from a deep sleep. She lifted her head and looked around stupidly. Mark and Jason had already pulled their clothes back on and were hovering uncertainly by the door, as if unsure what to do. Gradually, she began to collect her thoughts.

How the hell had she let this happen? It was too late to worry about that now. She had more important things to take care of. Somehow, she had to limit the damage. Her stomach churned at the thought of what might happen if any of this should get out. If Alec were to find out ...

She pushed Jonathan off, sat up, and stared across the room at the still wide-eyed onlookers.

'I think you should both leave now.' She held their stares. 'But, before you go there's something I want to say.' She did her best to look and sound stern. It seemed faintly ridiculous without any clothes on. Under the circumstances, however, it was a little too late for being bashful now.

'You will forget what you have just seen and done here.' Some chance of that! She only just stopped herself from giggling.

'You will not talk about it with each other and you most certainly won't breathe a word of it to anyone else. Is that quite clear?'

Jason and Mark nodded silently. Their faces told her that they were still enjoying the view.

'Because, if you do say anything,' she continued, 'if one word of this gets out, I shall make you both suffer in ways you can't even imagine. Do you understand me?'

She could feel her hands beginning to shake and she put them behind her quickly.

'Don't ever do anything like this again. Now get out.'

She didn't even hear them leave. She was vaguely aware of Jonathan going to the bathroom, then returning to begin gathering up his clothes. She ignored him completely, not trusting herself to speak to him yet. She could feel a deep sadness burning within her. A sense of loss that was suddenly almost more than she could bear.

It was all over. It had to end. Right here and right now. She couldn't risk it any longer. Jonathan wasn't a meek, pliable little boy any more. The cub had grown up into a lion. She had completely lost all her control over him and it was time to let go. She had Alec to think about now. Oh God, how she would miss Jonathan. She just hoped she could make him understand. She had to make him understand. For his sake and for Alec's sake.

'Jonathan. We need to talk. Come and sit down.' She realised that she was still naked and she reached out to pull her robe around her shoulders.

Jonathan sat down beside her, dressed only in his blue briefs. She tried not to look at his body.

'There's something I need to tell you,' he began, before she could compose her first words. Beth stared at him in surprise. Was he about to apologise and beg her to forgive him? Please, not now. It would only make things worse.

'There's no need to –' she began. Jonathan took her hand in his and pulled her round towards him.

'It's college,' he interrupted her. 'There isn't a good sixth form college around here so Mum's agreed to let me go up north and live with Dad.' He paused and his eyes filled with sorrow. 'She thinks it best if I move up there as soon as possible now that school's finished. I'm leaving next week.'

Beth stared at him in astonishment, her emotions jumbled. Relief washed through her. He was going away and their secret would be safe. Alec need never know anything about it. Sorrow engulfed her. She owed Jonathan so much. She would never forget him.

'It's probably for the best,' she replied softly. 'You and I, well, it had to end. You must see that. You should be with girls your own age.'

'I'll never forget what you've done for me,' he told her. 'I was so, I mean, I didn't know anything. The girls at school, all they do is giggle and tease. It's so hard when you don't know what's expected from you.'

It was all Beth could do to stop herself from laughing. He was thanking her for what she had done for him! She remembered how nervous she had been when she had first realised he was spying on her, recalled her terror the first time she had invited him round to her house to be punished. She had never been more than half a step ahead of him, if that! Yet, here he was thanking her!

'I'll never forget you either, Jonathan,' she whispered truthfully as he took her in his arms for one final kiss.

Visit the Black Lace website at
www.black-lace-books.com

FIND OUT THE LATEST INFORMATION AND TAKE ADVANTAGE OF OUR
FANTASTIC FREE BOOK OFFER! ALSO VISIT THE SITE FOR . . .

- All Black Lace titles currently available
  and how to order online

- Great new offers

- Writers' guidelines

- Author interviews

- An erotica newsletter

- Features

- Cool links

BLACK LACE – THE LEADING IMPRINT OF
WOMEN'S SEXY FICTION

TAKING YOUR EROTIC READING PLEASURE
TO NEW HORIZONS

LOOK OUT FOR THE BLACK LACE 15TH ANNIVERSARY SPECIAL EDITIONS. COLLECT ALL 10 TITLES IN THE SERIES!

All books priced £7.99 in the UK. Please note publication dates apply to the UK only. For other territories, please contact your retailer.

Published in March 2008

CASSANDRA'S CONFLICT
Fredrica Allen
ISBN 978 0 352 34186 0

A house in Hampstead. Present-day. Behind a façade of cultured respectability lies a world of decadent indulgence and dark eroticism. Cassandra's sheltered life is transformed when she gets employed as governess to the Baron's children. He draws her into games where lust can feed on the erotic charge of submission. Games where only he knows the rules and where unusual pleasures can flourish.

Published in April 2008

GEMINI HEAT
Portia Da Costa

ISBN 978 0 352 34187 7

As the metropolis sizzles in the freak early summer temperatures, identical twin sisters Deana and Delia Ferraro are cooking up a heat wave of their own. Surrounded by an atmosphere of relentless humidity, Deanna and Delia find themselves rivals for the attentions of Jackson de Guile – an exotic, wealthy entrepreneur and master of power dynamics – who draws them both into a web of luxurious debauchery.

Their erotic encounters become increasingly bizarre as the twins vie for the rewards that pleasuring him brings them - tainted rewards which only serve to confuse their perceptions of the limits of sexual experience.

Published in May 2008

BLACK ORCHID
Roxanne Carr

ISBN 978 0 352 34188 4

At the Black Orchid Club, adventurous women who yearn for the pleasures of exotic, even kinky sex can quench their desires in discreet and luxurious surroundings. Having tasted the fulfilment of unique and powerful lusts, one such adventurous woman learns what happens when the need for limitless indulgence becomes an addiction.

To be published in July 2008

JULIET RISING
Cleo Cordell
ISBN 978 0 352 34192 1

Nothing is more important to Reynard than winning the favours of the bright and wilful Juliet, a pupil at Madame Nicol's exclusive but strict 18th century ladies' academy. Her captivating beauty tinged with a hint of cruelty soon has Reynard willing to do anything to win her approval. But Juliet's methods have little effect on Andreas, the real object of her lustful obsessions. Unable to bend him to her will, she is forced to watch him lavish his manly talents on her fellow pupils. That is, until she agrees to change her stuck-up, stubborn ways and become an eager erotic participant.

To be published in August 2008

ODALISQUE
Fleur Reynolds
ISBN 978 0 352 34193 8

Set against a backdrop of sophisticated elegance, a tale of family intrigue, forbidden passions and depraved secrets unfolds. Beautiful but scheming, successful designer Auralie plots to bring about the downfall of her virtuous cousin, Jeanine. Recently widowed, but still young and glamorous, Jeanine finds her passions being rekindled by Auralie's husband. But she is playing into Auralie's hands – vindictive hands that drag Jeanine into a world of erotic depravity. Why are the cousins locked into this sexual feud? And what is the purpose of Jeanine's mysterious Confessor, and his sordid underground sect?

To be published in September 2008

THE STALLION
Georgina Brown
ISBN 978 0 352 34199 0

The world of showjumping is as steamy as it is competitive. Ambitious young rider Penny Bennett enters into a wager with her oldest rival and friend, Ariadne, to win her thoroughbred stallion, guaranteed to bring Penny money and success. But first she must attain the sponsorship and very personal attention of showjumping's biggest impresario, Alister Beaumont.

Beaumont's riding school, however, is not all it seems. There's the weird relationship between Alister and his cigar-smoking sister. And the bizarre clothes they want Penny to wear. But in this atmosphere of unbridled kinkiness, Penny is determined not only to win the wager but to discover the truth about Beaumont's strange hobbies.

To be published in October 2008

THE DEVIL AND THE DEEP BLUE SEA
Cheryl Mildenhall
ISBN 978 0 352 34200 3

When Hillary and her girlfriends rent a country house for their summer vacation, it is a pleasant surprise to find that its secretive and kinky owner – Darius Harwood – seems to be the most desirable man in the locale. That is, before Hillary meets Haldane, the blonde and beautifully proportioned Norwegian sailor who works nearby. Intrigued by the sexual allure of two very different men, Hillary can't resist exploring the possibilities on offer. But these opportunities for misbehaviour quickly lead her into a tricky situation for which a difficult decision has to be made.

To be published in November 2008

THE NINETY DAYS OF GENEVIEVE
Lucinda Carrington
ISBN 978 0 352 34201 0

A ninety-day sex contract wasn't exactly what Genevieve Loften had in mind when she began business negotiations with the arrogant and attractive James Sinclair. As a career move she wanted to go along with it; the pay-off was potentially huge. However, she didn't imagine that he would make her the star performer in a series of increasingly kinky and exotic fantasies. Thrown into a world of sexual misadventure, Genevieve learns how to balance her high-pressure career with the twilight world of fetishism and debauchery.

To be published in December 2008

THE GIFT OF SHAME
Sarah Hope-Walker
ISBN 978 0 352 34202 7

Sad, sultry Helen flies between London, Paris and the Caribbean chasing whatever physical pleasures she can get to tear her mind from a deep, deep loss. Her glamorous life-style and charged sensual escapades belie a widow's grief. When she meets handsome, rich Jeffrey she is shocked and yet intrigued by his masterful, domineering behaviour. Soon, Helen is forced to confront the forbidden desires hiding within herself – and forced to undergo a startling metamorphosis from a meek and modest lady into a bristling, voracious wanton.

ALSO LOOK OUT FOR

THE NEW BLACK LACE BOOK OF WOMEN'S SEXUAL FANTASIES
Edited and compiled by Mitzi Szereto
ISBN 978 0 352 34172 3

The second anthology of detailed sexual fantasies contributed by women from all over the world. The book is a result of a year's research by an expert on erotic writing and gives a fascinating insight into the rich diversity of the female sexual imagination..

Black Lace Booklist

Information is correct at time of printing. To avoid disappointment, check availability before ordering. Go to www.black-lace-books.com.
All books are priced £7.99 unless another price is given.

BLACK LACE BOOKS WITH A CONTEMPORARY SETTING

❏ THE ANGELS' SHARE Maya Hess	ISBN 978 0 352 34043 6	
❏ ASKING FOR TROUBLE Kristina Lloyd	ISBN 978 0 352 33362 9	
❏ BLACK LIPSTICK KISSES Monica Belle	ISBN 978 0 352 33885 3	£6.99
❏ THE BLUE GUIDE Carrie Williams	ISBN 978 0 352 34132 7	
❏ THE BOSS Monica Belle	ISBN 978 0 352 34088 7	
❏ BOUND IN BLUE Monica Belle	ISBN 978 0 352 34012 2	
❏ CAMPAIGN HEAT Gabrielle Marcola	ISBN 978 0 352 33941 6	
❏ CAT SCRATCH FEVER Sophie Mouette	ISBN 978 0 352 34021 4	
❏ CIRCUS EXCITE Nikki Magennis	ISBN 978 0 352 34033 7	
❏ CLUB CRÈME Primula Bond	ISBN 978 0 352 33907 2	£6.99
❏ CONFESSIONAL Judith Roycroft	ISBN 978 0 352 33421 3	
❏ CONTINUUM Portia Da Costa	ISBN 978 0 352 33120 5	
❏ DANGEROUS CONSEQUENCES Pamela Rochford	ISBN 978 0 352 33185 4	
❏ DARK DESIGNS Madelynne Ellis	ISBN 978 0 352 34075 7	
❏ THE DEVIL INSIDE Portia Da Costa	ISBN 978 0 352 32993 6	
❏ EQUAL OPPORTUNITIES Mathilde Madden	ISBN 978 0 352 34070 2	
❏ FIRE AND ICE Laura Hamilton	ISBN 978 0 352 33486 2	
❏ GONE WILD Maria Eppie	ISBN 978 0 352 33670 5	
❏ HOTBED Portia Da Costa	ISBN 978 0 352 33614 9	
❏ IN PURSUIT OF ANNA Natasha Rostova	ISBN 978 0 352 34060 3	
❏ IN THE FLESH Emma Holly	ISBN 978 0 352 34117 4	
❏ LEARNING TO LOVE IT Alison Tyler	ISBN 978 0 352 33535 7	
❏ MAD ABOUT THE BOY Mathilde Madden	ISBN 978 0 352 34001 6	
❏ MAKE YOU A MAN Anna Clare	ISBN 978 0 352 34006 1	
❏ MAN HUNT Cathleen Ross	ISBN 978 0 352 33583 8	
❏ THE MASTER OF SHILDEN Lucinda Carrington	ISBN 978 0 352 33140 3	
❏ MIXED DOUBLES Zoe le Verdier	ISBN 978 0 352 33312 4	£6.99
❏ MIXED SIGNALS Anna Clare	ISBN 978 0 352 33889 1	£6.99
❏ MS BEHAVIOUR Mini Lee	ISBN 978 0 352 33962 1	

☐ PACKING HEAT Karina Moore   ISBN 978 0 352 33356 8   £6.99
☐ PAGAN HEAT Monica Belle   ISBN 978 0 352 33974 4
☐ PEEP SHOW Mathilde Madden   ISBN 978 0 352 33924 9
☐ THE POWER GAME Carrera Devonshire   ISBN 978 0 352 33990 4
☐ THE PRIVATE UNDOING OF A PUBLIC SERVANT   ISBN 978 0 352 34066 5
    Leonie Martel
☐ RUDE AWAKENING Pamela Kyle   ISBN 978 0 352 33036 9
☐ SAUCE FOR THE GOOSE Mary Rose Maxwell   ISBN 978 0 352 33492 3
☐ SPLIT Kristina Lloyd   ISBN 978 0 352 34154 9
☐ STELLA DOES HOLLYWOOD Stella Black   ISBN 978 0 352 33588 3
☐ THE STRANGER Portia Da Costa   ISBN 978 0 352 33211 0
☐ SUITE SEVENTEEN Portia Da Costa   ISBN 978 0 352 34109 9
☐ TONGUE IN CHEEK Tabitha Flyte   ISBN 978 0 352 33484 8
☐ THE TOP OF HER GAME Emma Holly   ISBN 978 0 352 34116 7
☐ UNNATURAL SELECTION Alaine Hood   ISBN 978 0 352 33963 8
☐ VELVET GLOVE Emma Holly   ISBN 978 0 352 34115 0
☐ VILLAGE OF SECRETS Mercedes Kelly   ISBN 978 0 352 33344 5
☐ WILD BY NATURE Monica Belle   ISBN 978 0 352 33915 7   £6.99
☐ WILD CARD Madeline Moore   ISBN 978 0 352 34038 2
☐ WING OF MADNESS Mae Nixon   ISBN 978 0 352 34099 3

BLACK LACE BOOKS WITH AN HISTORICAL SETTING

☐ THE BARBARIAN GEISHA Charlotte Royal   ISBN 978 0 352 33267 7
☐ BARBARIAN PRIZE Deanna Ashford   ISBN 978 0 352 34017 7
☐ THE CAPTIVATION Natasha Rostova   ISBN 978 0 352 33234 9
☐ DARKER THAN LOVE Kristina Lloyd   ISBN 978 0 352 33279 0
☐ WILD KINGDOM Deanna Ashford   ISBN 978 0 352 33549 4
☐ DIVINE TORMENT Janine Ashbless   ISBN 978 0 352 33719 1
☐ FRENCH MANNERS Olivia Christie   ISBN 978 0 352 33214 1
☐ LORD WRAXALL'S FANCY Anna Lieff Saxby   ISBN 978 0 352 33080 2
☐ NICOLE'S REVENGE Lisette Allen   ISBN 978 0 352 32984 4
☐ THE SENSES BEJEWELLED Cleo Cordell   ISBN 978 0 352 32904 2   £6.99
☐ THE SOCIETY OF SIN Sian Lacey Taylder   ISBN 978 0 352 34080 1
☐ TEMPLAR PRIZE Deanna Ashford   ISBN 978 0 352 34137 2
☐ UNDRESSING THE DEVIL Angel Strand   ISBN 978 0 352 33938 6

BLACK LACE BOOKS WITH A PARANORMAL THEME

- [ ] BRIGHT FIRE Maya Hess — ISBN 978 0 352 34104 4
- [ ] BURNING BRIGHT Janine Ashbless — ISBN 978 0 352 34085 6
- [ ] CRUEL ENCHANTMENT Janine Ashbless — ISBN 978 0 352 33483 1
- [ ] FLOOD Anna Clare — ISBN 978 0 352 34094 8
- [ ] GOTHIC BLUE Portia Da Costa — ISBN 978 0 352 33075 8
- [ ] THE PRIDE Edie Bingham — ISBN 978 0 352 33997 3
- [ ] THE SILVER COLLAR Mathilde Madden — ISBN 978 0 352 34141 9
- [ ] THE TEN VISIONS Olivia Knight — ISBN 978 0 352 34119 8

BLACK LACE ANTHOLOGIES

- [ ] BLACK LACE QUICKIES 1 Various — ISBN 978 0 352 34126 6 — £2.99
- [ ] BLACK LACE QUICKIES 2 Various — ISBN 978 0 352 34127 3 — £2.99
- [ ] BLACK LACE QUICKIES 3 Various — ISBN 978 0 352 34128 0 — £2.99
- [ ] BLACK LACE QUICKIES 4 Various — ISBN 978 0 352 34129 7 — £2.99
- [ ] BLACK LACE QUICKIES 5 Various — ISBN 978 0 352 34130 3 — £2.99
- [ ] BLACK LACE QUICKIES 6 Various — ISBN 978 0 352 34133 4 — £2.99
- [ ] BLACK LACE QUICKIES 7 Various — ISBN 978 0 352 34146 4 — £2.99
- [ ] BLACK LACE QUICKIES 8 Various — ISBN 978 0 352 34147 1 — £2.99
- [ ] BLACK LACE QUICKIES 9 Various — ISBN 978 0 352 34155 6 — £2.99
- [ ] MORE WICKED WORDS Various — ISBN 978 0 352 33487 9 — £6.99
- [ ] WICKED WORDS 3 Various — ISBN 978 0 352 33522 7 — £6.99
- [ ] WICKED WORDS 4 Various — ISBN 978 0 352 33603 3 — £6.99
- [ ] WICKED WORDS 5 Various — ISBN 978 0 352 33642 2 — £6.99
- [ ] WICKED WORDS 6 Various — ISBN 978 0 352 33690 3 — £6.99
- [ ] WICKED WORDS 7 Various — ISBN 978 0 352 33743 6 — £6.99
- [ ] WICKED WORDS 8 Various — ISBN 978 0 352 33787 0 — £6.99
- [ ] WICKED WORDS 9 Various — ISBN 978 0 352 33860 0
- [ ] WICKED WORDS 10 Various — ISBN 978 0 352 33893 8
- [ ] THE BEST OF BLACK LACE 2 Various — ISBN 978 0 352 33718 4
- [ ] WICKED WORDS: SEX IN THE OFFICE Various — ISBN 978 0 352 33944 7
- [ ] WICKED WORDS: SEX AT THE SPORTS CLUB Various — ISBN 978 0 352 33991 1
- [ ] WICKED WORDS: SEX ON HOLIDAY Various — ISBN 978 0 352 33961 4
- [ ] WICKED WORDS: SEX IN UNIFORM Various — ISBN 978 0 352 34002 3
- [ ] WICKED WORDS: SEX IN THE KITCHEN Various — ISBN 978 0 352 34018 4
- [ ] WICKED WORDS: SEX ON THE MOVE Various — ISBN 978 0 352 34034 4
- [ ] WICKED WORDS: SEX AND MUSIC Various — ISBN 978 0 352 34061 0

BLACK LACE NON-FICTION

To find out the latest information about Black Lace titles, check out the website: www.black-lace-books.com or send for a booklist with complete synopses by writing to:

Black Lace Booklist, Virgin Books Ltd
Thames Wharf Studios
Rainville Road
London W6 9HA

Please include an SAE of decent size. Please note only British stamps are valid.

Our privacy policy
We will not disclose information you supply us to any other parties. We will not disclose any information which identifies you personally to any person without your express consent.

From time to time we may send out information about Black Lace books and special offers. Please tick here if you do not wish to receive Black Lace information. ❑

Please send me the books I have ticked above.

Name ....

Address ....

....

....

....

Post Code ....

Send to: Virgin Books Cash Sales, Thames Wharf Studios, Rainville Road, London W6 9HA.

US customers: for prices and details of how to order books for delivery by mail, call 888-330-8477.

Please enclose a cheque or postal order, made payable to Virgin Books Ltd, to the value of the books you have ordered plus postage and packing costs as follows:

UK and BFPO – £1.00 for the first book, 50p for each subsequent book.

Overseas (including Republic of Ireland) – £2.00 for the first book, £1.00 for each subsequent book.

If you would prefer to pay by VISA, ACCESS/MASTERCARD, DINERS CLUB, AMEX or SWITCH, please write your card number and expiry date here: ....

....

Signature ....

Please allow up to 28 days for delivery.